Darius Jones

Darius Jones

MARY B. MORRISON

Kensington Publishing Corp.
http://www.kensingtonbooks.com

DAFINA BOOKS are published by

Kensington Publishing Corp.
119 West 40th Street
New York, NY 10018

All Kensington Titles, Imprints, and Distributed Lines are available at special quantity discounts for bulk purchases for sales promotions, premiums, fund-raising, and educational or institutional use. Special book excerpts or customized printings can also be created to fit specific needs. For details, write or phone the office of the Kensington special sales manager: Kensington Publishing Corp., 119 West 40th Street, New York, NY 10018, attn: Special Sales Department, Phone: 1-800-221-2647.

Dafina and the Dafina logo Reg. U.S. Pat. & TM Off.

Library of Congress Card Catalogue Number: 2010926444

ISBN-13: 978-0-7582-2261-9
ISBN-10: 0-7582-2261-0

First hardcover printing: August 2010

10 9 8 7 6 5 4 3 2 1

Printed in the United States of America

To Michael Baisden
Thanks for all you've done for me and for the positive impact you have made
and continue to make throughout America.
Wishing you many continued blessings.

Acknowledgments

First and foremost, I thank the Creator for abundantly blessing me with many gifts. The publication of *Darius Jones* marks my tenth anniversary as a published author. I appreciate all of my fans for your unwavering support of my work over the years, especially those of you who bought my self-published version of *Soulmates Dissipate* in 2000. If you are new to reading my novels, I welcome you into the hearts, minds, and souls of my characters.

This tenth anniversary isn't about me; it's about each of you. I have so many people to thank for accompanying me through my first decade. My son, Jesse Bernard Byrd Jr., I love you. You're the best. I'm proud to be your mom. I enjoy our one-on-one time together when I am super silly or extremely serious. You embrace every facet of me including my animated character voices. Most important, I'm proud of you. You are living proof that we can have a plan for ourselves but God's plan supercedes ours. I had no idea that you're a better writer than I am. I'm ecstatic that you're on track to becoming one of the best writers for film and television instead of pursuing a career in basketball. I love you.

My mother, Elester Noel, and my father, Joseph Henry Morrison, will eternally reside in my heart. Although my biological parents did not rear me, I thank God my family is a village. I don't know where I'd be if it weren't for my great aunt, Ella Beatrice Turner, and her husband, Willie Frinkle, welcoming me into their home.

I've mentioned before and I must say it again, I don't know what I'd do without my siblings. My brothers and sisters mean the world to me. Wayne, thanks for coming to my Tasty Tuesdays and Tell It All Thursdays relationship venues in Oakland. Having you there meant so much. Andrea, my sister who diligently prays for every one of us, thanks for keeping me in your prayers. Derrick, aka Thundar, although our father wasn't the role model to teach you how to become a father, I admire your love and dedication to your wife and children. Regina, you are truly the strongest of us all and I'd wager to say the smartest too, chick. I'm in awe of how you've kept your family centered while simultaneously accomplishing your educational and professional goals. Margie, my sister with the spirit of an angel, you are absolutely beautiful. Debra, you are phenomenal. In spite of the plethora of obstacles you've encountered, you've overcome each one. You, my dear sister, are the essence of love.

When I self-published my first novel, *Soulmates Dissipate*, ten years ago, there were a considerable number of African-American bookstores in the United States. Whether or not your doors are open today, I am eternally grateful for your support. I must thank Michele Lewis, Emma Rodgers, Simba & Yao, Blanche Richardson, Karen Richardson, Vera Warren-Williams, Lori Carter, Bernard Henderson, Dominique, Doyna, and Donna Craddock, Carl Weber, and so many others for believing in me and giving me opportunities to succeed.

I'm blessed to have friends that I consider family. You have been there from day one of my literary journey and I thank you Felicia Polk, Vyllorya A. Evans, Carmen Polk, Micheala Burnett, Bennie Allen, Vanessa Ibanitoru, Brenda Clark, Malissa Walton, Howard and Ruth Kees, and Barbara Cooper.

To the friends I've met along my journey, I love all of my Facebook friends and fans, my Twitter peeps, MySpace crew, and my McDonogh 35 Senior High alumni. Then there's Richard C. Montgomery, always and forever you're absolutely special to me. To one of the world's greatest actors, Mel Jackson, I thank you for selflessly sharing your knowledge. To Sean Vaughn Scott, looking forward to the possibilities. Kelvin Powell, thanks for keeping it 100. I can't forget Jamaal Dennis, Kevin Stone, Sylvester Grisby, Belinda Walker, Onie and Diamon Simpson, Kent Lincoln, and Dr. Warren Strudwick.

To my author friends who started on this venture around the same time, I salute Gloria Mallette, Mary Monroe, Carl Weber, Karen E. Quinones Miller, Travis Hunter, Tracy Price-Thompson, Marcus

Major, Timothy McCann, Zane, Marissa Monteilh aka Pynk, and Victor McGlothin.

Then there's the group of authors who started before me whom I respect dearly, including Michael Baisden, Terry McMillan, Kimberla Lawson Roby, Eric Jerome Dickey, Francis Ray, Donna Hill, Tina McElroy Ansa, Margaret Johnson-Hodge, April Sinclair, Camika Spencer, and the late great E. Lynn Harris.

My publishing career has flourished in the hands of the scintillating pioneers of publishing at Kensington Publishing Corporation. Thanks to my editor and friend, Selena James, Walter Zacharius, Steven Zacharius, Adam Zacharius, Laurie Parkin, Karen Auerbach, Adeola Saul, Lesleigh Underwood, Mercedes Fernandez, John Scognamiglio, Daly Hernandez, and everyone else for taking excellent care of my career and me. I appreciate all the book tours, the Broadway plays, the Kensington family dinners, the birthday and Christmas gifts too.

To my family at Grand Central Publishing, you have been great to me with publishing the HoneyB novels. I thank Karen R. Thomas, La-Toya Smith, Linda A. Duggins, and Jamie Raab for supporting my career.

Well, what's an author without a brilliant agent? I'm fortunate to have two of the best agents in the literary business. I'm grateful to have Andrew Stuart and Claudia Menza for steering my career.

Wishing each of you peace and prosperity. Feel free to hit me up with a piece of your world at www.MaryMorrison.com.

Author's Note

Thank you for accompanying me on this journey through the Soulmates Dissipate Series and the Honey Diaries Series. Believe it or not, *Darius Jones* is the final book in both series. Don't panic. As promised, I'm still going to write the prequel to *Soulmates Dissipate,* entitled *Our Little Story.* In *Darius Jones,* I've brought together the main characters from both series.

Below, I have numbered both series in reading order:

Soulmates Dissipate Series

1. *Soulmates Dissipate*
2. *Never Again Once More*
3. *He's Just a Friend*
4. *Somebody's Gotta Be on Top*
5. *Nothing Has Ever Felt Like This*
6. *When Somebody Loves You Back*
7. *She Ain't the One*
8. *Darius Jones*

Honey Diaries Series

1. *Sweeter than Honey*
2. *Who's Loving You*
3. *Unconditionally Single*
4. *Darius Jones*

PROLOGUE

Darius

"Aw, shit! Baby! Watch out!" I stared in my side-view mirror. A white pickup truck rammed the back of our SUV, forcing us into the crosswalk on Sunset Boulevard. My wife slammed on the brakes. The pregnant woman in front of our SUV snatched her toddler into her arms, then jumped onto the sidewalk.

My four-year-old son screamed, "Daddy!"

Before I could look over my shoulder to check on him, the truck rammed us a second time, forcing us into the intersection beyond the red light. I stretched my arm across my wife's breasts, pushed her backward. Her forehead came one inch from hitting the steering wheel. If her seat belt hadn't locked and I hadn't caught her, my wife might be dead.

My son frantically kicked the back of my seat, yelling, "Daddy!"

"What the hell is going on!" The green light for oncoming traffic vanished. The yellow light beamed. I gasped, held my breath. An SUV sped downhill on Horn Avenue toward my wife's side of the car. It was coming too fast to stop. I saw the woman in the white truck behind us laughing, her head tilted down. Her truck bumped us again, putting us farther into the intersection.

"What the fuck are you doing?" I jammed my hand against the horn. *Honk! Honk! Honk! Honk!*

Fancy clenched the wheel, braced her back against the seat. I shouted, "Step on the gas!" as I reached for the steering wheel. I needed my wife to speed up. I lifted my leg, tried to place my size sixteen brown gator shoe over the gearshift to plunge the accelerator. My foot kicked our car into neutral. I put my foot on the floor in front of me just before—

Crash! The SUV slammed into the driver's side door. My wife's window shattered into tiny pieces. Glass showered her body. My wife's piercing scream penetrated like a thousand darts stabbing me in my head. Her forehead hit the steering wheel. Blood splattered on the windshield and on me at the same time. My wife's air bag deployed, flattening her body against her seat. The force of the last collision spun our SUV onto Holloway Drive.

"Jesus Christ!" I yelled.

I swore everything happened in less than sixty seconds. I wiped my face, praying the blood in my eyes and the nightmare I'd just witnessed was a bad dream. Reality told me this was no fucking accident.

The white pickup zoomed by us. The Arizona license plate was a blur. All I saw was . . . 777. Just as I extended my arms toward my wife, my air bag inflated like a parachute, jamming my body against my seat. "Ain't that a bitch?" My face was sandwiched sideways on the headrest. Blood oozed down my wife's hair, down her face, and onto her blue halter dress. I whispered, "God, help us."

"Daddy!" My son's screeching repeatedly pierced my ears.

Daggers replaced the feeling of darts. I couldn't help my wife or my son. My body felt numb from the waist down. A man was supposed to protect his family. I couldn't move. I closed my eyes. "God, give me strength."

I had to find the superhuman power I had when I was on the basketball court battling my opponents. That strength that exploded unexpectedly was still inside me. I knew it. Punching my way from underneath the air bag, I reached into the backseat and unbuckled my son. My legs were still numb. I pulled him into the front, stood him on my seat. I held him close trying to shield his face from Fancy.

He screamed. "Fancy's bleeding, Daddy," he cried, burying his face into my shoulder. "I'm scared, Daddy." His arms clamped around my neck.

Fuck! I didn't turn his face fast enough.

I wondered if his mother, Ashlee, was to blame for this accident. I had no enemies. Who else would do such an evil thing? At one time, I was almost in love with Ashlee for real, until she fucked my brother. I would've gotten rid of her pronto if she'd fucked any other man but I couldn't let my brother steal my money and my girl. So I'd kept fucking Ashlee until she helped me set him up. After I got revenge on my brother, I axed Ashlee. Maybe this was her idea of payback.

My thoughts raced but my wife wasn't moving. My son's hug strangled me. I could hardly breathe. All I saw was blood on her beautiful face. Her blue dress was now red. My limbs trembled uncontrollably.

Dragging my son's feet across my lap, I sat him on top of me. I yelled, "Somebody call nine-one-one!"

DJ screamed, "Ahhhh, Daddy! My legs!"

"Oh, Jesus!" I lifted my son. His blood stained my tan slacks. What the fuck was I thinking? I didn't know my lap was covered with glass. I'd accidentally cut my son's legs. I stood him in front me, tried but couldn't open my door. I reached to the floor. Searching my side of the car, I found my phone, dialed 9-1-1.

I held the back of DJ's head. Careful not to let him touch my shirt, I faced him toward my shoulder. "Oh, God." My stomach tightened. I heaved. Felt like I was about to puke. "Baby, I'ma get you out. Hang in there." My wife didn't respond. Her eyes were more closed than open.

I yelled into my phone at the operator, "Help us! She's not responding!"

A group of men pried open my door. I got out, ripped off my button-up shirt, took off my slacks, shook my shoulder-length locs, then picked up my son. His grip around my neck choked me. I couldn't breathe. DJ screamed directly in my ear. I tucked my phone into my fitted black boxer briefs.

"I got you, my man. Daddy's got you." I could no longer hold back the tears. This shit was fucked up. I'd gone from being the happiest man in the world to the most helpless man alive in a matter of minutes.

DJ cried, "I'm scared, Daddy. My legs hurt." He screamed again.

"Ease up a little," I told DJ. I checked his face. I removed his shirt, scanned his body. Slithers of glass were in his calves and the back of his thighs. I threw his shirt on the car seat, braced my arm underneath his butt to keep from touching the back of his legs.

I wasn't sure how but I made my way to the driver's side. Glass crunched beneath my hard soles. "That's my wife!" Pushing the men aside, I placed one hand on the dented handle and my foot on the smashed passenger door, then yanked as hard as I could. The door was stuck.

I snatched a crowbar from the man standing behind me. Son in one arm, iron in my other hand, I tried prying the door. Nothing worked. Spectators gathered. Cameras and cell phones pointed at me, below and above my waist, then at my wife. Fuck those inconsiderate bastards. What could I do except expect the photos to end up on Media TakeOut, TMZ, and everywhere else on television and online?

"Let us do this, Darius," one of the guys insisted.

Ignoring him, I cried, "I don't know what I'll do without my wife. Baby, hold on. I'ma get you out." I needed both hands. Unwrapping my son's arms from my neck, I said, "Son, stand right here. Don't move. Do not move."

He screamed again, touched the back of his thigh.

"Don't touch yourself!"

His body stiffened, mouth tightened, his innocent eyes stretched wide with fear. Looking up at me, he cried, "But it hurts, Daddy."

I didn't mean to yell at him. "Daddy's sorry, my man."

Jesus, they both need me and I need you.

CHAPTER 1

Darius

Two hours earlier . . .

At what point in a man's life was he ready to love and be loved? Sitting in the passenger seat of our SUV, I asked myself that question as I trailed my pointing finger from her kneecap, along her thigh, then up to the crevice of her crotch. I wanted her to park in the emergency lane, put on the brake, and turn on the flashers so I could bend her over the armrest and fuck her real good.

That was my fantasy but not a good idea with my son behind me in the backseat. I scanned from her succulent mocha lips, to her collarbone, to her cleavage, down to her lap where the seat belt hugged snug across her hips, keeping my pussy safe.

Damn, I love my sexy ass wife. Slugger could wait until we got home to slide his throbbing head inside our favorite hot spot. My wife was cool but her pussy seemed to have a built-in thermostat permanently set at a lethal body temperature of 106 degrees. Her good pussy was one of several reasons I hadn't fucked another woman since we'd gotten married.

I adjusted my partially erect nine-inch shaft, bit my bottom lip, shook my head. I was the luckiest man to have Fancy Taylor as my better half. She had what I called the magnificent five—brains, beauty, booty, breasts, and her own bank. The odds of finding all those qualities in one female were slimmer than winning California's Mega Millions lotto.

I texted her, I'ma beat that pussy up tonight!

Her iPhone dinged twice. My wife glanced at her phone, read her text, then nodded at me. When she tried to reply, I took her phone, placed it in my lap. "Not while you're driving." Careless shit happened when drivers didn't watch the road. Whenever possible, I was the passenger. Addicted to texting, tweeting, and Facebook—all that technological shit was my weakness—I had to have my hands free in order to communicate with my teammates and fans.

"I love you," my wife said, resting her hand on my thigh. In a sad tone, she added, "And I miss LA."

I agreed with her. Our living in Atlanta made us too laid back. Fame didn't excite folks in Atlanta. People in LA gave us that red carpet treatment. I replied, "No matter where we live, long as I've got you, I'm good. You are my everything, woman." Then I took a picture of the long line of cars on the 405 freeway in front of us.

"Am I your everything, Daddy?" my son asked.

My Facebook fan page automatically updated my Twitter page so I entered the caption, Only in LA, then posted the pic.

"Of course, my man. Daddy loves you unconditionally."

"What does that mean?" he asked.

"I love you no matter what," I said, reading the comments posted to my page. Most of my fans wanted to know where I was headed. Unbeknownst to my wife, my phone kept my dick out of a lot of chicks' mouths.

Pussy was deceiving. I wasn't banging, but every once in a while I'd let a chick blow me. The attitude I'd seen from women upfront wasn't what I'd gotten after cumming. I'd concluded that all females were either bipolar or straight-up undercover crazy.

Learned the hard way not to leave my cell phone unattended. One chick took a close-up of her pussy, texted the photo from her phone to mine, then replied from my phone back to hers, Can't wait to hit your pussy again. And she copied my wife. All that happened while I was taking a shit and a shower in my hotel room.

She was trying to get three minutes of fame. Shit backfired. When I got home, I told my wife my phone was stolen, asked her to buy me a new iPhone and change my number. Wasn't getting caught in a tiger trap. My wife had no reason not to believe me. I downloaded my data from my Mac computer to my new phone and kept shit moving.

I'd learned that each of my orgasms came with the hidden costs of a female's emotional distress. Ginger. Miranda. Heather. Zen. Maxine. Ciara. Ashlee. If I blended the best every woman I'd fucked had to offer and molded their assets into one woman, that one woman would not come close to being better than my wife. And the exact opposite of Fancy was my son's vindictive mother, Ashlee.

CHAPTER 2

Ashlee

Wham! I buried my fist in my pillow, wishing it were Darius's chest. Not a day went by that I didn't go insane missing our son.

"What did Darius do to prove he was a better fit parent? I'll tell you. Nothing, that's what!" I rolled onto my back, gave my down feather pillow the tightest hug. My fists pressed against my ribs. I kicked my feet high in the air, quickly sat on the edge of my bed, then closed my eyes. "I hate you, Darius!" I flung the pillow across the room, opened my eyes to the sound of perfume bottles crashing to the floor.

After having my son, my postpartum depression escalated to bouts of mania. I was happy before and when I'd met Darius. Cute little innocent adolescent Ashlee. That was me. The voice in my head said, "You know you should've aborted his baby." I thought keeping his baby would make him love me, make us a family. By the time I realized I was wrong, DJ was born.

I curled my fingers over my thumbs, squinted, rocked back and forth as I sat on the edge of my bed. "I did the right thing by keeping my baby. Darius still loves me."

My inner voice answered, *Keep believing that, you gonna end up in a psychiatric ward.*

"Don't say that," I told myself. "My mental instability isn't my fault."

My life changed forever when I became pregnant. I went from jovial to being depressed my entire pregnancy. Almost four years after giving birth, I was still on these antidepressant medications. I shook two tablets into my hand, tossed them in my mouth, then gulped a sixteen-ounce bottle of water without stopping.

I heard a car door open. "That's them." I placed the empty bottle on my nightstand, ran into my living room.

I snatched back my curtain, stared out my front window, and watched my ex's baby mama and her son enter Jay's house. Jay was my man until that bitch Tracy came back into his life. I hate weak men who let females control them. When I met Jay, he said he wasn't in a relationship. What he failed to mention was he wasn't over his ex. A man who was emotionally unavailable should keep his dick unavailable too. After I found out about Tracy, I leased this house across the street from Jay.

No man gets rid of me. I leave when I'm done.

Before Tracy closed his door, I opened mine. A burst of cold air clung to my virtually naked body. I yelled, "Bitch, you better watch your back! You and that trick ass baby of yours is next." Her son was a year older than mine. She needed to keep her ass at her own house instead of babysitting Jay's house while he was in jail.

Men were the root of all my problems. My daddy and Darius have moved on with their lives. *Slam!* I closed my front door, turned up the thermostat to reheat my home. I went back to my bedroom, sat on my bed. "Now, I hate Jay Crawford and Darius Jones."

I'd relocated from Dallas to D.C. shortly after the custody hearing. The worst day of my life was listening to the judge say, "Based on the caseworker's recommendation and the testimony given today, the court awards full custody to Darius. . . ." That bitch claimed I was mentally unstable.

The judge's decision to award custody to Darius numbed my compassion for men. Best if I didn't date another man anytime soon. I sat on the edge of my bed in my red boy shorts replaying that day in court over in my mind, trying to figure out what I'd done wrong besides fall in love with Darius. I flopped backward on the mattress.

Unlike with Jay, my heart had never stopped loving Darius.

CHAPTER 3

Darius

Jay-Z loved New York and Darius Jones loved Los Angeles.

The bumper-to-bumper traffic on the 405 didn't faze me. The LA sunshine beamed to a warm eighty degrees, my son chilled in the backseat, and my wife sat high behind the wheel driving us to BOA Steakhouse for dinner. The only person missing from my special evening was my mother. She'd insisted on attending a movie premiere with her new so-called fiancé, Grant Hill, and her new personal assistant, Bambi.

Hadn't met Bambi yet. Mom tried making me remember her from elementary, middle, and high school but I couldn't. Didn't matter. Bambi was Mom's PA, not mine.

I'd tell my mom that dude was all bad before she walked down the aisle. I'd paid for her wedding to see her happy again but I couldn't buy her happiness. I still had to look out for Mom but right now my mouth watered for two things, a tender medium bone-in rib-eye steak and the sweet taste of my wife's pussy. By nightfall, I would have devoured both.

I've got plans for you tonight, woman.

"What, Darius?" she asked, smiling at me with her curious brown eyes on high beam.

"You watch the road, Ladycat. I'll watch my . . ." I mouthed the word "pussy" so my son wouldn't hear.

My son chimed in. "Watch your what, Daddy? I'll help you."

"My man, what did I tell you about grown folks' convo?"

"Sorry, Daddy."

"You're up to something," my wife said, staring ahead. "I know that look."

"I'll tell you in a few." I had to savor what I was about to say and do for my wife. I wasn't good at prolonging surprises. If she asked again, I'd tell her. I stared out my window to avoid giving in to her.

Now I was really starving. Ready to sink my teeth into a tender juicy piece of USDA prime.

Tapping on my iPhone, I texted my secret to my teammate, K-9, along with a pic. Had to show and tell someone. He texted back, It's motherfuckers like you that make it hard for a single man like me to fuck for free. Congrats, D.

I didn't respond. I'd hit him back later.

I posted, Headed to BOA's with the Mrs. and my lil' man. Stay posted for pics. I included a link for the restaurant.

When a man had no interest in conquering new pussy, he was ready to tackle loving one woman. For once in my life, I was happy. I mean genuinely happy.

My mother, wife, and son were my world. My mother was my rock. My wife was my rib. My son kept me focused on what was most important in my life . . . family.

My phone vibrated. It was Ashlee. "What's up?" I answered, knowing she was going to ask to see DJ. I didn't want to get into it with her, so I cut her off with, "Let me call you back," and hung up.

"Who was that?" my wife asked.

I spelled the word visitation. Glancing over my shoulder, I winked at my son. He gave me an upward nod. That was his way of signaling he was good. I held my wife's hand, then became quiet. I loved her ass so much I felt that shit from my fingers all the way up in my chest.

She was the only woman who told me to my face when I was wrong. Sometimes she yelled at me but when her voice was barely above a whisper, or when she called me Darius Henry Jones, I stopped whatever the fuck I was doing and gave her my undivided attention.

"I get so caught up in your basketball games, I forget about her every other weekends. I'll do it after the Cleveland game. Baby, when you win MVP, you should tell your agent to look into trading you from Atlanta to LA," my wife said. "This is your hometown."

Aw, man. My lips curved to the side. "Nah, it's best we stay put for another year." Moving wasn't a bad idea. Moving back to LA was a bad idea. I might give in and fuck one of these LA glamazons.

I asked my wife, "Why did I have to go there? I wish I'd never met her."

I appreciated that my wife never emasculated me like my son's mother. Never understood why my son's mom verbally castrated me, then thought I'd ask to marry her ass. What dude in his right mind would volunteer to be humiliated twenty-four-seven? That was some backward bullshit thinking.

"Go where, Daddy? Who, Daddy?"

My wife tapped me on the thigh, shook her head, told me, "Don't say things like that," then spoke to DJ. "Your dad was just thinking out loud."

Some thought me to be arrogant, cocky, a shit talker, an asshole. Others thought of me as *the shit*. Regardless of their opinions, they didn't know me. My wife, she knew me.

CHAPTER 4

Ashlee

"Let me call you back," Darius said, ending the call. And he wondered why I hated him. At times I wished he were dead. I wished they were both dead. Jay and Darius.

Dating Jay helped take my mind off my problems. Helped me to temporarily forget about Darius. Jay sexed me crazy just like Darius. If he hadn't left me for Tracy, I wouldn't have lied and said he'd raped me. Without Jay in my life, I had to go back to Darius. Why did the roads in my life keep leading me back to Darius? Maybe we were meant to be together.

I rolled out of bed, showered, dabbed The One perfume by Dolce & Gabbana behind my ears, put a little inside my navel, and trailed a line between my breasts. I put on my black catsuit and my black fur-collared button-up fitted sweater. Zipped up my thigh-high boots. I fingered my natural hair creating wide waves that flowed over my shoulders. Put on my cherry dick-sucking lipstick that men couldn't resist.

My cell phone rang. Hoping it was Darius calling me back, I glanced at the caller ID. It was Bambi.

As I locked my front door, I answered, "I'm not selling my tickets to see Darius play in Cleveland next week."

She laughed. "Hey, Ashlee. Trust me, I understand. I've got tickets for that game but I get that a lot now that I'm Jada's *personal* assistant."

Whoa, wait a minute. Low self-esteemed, overweight all her life, unattractive Bambi was what? "You're Jada Diamond Tanner's *personal* assistant?"

"As in Darius's mother. That's me. You know I was Darius's number-one fan before you got knocked up."

"And that would make me his son's mother for life. So why are you calling me? I haven't heard from you since high school." Graduation was five years ago. When I told Bambi I was pregnant with Darius's baby, she cursed me like he was her husband.

I guess Jada felt sorry for Bambi the way I had. I was Bambi's only friend in elementary and junior high. She was the only obese girl in our elementary school. She'd gained more weight in middle school. By the time we were seniors, Bambi was close to weighing three hundred pounds.

Bambi was infatuated with Darius since we were six years old. Told me her parents were to blame for her obesity because they'd started overfeeding her at birth. She hated her parents. Whatever. If she was still fat, she couldn't use that excuse.

"You gained any weight? Darius probably didn't recognize you when he saw you, huh?"

"Did you take your medication today? Darius knows but he hasn't seen the new me yet. Now that I'm closer to Darius than you are, are you jealous?"

Okay, Bambi was officially my enemy. She was never smarter or prettier than me. She had called to get all up in my business and steal Darius from me. I wanted to curse her out but she wasn't worth it. The only place Darius would sex her was in her dreams.

I tossed my purse on the passenger seat, got in my Benz, started the engine.

"Listen, Ashlee. I'm in LA with Jada and Darius. Jada invited me to a movie premiere tonight so I don't have much time for you. Jada asked me to call and confirm your address so she can send you an invitation to her wedding."

Jada was getting married a third time and I hadn't been married once. No way. "You're lying. Jada would never hire you. What are you up to?"

"You want an invite or what?"

"I'm good." Jada already had my address. "Don't put me on any list of yours. By the way, how're your parents?"

"Dead," she said, then ended the call.

CHAPTER 5

Darius

"**B**aby, I love you so much." I never got tired of telling her that shit because it was my truth. *What the hell. Let it rip.* "I can't hold it any longer. Baby, I want to marry you again." Hell, if T. Parker could marry Eva twice, I could give my baby the big ass wedding she'd dreamt of.

Her hand was at the top of the steering wheel. She slid her hand down to the bottom. Damn, she had the sexiest mannerisms doing the simplest things. Her long straight dark hair flowed over her bare shoulders. Her titties were perched high under her aqua blue halter dress. Her hair, her breasts, all of that shit right there was mine.

My wife made a smooth U-turn, parked at a meter in front of 9200 Sunset. "I'd marry you again in a heartbeat," she said, smiling back at me.

Valet parking for BOA was less than fifty feet away. My wife was one of those women who believed in holding on to what was hers. She preferred self-parking and keeping the keys.

"Then let's do it," I told her.

Her eyes lit up like diamonds. Her smile melted my heart. "Are you serious, Darius? I can have the wedding I've always wanted?"

"Yes, baby. Yes, you can have whatever you want this time."

"Darius Henry Jones, do not tease me."

"Baby, plan it. Honeymoon and all. Let's do it right after the season is over."

The first time we were married we invited family, close friends, and a few of my teammates. My biological dad wanted me to wait until I was thirty before considering marriage. I wasn't letting Fancy leave me twice. He was more concerned with my earnings supporting his future. He didn't understand that by marrying Fancy I was investing in my future. I didn't want to invite a ton of spectators to our ceremony. Unless I was on the court ballin', I never liked witnesses or a crowd.

"Daddy, I want you to marry my mommy. Can you marry her too?" my son asked. "Please. That would make my mommy happy too." His small foot kicked the back of my black leather seat as he waited for me to answer. I had to say something or he'd ask again and kick again.

Kids said the darnedest things, but my son was brainwashed by his mother. Most of what came out of his mouth was his mother speaking through him. No telling what he'd say next. Ashlee had drilled in his head about our one day being a family and how he shouldn't call my wife "mother" or "mommy" but to call her by her first name, Fancy. My wife was okay with DJ calling her by her first name. She wasn't trying to replace Ashlee. My wife was making sure my son had a healthy and happy home. I'd given up on trying to build a relationship between Ashlee and Fancy.

Ashlee was one unfit chick. She was gorgeous on the outside but, man, the demons had invaded her mind. My mom was good at letting DJ talk to Ashlee a couple of times a week, saying, "Darius, you can't change the fact that Ashlee is DJ's mother. He needs her too." Yeah, right. Whatever. Mom hadn't experienced Ashlee the way my wife and I had.

Fancy chuckled at DJ. I lifted my brilliant soon to be four-year-old from his booster seat, and said, "My man, marrying two women would send your daddy to jail. You don't want me to go to prison, do you?"

"Nope, but Mommy does. Mommy said she's going to set you up and send you to jail just like she did Jay."

CHAPTER 6

Bambi

Jada texted me. I've decided not to meet Darius and Fancy for dinner at BOA's. Change the reservation from five to three. See you at the premiere.

Before working for Jada, I slept with my cell phone so I wouldn't miss any of Darius's postings on Facebook or Twitter. Soon as Jada hired me, I searched her files. I stored Darius's home addresses and his cell phone number in my phone.

I'd heard the way to a man's heart was through his stomach. Truth was, the way to a man's heart was a journey through his mother's stomach. I had to become more than Jada's assistant. I had to make her dependent upon my services.

I changed the reservation as requested but I was already in motion to BOA's for Jada to introduce me to Darius. I drove to the corner, whipped a U-turn behind Fancy. I made another U-turn at Doheny Road, then parked my silver convertible rental at the only metered space in front of where Blowfish Sushi to Die For used to be. Contractors were renovating the space for another upscale LA nightclub. I turned off the engine, then watched Darius carry his son to the door of BOA. Darius opened the door, stepped aside, then entered after Fancy.

A walnut-size lump lodged in my throat. I longed for the day that I'd be the woman in front of him. I tapped on my cell, waited a few seconds, then heard, "Thanks for calling BOA Steakhouse. How may we serve you?"

I swallowed my envy, then answered, "I'd like to change the reservation for Darius Jones from five to three please."

"The party of three is being seated now. Is there anything else I can help you with?"

"That'll be all," I said, ending the call.

Working for Jada allowed me to use her name or Darius's name for my personal reservations too. For the first time in my life, I was an extension of celebrity. I was above Ashlee.

I had kept every news article on Darius Henry Jones since he'd played high school basketball. Fell in love with him in kindergarten the first day his mother brought him to school. I was the quiet overweight girl at St. Boniface. The boys gave me their food; the LA girls gave me attitude.

Ashlee's dad Lawrence and Darius's mom started dating when we were all six years old. Darius never considered Lawrence his dad. I felt bad for Darius when the media announced he'd changed his name to Williams, then changed it back to Jones. His mother was wrong for lying to him about who his real dad was. Most of what I knew about Darius before working for his mom I'd read in the paper or saw on the news.

It didn't take Maury to say, "Wellington Jones, you are not the father." Darius looked exactly like Darryl Williams and nothing like his so-called dad. I wasn't hating on Jada for lying but she'd stepped to the left on that one. Right or wrong, sometimes a woman had to make the best decision for her life and not give a damn about what a man thought.

Removing my sunglasses from my purse, I placed them on my head, then refreshed my lip gloss. My first day working for Jada, I'd memorized Darius's personal profile on her computer. I knew a lot more about my Darius, like his favorite steak was rib-eye cooked medium. Under intimate apparel his preferred underwear were black boxer briefs.

One day I'd persuade Darius to divorce Fancy and marry me. Waiting for Fancy to cheat on Darius hadn't worked thus far. Her ass showed up courtside at every damn game with Darius's son. I had to find a way to convince Darius that divorcing Fancy was his idea. I stood next to the hostess, scanned the room, then opted to sit at the bar facing the booth where Darius and his family were seated.

En route to the bar I saw Lamar with that Khloe chick and a few other folk seated at a booth on the patio. Marrying money didn't upgrade every woman. That shimmering silver long-sleeved mini-dress she'd worn to the Grammys after-party was bangin' but not on her body. Besides, why was she in line with the ordinaries? Bet her sister Kim wouldn't have stood in line to get in.

Scanning the patrons, Adam Zacharius, one of the youngest men in Hollywood to manage a media company, was seated at the opposite end of the bar chopping it up with his fiancée. He'd recently finished the film *The Company We Keep,* based on the novel written by Mary Monroe.

"I'll have a vodka martini stirred," I told the bartender, then picked up the menu.

Glancing over my shoulder, I admired Darius for three seconds. I had videos of all his games and of his wedding when he married that bitch Fancy. *Look at her ass all happy and shit. Your meter is expired. Time up. Bitch, you have got to go!*

I was at Madison Square Garden when Darius was drafted, went to all of his home games in Atlanta, traveled to all his away games. I'd saved photos from the Internet in my phone of his son, his ex-wife, his new wife, his mother, his step and biological fathers, and Ashlee. That trick was almost crazier than me. Bet she was still trying to figure out how I'd gotten her number.

"Um, um, um. You are the best," I told the bartender. Before taking another sip of my martini, I said, "I'll have a half dozen oysters on the half shell," to spike my libido.

Until I married Darius, I had to get my fuck on just like him. I rummaged through my purse, made sure my bottle of five-milligram Cialis was in there. Had to keep track of my pills. Without hesitation I'd slip a penile enhancement pill on a man in a minute. I took fucking seriously and wasn't taking any chances on a limp dick or premature ejaculator leaving me with an angry wet ass.

The fucking around Darius had done on Fancy was coming to an end when we got married. Let me catch him with my dick on any parts of another chick, I'd fuck him up worse than Ashlee had done Jay.

But Ashlee had better not think about coming between Darius and me or she'd turn up face down floating in the Potomac River. The president would find Osama bin Laden before anyone would find her depressed miserable ass.

Exhaling, I gulped the remainder of my drink, balanced the olive on the tip of my tongue, then swallowed it whole. "Bartender, another, please." The sight of Fancy angered the hell out of me. If I could pick up this black granite countertop and drop it on her head, I would. I didn't have an affinity for kids but Darius was too close to both of them for me to try anything violent.

I had a life-size six-eleven body-length pillow made in the image of Darius. Every home love potion I'd created to make Darius fall in love with me had failed. My last chance was to visit the two-headed lady. I'd found her web site online, e-mailed her my information. For five thousand dollars she'd agreed to cast a surefire love spell on my Darius. He was worth every penny. Next week I had an appointment to take Darius's loc to the two-headed lady down in New Orleans. I'd picked up the dreadlock that fell from his head when he was sitting on the sidelines at one of his games.

The two-headed lady told me, "Don't contact me again. Just come. I will know when you are here. When you arrive, come to the French Quarter."

I prayed she wasn't scamming me. She was my one last chance to cast a spell. If her spell didn't work, I'd do the unimaginable. I'd kill Fancy.

I was Darius Jones's number-one fan. He just didn't know it . . . yet.

CHAPTER 7

Fancy

She was eerie. The woman seated at the end of the bar. The sound of acrylic nails slowly scratching along a chalkboard pierced my eardrums when she stared at me.

I didn't want to stare back at her. I was temporarily paralyzed. I'd seen those morbid deep-set eyes before but couldn't recall where. Her pupils seem dilated. Her eyes were darker than her black hair and brows. She was five-feet six or seven without her high heels. Her curly shoulder-length mane was shiny. She was so pale she could pass for black, white, or Latina. Her thick lips were plastered with a vibrant watermelon shine. Could've been permanent lipstick layered with a gloss. Her lips were too perfect to tell. She was a B cup, with a flat stomach and narrow straight hips. She was a comfortable size six, maybe a eight.

I noticed two distinct things about her. Her raspy voice, and the fact that her pointed nose had a flat bridge. The sunglasses that she removed from the top of her head, then sat on the counter wouldn't fit her face unless she'd worn an adjustable strap or had a nose implant.

"Baby, please, can you stop texting for a minute?" I needed my husband's attention.

"Two more minutes and I'm done," Darius said, rapidly pressing keys with his thumbs.

One thing I learned the short time I'd lived in the City of Angels (before relocating to Atlanta with my husband) was most women in Los Angeles were anything but angels. I'd mastered the LA body scan. Took me three seconds to check out a person. First, I'd flash the person's face, then I'd notice their shoes. Finally, I'd quickly scroll my eyes back up to their face.

In those three seconds I could vividly recall a person's eye color, nose, lips, forehead, cheeks, shoes and style, ankles, body size, hips, hands, nails, waist, breasts, and clothes. My karate skills sharpened my memory of people and places.

Knowing karate had saved my life when my mom's ex-man tried to kill me. When I was a little girl, I'd lied on Thaddeus. Told the police he'd raped me. Unlike Ashlee's lying on Jay, I'd done it to save my mother's life. My mother was afraid to tell the police Thaddeus had beaten her. I was a kid trying to be an adult when I had him arrested but I had no indication he'd get out of prison and come after me.

Two years ago Thaddeus broke into my apartment, tried to kill me, and Darius killed him. No doubt my husband would die for me. That woman at the bar, her spirit haunted me like she was Thaddeus. I wondered. Could a dead person seek revenge though another person's soul?

I'd definitely seen that woman before. Eventually it'd come back to me. I wasn't insecure or paranoid but whosoever she was she'd given me bad vibes. I'd felt that gut-wrenching feeling before. Most of the times my stomach churned like that at Darius's games. Sometimes I felt it at the park when playing with DJ. Today, I felt it on our way into the restaurant. It was as if someone was stalking us.

CHAPTER 8

Bambi

Keeping track of Darius, I picked up my spy sunglasses, activated the video record button, sat my black glasses on the edge of the bar facing Darius, Fancy, and DJ, then proceeded to suck an oyster off the shell.

"Um, um, um." The natural sea salt flavor of oyster juices trickling down my throat reminded me of the taste that oozed from the pores of Darius's dick onto my tongue right before he came in my mouth. That was after Ashlee, before Fancy. Jada had no idea how close I was to her son.

It was no accident that I'd gotten this job working for Jada or that I was attending the movie premiere later tonight for *Something on the Side*, starring Velvet Waters. It was by accident that I'd found a background check in Jada's archives for a Lace St. Thomas, also known as Honey Thomas.

Fancy stared at me. I stared back. *Bitch, you don't scare me. Best keep your eyes on my man while you got him.* By the time Fancy realized who I was, I'd be laying on her side of the bed next to Darius.

The little boy sat in a booster seat between them hugging Darius's neck. He was cute. *Enjoy the ride, kid. Your days are numbered too.* I'd find a way to detach DJ from Darius and send DJ to live full-time with Ashlee. Parenting should keep her occupied.

Anyone attached to Darius Jones, directly or indirectly, was also attached to me. My list, including Jada, Honey, Fancy, Ashlee, Grant, Velvet, Valentino, Rita, Jean, Sapphire, Benito, Summer, Ciara, and Maxine, were all on speed dial. I'd done background checks on all of them. It was ridiculous how Jada's executives—Ginger, Heather, Zen, and Miranda—had fucked my Darius. I had those cougars' numbers too.

I picked up my sunglasses to make sure the recorder was on, placed them back on the bar facing Darius, then sucked up another oyster. Imagining Darius's tongue was in my mouth instead of in his wife's, I closed my eyes and let the juices saturate my palate. I opened my eyes. I couldn't stand watching him drool over Fancy. What made that trick so special?

Fancy disgusted me. I'd seen enough. *Enough!* I picked up my glasses, dropped forty on the counter, then stormed out of the restaurant. Two weeks on the job and I was ready to give my two weeks' notice. Wasn't sure how long I could tolerate working for Jada. I had to execute my plan quick.

Sitting in my car, I made a call. "Meet me right now," I said, giving her my location. I ended the call, walked to the corner, entered City National Bank and made a sizable cash withdrawal.

I went back to my car, turned on my radio, listened to KJLH. Thirty minutes later she parked her white pickup in the yellow zone in front of my car. I motioned for her to come get in my car.

She dragged her feet, draped her purse across her shoulder. A resounding, "Hey, Bambi," escaped her mouth when she climbed in.

For a small woman, Rita sure was loud. Pointing across the street, I told her, "That's Darius's SUV. I need for you to take care of the woman who gets in the car with him."

"Take care of her how? In a good or bad way?"

"In the worst way possible," I said, staring at their SUV.

I'd found Rita's information in the background check on Jada's computer for Honey. She was from the small town of Flagstaff, Arizona. The first time I spoke on the phone with Rita, I instantly realized she was easily persuaded. The envelope I handed her, containing five thousand dollars, would convince her to get my job done.

"Oh, this sure is a lot of money," she said, stuffing the cash in her purse. She gave me the empty envelope. "Thanks, Bambi. How you want me to do it?"

Clenching my teeth, I told her, "I don't care how, but make it happen today. If you do a good job, I'll give you another five grand in the morning." With Rita doing my dirty work, I'd be out of the picture. Hopefully Fancy would too.

I waited for Rita to get out, dropped my convertible top, revved my engine, then sped to my hotel room for a quick change of wardrobe. In no time I was off to the premiere of *Something on the Side.*

CHAPTER 9

Fancy

Glad he'd put his iPhone in his hip case, I asked Darius, "Baby, did that woman seem strange to you?"

Hunching his shoulders, he asked, "What woman?"

"The one who just left the bar. She had on white low-rise jeans, a white silk tank, a brown Gucci belt, brown slip-on Gucci heels, a real Gucci handbag, and she put her sunglasses on the counter facing us. She was sitting on the end," I said, pointing to the stool where a man was now seated.

He laughed. "Man, you were all over her. This is our day, not hers. Stop tripping. There's lots of women at the bar," he said, lightly kissing my lips.

Struggling to dismiss the feeling, I kissed him back. Perhaps I was tripping, but her bad vibes crept through me. Fearing things with my husband were too good to be true, I exhaled, trying to relax and enjoy my family.

I smiled, then said, "I want SaVoy to be my matron of honor. My mom is going to be so excited and my little sister is going to be our flower girl. DJ, you are going to be the ring bearer. I'm going to fly in my favorite makeup artist, Kim May, from D.C. And I have to ask G. Garvin to cater the reception." I bounced in my seat trying to shake off the negative energy. The feelings stuck with the adhesiveness of Krazy Glue.

Darius nodded as I continued. "I'm inviting all my clients and I want your entire team to be at our wedding. I'm inviting the media too. And hopefully your mom won't mind handling the publicity so we can be on *Wendy Williams, Mo'Nique, Tyra,* and hopefully we can do *Oprah* before she ends her show—"

"Whoa. Baby, baby. Exhale. Whatever you want, Ladycat. This is your fantasy wedding come true," Darius said. "But."

I gasped, braced my back against the booth. "No, 'buts,' honey." I hadn't eaten all day. My stomach churned, then growled to the movement of trapped air. "Don't say it. I don't want to hear any 'buts.' "

He licked his lips, then smiled. "You can't marry me again until I propose again," he said.

Darius stood on the chocolate leather seat, tapped a spoon against his half-full water glass. DJ sprung from his booster seat, stood on the seat next to his dad. I was embarrassed and proud at the same time. The two most important men in my life were with me. Finding a husband was easy. Finding a man who loved me for me was a blessing. Darius reached into his pocket, pulled out a white box.

I held my breath, covered my mouth.

"I want everyone here to witness this. I love my wife so much, I'm proposing to her again."

Stepping from the booth to the floor, Darius knelt before me on one knee. DJ jumped off the booth, placed his hand on his dad's shoulder. I slid to the edge. Darius stared into my eyes, then said, "Fancy Taylor Jones, will you marry me, again?"

My body trembled uncontrollably. I felt like Disney's next black princess. I'd go anywhere with my husband. Do whatever for him. For a moment I questioned if I deserved this much happiness. I'd disrupted Byron's marriage, ruined my ex-boyfriend Desmond's belief in women, and . . . I didn't want to conjure emotions about Thaddeus or that strange woman but they'd surfaced for a moment until Darius opened the ring box.

First, I was speechless. The diamonds set in platinum blinded me. I hugged Darius, then screamed.

DJ patted me on the thigh, pressed his pointing finger to his lips. "Fancy, use your indoor voice."

"My man."

"Grown folks' convo, Daddy?"

"You got it."

I swore the entire restaurant could see the diamond's shine darting from my eyes. I cried, covered my mouth, cried, nodded, then cried some more. "I love you, Darius Jones." In part, my tears were to cleanse my spirit of the unhappiness I'd caused others.

Darius kissed my tears, then placed the ring on my finger. "This two-carat pear-cut diamond that points toward you represents a teardrop from my heart to yours. The one that points toward me represents a teardrop from your heart to mine. The three-carat heart-shaped diamond in the middle is a symbol of our infinite love."

I thought I'd die from joy. He'd put a lot of thought into this and kept it a secret until now. Wow.

Gliding the ring on my finger, my husband said, "No matter where we are, we will always be together. The seven total carats mean we are indivisible. Divorce is not an option."

Everyone in the restaurant applauded us. I hugged my man. I kissed my husband. Told him, "I love you," repeatedly.

DJ leapt onto the booth, tapped Darius's side. "Daddy." He shook his head, then said, "Mommy's not gonna be hap—"

Why should Ashlee be happy? It was her mistakes that allowed me to have her son's father and custody of her son.

Darius quickly covered DJ's mouth. "My man, right now I need you on my team." Darius removed his hand, then gestured for a response from DJ. Darius stood, placed his huge hand on DJ's chest, then eased DJ's back against the booth.

DJ's eyes scrolled all the way to Darius's. "I am on your team, Daddy. I'm the sixth man, remember?" He nodded upward. His hands moved up and down as he tried his best to explain. "Mommy said I have to look out for you because you always make mistakes. Like when that lady sucked your—"

Darius interrupted, "Check, please."

CHAPTER 10

Darius

Sho nuff this is my DNA.

I shook my head at my son. "My man. Chill for a sec."

Thank God Fancy didn't address anything DJ had said. My wife found out firsthand how crazy my son's mother was when Ashlee slipped her an abortion pill. Ashlee killed our firstborn while it was still in Fancy's womb.

Another lesson I'd learned. After a breakup, change all the locks to my house. Ashlee had entered my house, replaced my aspirin with abortion pills, then drove my wife insane enough for Fancy to take what she'd thought was aspirin. I hated thinking about that shit. I told my wife, "We're celebrating the rest of this day.

"Hold your hand up." I took a picture with my cell phone, posted it on Facebook with the caption, Just proposed to my wife again. We're doing it huge this time!

I kissed my son. "Give your dad a hug." It wasn't his fault his mother had brainwashed him. I wished my mom would stop calling Ashlee for DJ and letting her fill his head with all that foolishness. Bad enough Ashlee's weekend visitation was coming up. I dreaded calling her back.

Ashlee was bitter. Her life's mission was to destroy men, myself included. This guy Jay who my son mentioned earlier, I wasn't sure who he was but I knew it was in my best interest to find out. Wasn't sure I wanted to know why he was really behind bars but I had to know if Ashlee was responsible. I'd bet money that Ashlee woke up angry, went to bed mad at the world, and spent her day contemplating how to break up me and my wife. I was already knowing Ashlee was going to explode atomic bomb style when she saw Fancy's second engagement ring. This was my life and my wife and I couldn't care less what Ashlee felt or thought.

"Make our order to go and toss in a bottle of champagne," I said, handing the waiter my credit card. I dialed my mom to give her the news about our second wedding. Solemnly she answered, "Hey, baby."

Was there a full moon coming tonight or what? I'd heard something about a full monster moon. My mom didn't sound happy, and earlier, Fancy was tripping over the chick at the bar. Of course I saw her—who didn't? My peripheral vision was spectacular on and off the court, but I wasn't insane enough to say, "You mean the fine ass bitch sucking up oysters like she was sucking up dicks?" She was a 909.

My teammates came up with a coding system for females. Nine being the highest, the first number represented a woman's face. The second number had to be zero or one. Zero meant we hadn't fucked with her. One meant we had. And the last number represented her body.

I asked, "Ma, what's wrong now? I knew you should've joined us."

Fancy looked at my face. Frowned. "Your mom okay?"

I held up my hand toward my wife. "Hold on a minute, Ma." Pressing mute on my cell, I told Fancy, "Sign off on the bill. We'll be in the car."

I walked outside, strapped DJ in his booster seat, doubled-checked to make sure the seat belt was snug across his shoulder, then sat in the front passenger seat. "Ma, give it to me. Straight."

"It's nothing for you to worry about, sweetheart."

"Is that Grant guy disrespecting you? Is he tripping? If so, we can cancel the wedding and I can make him disappear from your life permanently." Not the way Ashlee might do. I'd never send an innocent man to prison. I wasn't that devious.

"It's okay. I can handle him, sweetheart. He wants me to go to the movie premiere with him tonight. I wouldn't mind if his ex, Honey, wasn't going to be there. Just not sure I'm feeling up to any ghetto drama, that's all."

Truth be told, sometimes men liked a little fire in our women. I loved how my wife was nice, strong when necessary, and if she got a head start, she could drop a dude my size. Bring him crashing to his knees. My mom was strong in many ways but she was weak for men. Wellington. My dad. This dude Grant.

"I'm sending a car for you, Ma. Come hang out with us. We're taking our food to go. If you're hungry, I'll have Fancy order whatever you want. I want to see you smile. Hear your happy voice. Besides, it's not often we're back home in LA at the same time."

LA was special. I loved coming back to my house in the Valley. I had my fully furnished spot, my sports cars, the SUV we were rolling in, and my business here. My mom had the same but tonight she was in tow with dude and I didn't want her to feel obligated to hang with him if he was making her miserable.

I had to give Mom a lot of the credit for my happiness. Coast to coast my face lived on billboards. My new office building, Somebody's Gotta Be on Top, was state of the art and I was fully staffed with a hundred and one employees. I was so big in the industry I was the first baller to endorse myself.

"I'm okay, sweetheart. We're heading out in a few. Bambi will be there if I need anything. I'll call you later tonight after it's over. Give my grandson a kiss for me."

"That I can do. Ma. I love you. Thanks for always being there for me. You don't always have to be Superwoman. You don't need Bambi. Let me be here for you."

Mom sniffled, then said, "I love you too, sweetheart. Bye."

DJ was too far away for me to kiss him, so I kissed my hand, touched my son's leg, then said, "My man, that's a kiss from your grandma."

I had no problem showing my son love and affection. Had no problem keeping him in check either. Didn't want him to become the spoiled brat I was. I'd had so many women, I'd lost count by the time I'd met Fancy.

"Your mom okay?" Fancy asked, placing our food and champagne behind her seat. She settled in behind the wheel.

"She's good. Just wish she'd stop seeing that dude. She's not happy with him. Why do women cling to men who make them unhappy?"

"Darius, stop acting like you're the parent. They're not dating. They're engaged." My wife reminded me of what I knew but didn't want to acknowledge.

My mom was holding on to Grant the way Maxine had held on to me. I was happy as hell I hadn't married Maxine. She was one of those ultra-conservative boring females. I'd heard that madness that a good girl was the kind of woman a man should marry. Bullshit. Boring wives deserved to get cheated on.

Sometimes I wondered if it was my fault Maxine had contracted HIV. Wasn't sure Maxine would've cheated on me had I not cheated on her. Payback was a dumb reason for any woman to open her legs. With my promiscuous ways, one would think I would've contracted the disease, not her. Maxine had two lovers: me, and the dude who infected her. I was the male whore, so to speak, and not ashamed of my past, mind you. My whoring around before settling down made me a better man and a damn good husband.

Fancy started the engine, left the car in park, then said, "Oh, Darius, should we fly everybody to Paris? Spain? Italy? Should we get married on a yacht on the French Riviera? What about one of New York's garden rooftops?"

"Whatever you want, Ladycat. Whatever *you* want."

I gloated reading the comments and tweets.

You the man, dawg!

I want one, Darius. I'll marry you too!

If I get one of those, you can have whatever you like.

The last comment was from a dude and had to be removed.

"For real, Darius. You just gave me this ring and your head is buried in your phone."

"Sorry, baby. I'm just reading the responses." Three hundred fifty-six comments in less than a half hour after posting. Damn. I could have a thousand tricks hitting me up before midnight.

The women I'd fucked, including my son's mother, had come to me with their pussies on silver platters. Well, that wasn't exactly true about Ashlee. I pursued her. There was something pure, innocent, and naïve about her at first. She believed in me, like my mom.

Fancy turned off the engine, opened her purse, got her phone, started texting too. I hated that shit. Watching my wife out the corners of my eyes as she texted made me jealous. Who the fuck was she texting? What messages was she sending? She scanned her surroundings, then looked at me as she tapped the keys. She only looked down to read a response, then she was at it again. Typing, faster.

I couldn't match her speed so I laughed knowing I'd interrupt her thoughts. I kept reading my messages. My son was quiet. Probably asleep.

"My mom should've come. She's going to love your ring."

Fancy was quiet. Sometimes her emotions went from hot to cold but her pussy was always a hundred and six. She couldn't outdo me with texting. She only had one close girlfriend and a bunch of clients. If I showed my wife the postings that just came in, her blood would boil. She'd lose her mind. That's what happens when girls sign up for the boys' club. They get burned.

A person would have to be slick times ten to get over on Darius Jones.

CHAPTER 11

Bambi

I sat at the computer desk in my hotel room at the Hollywood Renaissance braiding my naturally curly black hair into eleven corn-
rows wondering if women in prison resembled me.

Not wanting to drive to my parents' house in Long Beach, I'd
checked into this hotel. Technically their house, free and clear, was
now mine. I'd lived with my parents until the double-assisted suicides
happened a year ago.

I stared in the mirror, covered my forehead, eyes, and nose with a
mesh net stocking cap, then called Ashlee.

She answered, "Stop calling me!"

"What's up with the yelling? I thought you might want custody of
your son. I could help you get DJ back. You want in on my plan?"

"What are you up to?"

"In or out?"

"Out," she said.

"Sleep on the idea, kiddo. I'll call you with details," I said, ending
the call. She knew she wanted her son back. Couldn't blame her for
not trusting me. My being weird was my parents' fault. My obstacles
taught me how to be hardcore effective.

My childhood was abnormal. Too many unspeakable things happened inside my home. I believed school was my escape, until my first

day. Why was I a doughnut when the other kids were shaped like Twinkies?

My classmates teased me about my weight. The pretty girls like Ashlee Anderson befriended me so I could be their ugly girlfriend and they could get all the attention from boys. Outside of school, I wasn't permitted to socialize. Ashlee was my friend at school. I liked her until she made me hate her. Why did she have to have Darius's baby? She had to take DJ because he wasn't living with Darius and me.

Properly placing the stocking cap atop my head, I smiled. A million-dollar payoff to the coroner and my parents' causes of death were documented as cardiac arrest. Their cases were closed, and I got what I deserved, a twenty-million-dollar cash settlement, the house, and my parents' interest in their law firm. In exchange for leaving my parents' financial interest intact, the remaining partners agreed to provide me with pro bono legal services and representation in perpetuity.

The amazing things one could do with money. I hired a personal trainer, lost a hundred pounds, and had a few nips and tucks. I looked so good I doubted anyone from elementary, junior, or high school would recognize me when they saw me, including Ashlee and Darius.

I applied a small amount of eyebrow glue to the back of my 100 percent human hair brows, then looked into the magnifying mirror, and perfectly layered each blond-colored brow over my jet black brows. I glued on my light brown eyelashes. Just as I finished trailing a thin line of glue along the edge of my hairline, my cell phone buzzed.

"Make it fast," I said. I had to apply my full lace wig before the glue got tacky.

"Bambi, it's done," she said. "I got her good, Bambi, but I think I—"

Country bitch. I hissed, "Not on the phone. Tell me in person. I'll call you after the premiere and tell you where to meet me tomorrow morning. I want full details." I ended the call.

That woman was so desperate for a dollar she'd throw her firstborn under a bus, then roll over them. When I hired her she told me there were two things she'd never do and that was kill or steal. For the right price, she'd do both. The services Rita provided were worth more than I agreed to pay her. The fact that she didn't know her self-worth wasn't my responsibility. She'd get what she'd negotiated.

Securing my twenty-two-inch blond wig along my hairline, I waited fifteen minutes, stood, held my head upside down, brushed, then fluffed my hair.

I applied my concealer, foundation, and brown eyeliner. I stroked on various hues of sparkling green eye shadow, toned it down with a hint of jade, and brushed on a cotton-candy pink lipstick. I inserted my light blue contacts. After easing into my padded butt panties that would make Serena Williams jealous, I stuffed silicone breast pads into the sides of my bra to sandwich my B cups into a facade of perfect DDs that gave me amazing cleavage. My beaded forest green designer gown hugged my curves. I stepped into iridescent stilettos, picked up my purse, then double checked to make sure I had my ticket.

Instantly I went from being a fair-complexioned African-American woman to looking like Anna Nicole Smith with a perfect tan. I kissed the plastic covering on a photo of my Darius, then placed it back in my purse. His picture was my good luck charm. With Darius by my side, all things were possible.

Slipping my room key into my handbag, I grabbed my Ho-on-the-Go travel bag (filled with a complete change of clothes), left my suite, and made my way to the lobby. The bellman smiled at me. "You are one gorgeous woman. Can I, make that, *may* I assist you with your bag?"

"Thanks, but no thanks, handsome. My driver is right there," I politely said. Easing into the backseat of the black stretch limousine, I thought, *Neither the offer nor the compliment would've been extended a hundred pounds ago.*

I gazed out the window, then became lost in Bambiland wondering how I'd use Darius's mother tonight. There was a thin line between being professional and personal. Since I had access to Jada's company's files, the choice was mine.

I'd come up with something.

CHAPTER 12

Bambi

A long line of limos led to the theater. My driver opened my door. "Make sure you transfer my black leather bag to the Town Car that's picking me up. Have the other driver here in thirty minutes."

I swooped my thick wavy tresses to one side, thrust my breasts forward, arched my back, and smiled as though I was Mrs. Darius Jones. An usher escorted me to my seat. I sat one row to the right behind my future mother-in-law. By the end of the night, I would become Jada's newest best friend or she would be my worst enemy. Getting past Jada to get to Darius wasn't going to be easy but I refused to let her stop me.

The lights slightly dimmed. Jada glanced over her shoulder, looked directly at me. Quickly I turned my head, fingered my hair down my cheek so she couldn't see my face.

She tapped my leg, then said, "That seat is for my assistant. You'll have to—"

A very pregnant woman being escorted by a tall thin man with a long ponytail stepped sideways in front of Grant and Jada, commanding Jada's attention. When the pregnant woman sat down next to Jada, Jada turned to Grant, stared into his eyes, squinted, then frowned. I noticed Jada's jaw tighten like a nutcracker cracking a walnut.

Aw, damn. That's Honey. Her pictures on Google didn't do her justice.

Honey was gorgeous and pregnant. And she was with Valentino? Once I make a few phone calls, Valentino will be back behind bars where he belongs. Pimping and pandering, Valentino had had one foot in prison all his life except he'd managed to keep both of them free most of the time to trample on his prostitutes. He was a slick motherfucker and a slick motherfucker like him could interrupt my flow if he got too close.

Halfway through the movie, Honey moaned and held her stomach but continued watching the movie. *Here we go.* Something was about to jump off. I clutched my purse, held my phone, prepared to make a move.

Ten minutes went by. I decided to monitor my home in Long Beach from my iPhone. Outside there was nothing unusual. I checked my bedroom. Normal. I turned on the back porch and kitchen lights, turned off the living room lights, then peeped inside my parents' bedroom. The coffins were closed just like I'd left them.

After the credits rolled, the director proposed to Velvet. Right as Honey's water broke, Velvet accepted his marriage proposal, then Grant asked Honey, "Is that my baby?"

My jaw dropped. Jada stood, did the pee-pee dance. Jada was truly going to need a friend. I thought I was on top of things, but this was new and valuable information. Jada's cell phone rang, temporarily interrupting the flow of things.

Honey answered Grant, "It's not your child, but these babies are your twin boys."

Well, thank God they weren't Valentino's. He already had three children he wasn't taking care of. Left his wife and kids, for what? To try to be the man for another woman? To raise Honey's babies? How he gon' put an engagement ring on Honey's finger when that fool was still legally married? According to Jada's file on Valentino, Summer was the best thing that ever happened to him. Hopefully Summer won't come running to bail him out this time.

Jada stopped speaking into her phone long enough to call Honey a liar. Jada walked away, returned, then cried to Grant, "Fancy was hit by a driver. We've got to go to the hospital."

Bingo! I said to myself. That was what my contact meant when she'd said, "I got her good." *Yes!*

Jada yelled, "Grant! Did you hear me? Darius's wife was hit by a driver! Let's go!"

I guess people had the right to be consumed with their issues. Jada was worried about Fancy. Grant was worried about Honey. And I was concerned with my Darius. He needed me to console him. I had to find out what hospital they were at.

My intention to get Darius was no fly-by-night suck-his-dick groupie trick. Oh, no. I'd already sucked his dick twice but he wouldn't remember. How could he? I was never the same woman twice. I was determined to either marry him or massacre him. If I couldn't have Darius Jones, no woman would, especially Fancy.

I had to make sure Fancy's hospital stay was permanent.

CHAPTER 13

Jada

My heart dropped to the floor when Grant didn't move a step. I had two choices. Drag him or leave him. I glanced at the woman sitting in Bambi's seat. Maybe Bambi had changed her mind about coming and gave her ticket to the white woman behind me. Refusing to make a spectacle of myself, I hiked up the hem of my gown, then stormed out the theater.

One heel clicked in front of the other. My pace increased to a light jog down the aisle and out the back exit. Frantically I searched for Grant's driver's limo. Rows of black stretch Escalades, Hummers, Lexuses, and Tahoes lined the parking lot. Holding my gown inches above my ankles, I gulped the warm car exhaust air in attempt to prevent an anxiety attack.

I turned 180 degrees and bumped into the white woman in a green gown who was practically on my heels. "I'm so sorry," she said, then asked, "Are you okay? I overheard you say someone was in an accident. Is there anything I can do to help you?"

Her Valley girl tone made me frown. She was extremely buxom for a woman of her race, like she was a black woman trapped in a white person's body. Her blue eyes stared into mine. I turned another 180 degrees. "Where is his driver?" The line for taxis was unbelievable. I couldn't give up. Darius and Fancy needed me. Panting, I leaned forward, placed my hands on my knees.

"I can give you a ride to the hospital," the woman said. "I'm headed that way and my driver is right there." She pointed at a black Town Car less than a hundred feet away. I didn't want to leave Grant with Honey.

Beep. Beep. I glanced up but didn't straighten up until I heard Grant's voice. "Jada, over here."

Thank God. I told the woman, "I appreciate your offer but I have a ride."

I hopped in the back of Grant's limo, sat beside him, then told the driver, "Take us to Cedars Hospital quick. It's an emergency."

My body shivered but I wasn't cold. I was worried about Fancy, Darius, my grandbaby, and my relationship. I was terribly upset with and disappointed in Grant for believing Honey but grateful that he hadn't abandoned me.

"Can't you find a faster way out of this jam, driver?"

"Doing the best I can, ma'am, without going over the top."

Grant laughed. I didn't.

Timing was horrible but I had to ask Grant, "What is your obsession with her?"

"Her? I'm here with you, aren't I?"

He was with me but he was torn between her and me. I wasn't going to be Grant's rebound. "Her, yes, her. Honey. That 'her.' Now answer the question."

"What was the question, again?"

"Don't play with me."

Grant turned away, stared at the black tinted window. I stared at his reflection. He couldn't escape me or my question.

"Look, it's not an obsession. I know Honey. I'm the father. She wouldn't lie to me," he said, still looking away.

Men. Grant didn't want me to see the uncertainty in his eyes. He prayed he was the father because he wanted Honey. Otherwise, he'd be on my side. He had to choose. No way was I signing up for a three-some or a five-some.

I demanded. "Look at me." I waited, made an eye-to-eye connection, then continued, "Oh, but you lied to me." I searched for answers I already knew. "How did she get pregnant if you claimed you used protection? Huh? We could've ended this relationship nine months ago."

Grant stared at the floor, shook his head. "Jada, we've got more important things to concern ourselves with. This is not the time to argue."

"Oh, so now I'm Jada and not 'baby.' Admit that you lied to me, Grant! Admit it, damn it!" Maybe I should've accepted that ride from that nice lady.

"If it'll make you feel better, okay, you're right. You're always right. Satisfied? I lied to you but that doesn't change the fact that Fancy is injured and Honey is about to deliver *my* boys. Driver, please hurry. I don't want to miss my sons being born."

I slid closer to him. My thigh touched his, reminding me how muscular his body was. How great his naked body felt lying next to mine. This man had sexed me senseless. Made me feel young again.

"No, Grant. She's about to deliver her babies. Until we have a paternity test, I consider this one more lie to add to her list of trifling ways. Maybe I should call the police and tell them where to find Ms. Prostitute. Huh? Ms. Madam. Huh? Save you the disappointment. She's unfit and you know it. How about I do you that favor?"

Grant became quiet. His jaw flinched. He sucked then licked his upper teeth. "How about I tell you that"—Grant paused, looked me in the eyes, then continued—"I'm still in love with Honey."

Smack! My involuntary reflexes hit him. I went to slap Grant's face again. He grabbed my wrist.

"Stop it, Jada. Don't you ever, ever hit me again. I'm trying to be honest with you. I thought I'd gotten her out of my system by not seeing her for nine months but—" He stopped speaking midsentence. A tear fell. He blinked.

I knew that feeling all too well but wasn't going to admit it to Grant. I told him, "I'd be lying if I said I understood. I don't. Why am I wearing this?" I asked him, wiggling my engagement ring in front his face. "What about the million dollars my son has already paid for our wedding? I didn't pursue you, Grant. You—" I stopped speaking.

I wanted to slap his face again. I wanted to push him out of the moving limo. I wanted to hurt him more than he'd hurt me. I deserved somebody to love me the way he loved Honey. My Wellington was my soul mate. He loved me like no other man but I couldn't bring him back. I had womanly needs that I wanted Grant to continue fulfilling.

Wellington and I had lots of great days but over time they were always interrupted by that no good Melanie Marie Thompson. There was always a woman lurking in search of destroying my good relationship. When Wellington and I were engaged, Melanie had lied and said she was pregnant with his triplets. She knew damn well her babies weren't for him. But like a fool (or a good man), Wellington believed her and did what he thought was right. He married her. So I left them in the Bay area and moved from Oakland to Los Angeles. After Wellington found out the truth we reunited and eventually married. Years later, when he was in the hospital dying, I wished I'd never found out that he'd never stopped seeing Melanie.

Why do men lie so damn much? Why do I keep falling in love with the same type of man? Maybe I should just let Grant go. He's already telling me he's never going to give up Honey. What was more important was for me not to take him back when he finds out those babies aren't his.

I was glad the driver was on La Cienega Boulevard in front of Bloomingdale's at the Beverly Center. "Go down Beverly and drop me off at the Emergency entrance." I needed to get away from Grant and inhale fresh air before I passed out or knocked him out.

"Hey, I'm sorry," he said, holding my hand. "I never meant for this to come out, not this way. I have too much respect for you. It's just seeing her and not knowing, you know?"

I wasn't about to accept his indirect apology. He'd known she was pregnant. When was he going to tell me? That was the question. In his heart, he knew he wanted her and not me. That hurt.

I removed his engagement ring from my finger, placed it in his hand, and said, "You owe my son a million dollars. Take your ring and save your apology for Honey. We're done. No, make that, I'm done with you and your lies. And one more thing. Don't ever call me again. And another thing, I hate you! And . . . and . . ." Wow. In less than five minutes after giving back his ring, I'd run out of negative things to say to Grant.

But I wasn't done with him yet. Oh, no. I was just getting started.

CHAPTER 14

Bambi

"**G**et out the goddamn car, tricks." What on earth were Jada and Grant doing? Women. Damn. She was probably tripping because those babies might be his. Not like his sperm could crack her mother hen eggs. "Get out of the damn car!"

"Stop here at this street meter," I told the driver. Didn't want us to create a *Coming to America* scene with multiple luxury cars in front of Emergency, thinking we were lost shopaholics who were supposed to be across the street at the Beverly Center.

En route to the hospital I'd done a quick wardrobe change in the car. Wasn't much I could do in the short time frame to alter my blond hair and brows so I gathered my hair on top of my head and covered it with a charcoal Yankee baseball cap. Each time I wore this cap it reminded me of Jay-Z's and Alicia Keys's "Empire State of Mind."

Yanked out my silicone pads, kept on my butt pads. I threw on my plain gray sweats and a matching T-shirt. Now I resembled a fair-complexioned black woman with itty-bitty titties and big booty.

I'd replaced my blue contacts with gray, removed my eyelashes, changed my makeup to a fresh clean earth tone. Slipped on my socks and gray tennis shoes. At times, I preferred gray because unlike wearing all black or white, not many people noticed the color gray or the person wearing it.

"Damn. It's about time." Tossing my binoculars on the seat, I got

out of my Town Car. I eased on my sunglasses, snapped on my eaves-
dropping Bluetooth, turned up the volume as I raced across four
lanes of traffic on Beverly. I slowed my pace, trailed a short distance
behind Jada and Grant. Grant smelled good and looked great.

I stood on the opposite end of the lobby listening to them speak
with the intake nurse who was behind the desk. Grant reminded me
of a lighter skinned Dwight Howard. If I weren't loyal to Darius, I'd
snatch Grant from Jada and Honey. His broad shoulders were the
kind I could hug for hours. That black tuxedo with the red wing collar worked. I checked out his shoes. Thank God they were black and
not red. I didn't like men who were ultracolorful head to toe.

Jada's gear was glam but her face was garbage. The way she sucked
her lips in so damn far I thought she'd choke on them. Good for her
she had that black-don't-crack dark radiant skin. If her face were dry,
the way she was all twisted, those hazel eyes would've caved in behind
cracked crow's feet. As they faced my direction, I turned my back,
walked a few feet away but heard every word.

"Are you coming with me?" Jada asked Grant.

"Coming with you where? You heard the receptionist. Fancy isn't in
her room yet." Grant shook his head. "But Honey is in labor. I hope
she'll let me watch our boys being born. I missed her whole pregnancy. Can't miss the delivery too. But I'll find you later. Don't leave
the hospital without calling me."

All I needed was the room number for Fancy but I overheard the
receptionist say the number for Honey's birthing room too. She'd be
in that room the remainder of her stay, the woman had said. Fancy
was assigned to a room on the third floor; Honey on the ninth, both
in the north tower.

After Jada and Grant got on the elevator, I roamed the lobby letting
fifteen minutes pass before approaching the intake nurse. "Excuse
me. I'm here for the birth of my nephews. My brother-in-law said my
sister Honey Thomas is in room nine-one-oh-nine."

"She's got a sizable support group up there already. I'm not sure if
there's enough space in her room for you but you can try. If the room
is overcrowded, there's a family waiting room down the hall," she said,
handing me a peel-and-stick badge.

"Thanks," I said, pressing on my visitor's pass.

I went to Fancy's floor first. Found 3117. Peeped inside. The refrigerated room was empty. The gust of air gave me chill bumps.

"Excuse me, miss, you can't go in there. We're preparing that room for a patient."

I turned around. The nurse proceeded to step in front of me, then close the door. She wore a white cotton short-sleeved V-collar pullover with random pastel hearts scattered about. Her pants were solid white and she had on those white leather oxfords. I noticed she wore a name badge, Anita Harris, RN. Her short hair was auburn, brows black, lips wide, and pumpkin-seed-shaped eyes. I could easily apply a wig and my theatrical makeup to resemble her features.

"Oh, I was looking for my friend. The receptionist told me she was here," I lied.

Quickly, she asked, "What's your friend's name?"

"Fancy Taylor."

"What's your name?" she asked, setting a teal tote with lavender straps inside the room by the door.

She sure had a lot of questions. Bitch was lucky I left my Mace in the limo. I told her, "Bambi."

"Yeah, right. Miss, don't come up here trying to get an autograph from Darius Jones. His wife is in critical condition. Please, leave and don't let me see you up here again." She entered the room, then mumbled, "Damn, groupies done started already."

Who in the fuck she calling a groupie?

Leaving wasn't a problem. And I'd be back but she wouldn't see the real me. I'd seen the sizable room reserved for Fancy. I wasn't concerned with seeing Fancy right away. Wasn't like she was going anyplace soon. Plus, the situation was too fresh for me to make a move.

Darius probably wasn't leaving Fancy's side tonight but he had a game coming up in Cleveland in a few days and he was scheduled to return to Atlanta after that game. Wish it were play-offs instead of preseason. His team could do without him this early in the season. *Damn.* I checked out the floor plan, the location of the nurses' station, and noted where the nearest stairway exits were in relation to Fancy's room. I trotted downstairs, sat in the lobby for thirty minutes, then took the stairs back up to bypass the nurses' station.

I checked the ninth-floor exit door entrance from the stairway to see if I could gain access to the floor. The door was unlocked. I trotted to the third floor, entered through the exit door. The door to room 9109 was closed.

Now that I had the lay of the land, I'd come up with a brilliant idea.

CHAPTER 15

Darius

First detained by a cop to answer questions about the accident, now I paced the hallway outside of ICU waiting to hear my wife's fate. I hugged my son to my chest. His legs were wrapped in bandages. The doctor said he had abrasions, no deep wounds. Lil' man would be okay in a week or two. He was released to me but I couldn't take care of him that long.

"We need to check on Grandma, my man."

"I want my mommy."

"Me, too. But we have to wait until the doctor says it's okay to go in."

"No, Daddy. I want my mommy, not Fancy. I'm scared."

I kissed my son. He didn't understand that Ashlee was awarded every other weekend visitations. Letting him stay with his mom in D.C. would be voluntarily breaking the court order. I hadn't violated the Dallas custody order in three-plus years. Wasn't going to do it now. I dialed my mom's number. DJ could stay with her until Fancy got better.

Mom answered, "Hey, baby. I'm here. I'm on my way up. What floor are you on?"

"Third. I'm in the hallway. They haven't let me see her yet. I need you to come get DJ."

"I just got off the elevator. I'm walking up behind you."

"Grandma! You made it."

"Yeah, baby. Grandma made it."

Mom touched DJ's bandages. Her brows raised, eyes squinted. I told her it wasn't that bad. She exhaled, kissed DJ, rubbed his back.

"Why you all dressed up, Grandma?"

"Grandma had to get here fast to get you, sweetheart. You are more important than me changing my clothes. Come here, Grandma's baby."

Relieved Mom had taken my son, I hugged them both. My tears flowed. I tried hard to stop. Didn't want my son seeing me break down like this. I felt a tap on my shoulder.

"Excuse, me. Darius, man. I heard you were here but didn't believe it," a man dressed in blue scrubs said. "Can I get your autograph?" His smile was wide. Swore I saw and wanted to knock out all thirty-two of his teeth. He stood there grinning and shoving a pen and pad in my hands.

I looked down on him and asked, "You know if my wife is dead or alive in there?"

His smile disappeared. Before he replied, a nurse opened the door, saving his life and mine. "Mr. Jones, you can come in now."

"Ma, don't leave yet."

"I won't be far. Honey is upstairs supposedly delivering Grant's babies."

Honey? Grant? Babies? I shook my head. Quietly I entered Intensive Care, followed the nurse to my wife's bedside. Bandages surrounded my wife's head and face like she was a mummy from the chin up. I couldn't tell if the bandages made her head bigger or if her head was swollen.

She was connected to a breathing machine. IVs and shit were in her arms. A monitor was strapped to her middle finger. "Baby, if you can hear me, hang in there. I love you," I said, gently touching her hand. Maybe if I hadn't been texting she wouldn't have been upset with me, and the accident wouldn't have happened. They let me see my wife for fifteen minutes while they prepared room 3117.

I asked the nurse, "You sure you can move her in her condition?"

"Your wife is at the best hospital. We have a state-of-art room that she'll be in. You'll see." The nurse spoke in a soft tone. "Don't take this the wrong way but I wish the media would show this vulnerable side of you; however they're not allowed on this floor. They're so quick to condemn, but you're one special man, Darius Jones. I can vouch for that. You have no idea how many injured people are admitted here and their so-called loved ones don't visit them at all."

Her words were comforting but she couldn't vouch for shit about me. Like the groupies and the media, she didn't know me. I'd only seen Anita Harris for a few minutes. My eyes drifted away from her. The numbers 777 and Arizona flashed in my mind. I looked at my wife. *The person responsible for this is going to pay.*

Nurse Harris entered information into her electronic device. I stood by my wife's side.

"You can go to room three-one-one-seven now. We'll bring her there soon." The nurse ushered me from the room.

Mom was gone. I didn't know how but I made my way to 3117. I sat in my wife's room waiting for them to bring her in. "Damn, it's cold in here." The room had a sitting area off to the side, away from the patient's bed. A small circular coffee table with magazines was between two chairs. I sat in a low-back bucket-shaped lime chair next to my wife's bed.

I posted to my Facebook profile, What would you do if the one you loved was instantly taken away from you? Pray for my wife and my family. Scanning my iPhone applications, I pressed TVU Player to watch live television. See if the news was reporting my situation accurately.

The news reporter said, "Darius Jones just posted to his Facebook page a comment that has condolences pouring in from his fans. Is Darius Jones's wife dead? Stay tuned for up-to-date news on the number-one news station in Los Angeles."

Fucking idiot reporter. I posted, My wife is NOT DEAD!

Mom texted, We're in the waiting room on the ninth floor.

Honestly, I'd hoped that Moms would be here for and with me when they brought my wife to the room, but she was keeping that hawk watch over Grant. Time alone for me was good and bad. Too much had happened in a short time. I wanted to yell, "This is fucked up! Why? Why did this fucked up shit happen to us?" I kept replaying how that white pickup truck forced us into the intersection but had no idea why. Worse, didn't know who'd done it. Made a mental note to ask Nurse Harris what room the woman in that SUV was in.

A woman in gray sweats entered the room, stood a few feet in front of me. "Hey, you okay?" she whispered in a raspy voice before closing the door.

"Nah, I'm fucked up in the head right now. You work here? Where's my wife?" This chick was dressed too casual to be on staff. Yankee cap on her head, sunglasses. Wondered if she was a jump off. For her sake I prayed she wasn't, 'cause I'd lose it.

"It's my day off. I heard about your wife's accident. Came by to help you any way I can. Here's my card. If you need anything, call me."

I put the card on my wife's stand without looking at it. "No disrespect, but could you please leave?" I sensed she was lying but didn't want to offend her if she were telling the truth, and if she'd have to take care of Fancy tomorrow, didn't want her having no attitude.

"Oh, look. They forgot the other patient's bag in your room." She walked toward the door, picked up a teal bag with lavender straps that was next to the door. "I'll get rid of it. Don't forget to call me if you need anything. I'll do anything for you," she said, closing the door.

CHAPTER 16

Darius

Glad the woman in sweats left, I had time to reflect. How did I go from proposing to my wife to praying for her life? I sat by my wife's empty bedside thinking, *I came from a broken family. I refuse to have one.* I always had money. I was never broke. But Moms was Mom. She had her struggles. I'd forgiven her for lying to me about my biological father.

Forgiveness eases the pain; it didn't erase the pain. Had Maxine, Ciara, and Ashlee forgiven me? Should I care? Of the times I'd cried, I'd never cried for any of my exes. I cried when MaDear died, and now. I'd never cried this much in my life. I wondered how many tears my exes had shed for me.

The door opened again. This time it was Ladycat. Two nurses rolled her in. They slid her body from a smaller bed to a bed the size of a twin. Disconnected and reconnected her oxygen tank. Made certain all of her machines were functioning properly. Raised, then locked the guardrails. I didn't want to be rude but I wanted them to leave so I could be alone with my wife.

Nurse Anita said, "The doctor will be in shortly. Your wife's belongings are in—" She paused, then asked the other nurse, "Did you move the teal bag that I put Mrs. Jones's belongings in?"

"Oh, the one with the lavender straps?" I asked.

"Oh, thank God. You have it already," Anita said.

I shook my head. "No, the other nurse said that bag belonged to someone else." Wishing they'd leave, I didn't give a damn about that tote bag.

The nurses exchanged blank stares. Nurse Anita said, "We'll find her bag."

I'd never seen that bag before. "My wife's purse was—" Fuck, in our SUV. I needed my mom. I was in no condition to call credit card companies. Besides, I didn't know what numbers to call. It was too late to call my banker. I prayed no one would steal my wife's identity.

As the nurses exited the room, I whispered, "Thanks." Couldn't get any other words out before the tears gushed again.

I wasn't much of a prayer man but I needed God. MaDear told me, "Baby, God always has open arms. His arms are wide enough to hug us all at the same time. Don't you ever be too prideful or too ashamed to call His name."

Kneeling beside Fancy's bed, I wanted to pray silently but the loudest, "Dear God, please don't take her from me!" belted from my gut. "Please, I'm begging You." My tears streamed over the mucous escaping my nostrils. I didn't care.

I pulled my chair closer to her bed, sat by her side, then held my wife's hand. Her hand was cold, mine too. Wish they could turn on some heat. I stared at Fancy. She slept like an angel. Her eyes and nose were all I saw. She didn't move her hand, didn't open her eyes. She lay there motionless.

"Baby, do you remember the night we met? I do. New Year's Eve. Of all places, church. When I saw you standing in the doorway soaking wet in that sexy designer gown and"—I laughed, then continued—"with your weave dripping water to the floor. You were gorgeous then and you're more beautiful now. You were tough then and you're tougher now. I remember how I wanted you to come to my house that night or invite me to yours and you made me drop you off at your place.

"I knew I liked you then. I'd wanted to get at you for over a year before you gave me a chance. Waiting one more night was cool but you made a brotha put in OT. It was worth it. You're worth it. And, baby, do you remember the time you got me off in the hallway at your condo building? That's when I knew for sho you were the one. And what about that day we met that psychic lady in Berkeley by Skates? She was the real deal. I could use her help now and you know I don't believe in psychics." I paused, then whispered, "I love you, baby."

Recalling what that psychic lady told me, "Death follows you," my breath stopped at the edge of my nostrils. Was this accident God's plan? Was He breaking me down to build me up? Was he going to take from me the person I loved most? The psychic lady had also said, "You'll be happy again."

Until a couple of hours ago, I was happy. "Lord, I'm begging You. Please don't do this to—"

The doctor entered the room interrupting my flow but that was cool. His role was more important than mine. My mother entered behind him carrying DJ. Thankfully DJ was asleep and Grant wasn't with them. I hugged my mom tight. Didn't want to let her go but had to.

Mom covered her mouth when she saw Fancy. "Oh, Darius. What on earth happened?"

I knew Mom seeing Fancy was a shocker considering DJ had surface scars and I had none. "Not now, Ma. I'll tell you later. I'm glad you're here." I hugged my mom's waist, then asked, "Doc, give it to me straight."

"I'm Doctor Duke. Mr. Jones. Your wife has to remain in guarded condition because she's in a coma. We're doing all we can to bring her out. Temporary comas are not uncommon for auto accident victims. Those air bags and seat belts saved both of you. Don't know how you walked away or how your wife doesn't have any broken bones but someone up there is looking out for your family."

I looked at Mom. "We know exactly who."

The doc continued. "Your wife responds to pain by opening her eyes but she doesn't respond to light touches or sound. When the minor swelling in her brain dissipates, that should relieve pressure on the stem. Accident patients sometimes regain consciousness within a few days, or it could be several weeks. Or sometimes not at all."

I never imagined being a single dad or having to make it on my own without Fancy. Maybe if I did some good in the world, the way

Shaq and LeBron always gave back to their community, God would heal Fancy. Maybe if I donated a few million to the people in Haiti or built a few homes for the forgotten Katrina victims, my wife would regain consciousness. And if I apologized to my exes, would God let my wife be normal again? Damn, what if she suffers permanent brain damage? Will she remember me? Will our lives be the same if my wife is permanently disabled?

"Your talking to your wife is good. Do that as much as you can. She may be hearing you, though I'm not sure because she's not responding at a high level. But she is responding. If you want to spend the night, I can have another bed delivered immediately."

I nodded so as not to interrupt him, then glanced at my son. DJ was still asleep. How could my wife be fighting for her life while we were healthy enough to go home?

"We'll check on her around the clock. I'm staying the night just in case an emergency develops. Any questions?"

I had mad love and respect for Doc. I had to do it. I hugged him. "Thanks, man."

Mom asked, "Can I stay with her when my son is not here?"

"Afraid not," the doctor answered. "Under her circumstances I shouldn't allow Mr. Jones to stay overnight." He paused, looked up at me, then said, "but he is the league's MVP. I'm personally making this exception for you, Darius." He patted me on the back, then left the room.

"Ma, when I'm not here, stay as long as they'll let you. Please. Right now I need for you to take DJ home." Who would watch DJ, when I was traveling and my mom was here with Fancy?

DJ opened his eyes. "Daddy!" he said, reaching for me. I held my son. "Who's that?" he asked, looking at the bandages around my wife's face.

"That's Fancy, my man." Handing my son back to my mom, I said, "Get him outta here, please."

"Of, course. Anything for you, hon—baby," she said, changing her word. My mom hugged me, told me, "I love you," and left.

I pressed my fingers deep into my eye sockets. Something so soft, tears, still managed to escape. My wife was gentle and strong like that.

She held it down when I was a boy trying to be the man. When I didn't understand what it meant to be a man. I'm so glad I didn't take my wife for granted. My tears were partially out of regret. I wished I had given her the attention she'd deserved instead of texting.

I kissed her bandage, then whispered, "Baby, hang in there. I need you."

CHAPTER 17

Jada

I was trying not to come undone. Two events changed my life. I knew we shouldn't have gone to that premiere. If we had stayed in Atlanta, if we had gone to dinner with Darius and Fancy, maybe Fancy wouldn't be hospitalized, and Grant and I would've been happy not knowing Honey was pregnant.

I dialed Bambi's number. She never did answer my question yesterday when I asked where she was.

"Hi, Jada. How's Fancy?" Bambi asked.

"Too soon to tell," I said.

"I'm here for you. What do you want me to do?"

That was why I'd hired her. Bambi was eager to complete any task. She'd made a drastic change from when I'd seen her at Darius's high school graduation. I still had to introduce her to Darius. Maybe Bambi could stay at my house here in Los Angeles and watch DJ while I went to the hospital.

"Come by my house," I said, giving her my address in the Valley. "I need you to pick up my key card, go to Grant's hotel room, get my things, and drop them off here. And I might need you to stay here with DJ for a few hours while I go check on Fancy."

"I'm on my way, but I should let you know I've never watched any kids. I'm sure I can manage though."

I hadn't thought about Bambi not having any siblings or kids. DJ was a good kid but I shouldn't have expected Bambi to watch him on a regular basis the way I'd expected Grant to.

Secretly Grant had hoped he'd see Honey yesterday. Whether or not he knew she was pregnant was irrelevant. My heart was with Darius, my prayers with Fancy. Hadn't heard from Grant since last night. Felt foolish sitting in that waiting room for hours. I had to find a non-confrontational way to make Grant have a paternity test.

He refused to ask Honey to let me watch the birth. He insisted on staying at the hospital in the room with Honey. Guess he was standing in the viewing window right this minute basking in the moment of believing he was a father.

Having my grandson was a delightful detour to obsessing full-time over Grant's inconsideration. I set a poolside table for two. While my chef prepared breakfast, I decorated the round glass top with black and blue Batman placemats, gold silverware, Batman plates, bowls, and eight-ounce glasses.

DJ ran out of the house onto the patio. "Can I swim a little while, Grandma, till the food is ready?"

"No, baby. Not with your bandages on."

"Please, Grandma? Please?"

I exhaled. "Okay. Just a few minutes. And right after breakfast I'll have to clean you up and change your bandages." Somebody should have fun. I sat close to my pool, in case I had to dive in. Next to being a mom, being a grandmother was my greatest joy. DJ was adorable. He ran toward the deep end, jumped off the side, bent his knees, then made a big splash.

I missed LA. If things didn't work out with Grant, I was staying in LA and selling my house in Atlanta. Darius was grown. He didn't need me at all of his games. I checked my cell hoping I'd missed a call, text, or e-mail from Grant. Opening his e-mail, I started to delete the picture of the twins. I placed my phone inside the towel beside my chair.

"Get in with me, Grandma!"

Normally I would but I wasn't in a good mood, wasn't up to faking it. "Let Grandma see you float."

Fancy had taught DJ how to float, swim, and dog-paddle. She was great with DJ. After what Ashlee had done to Fancy, I was shocked Fancy was so forgiving. No way would I raise a woman's child after she'd killed mine. Maybe taking DJ away from Ashlee was Fancy's way of adopting a child. I asked God to bless Darius and Fancy with a child of their own and Ashlee with peace of mind. I knew Darius had driven Ashlee insane, but there was nothing I could do to protect that child's sanity.

The sun beamed brighter than yesterday. Silently, I prayed. "Dear God, I know with you all things are possible. Please lay Thy healing hands on Fancy and Darius. I know You won't give us more than we can bear. I know my son has caused a lot of women tremendous pain but I ask that You be merciful, Jesus."

Hopefully God would show my son favor and not let him suffer long. Before the accident, I hadn't seen my son that happy in his life. I looked up to the sunshine as a good sign for each of us.

My phone rang. I held up the cell and called out to DJ, "It's your daddy."

He came running. "Stop. What did I tell you about running by the pool?"

"Sorry, Grandma. Oh, give me the phone. I wanna talk to him."

"Just a moment. Dry yourself off first," I told DJ, then answered my son, "Hi, sweetheart."

"Ma, she opened her eyes to the sound of my voice," he cried.

Holding back my tears, I said, "Baby, that's wonderful news."

"I know, Ma. I think she's going to make a full recovery. I need your advice. What should I do about my game coming up? I was supposed to leave today. I mean, I can miss this one day but at some point in the next two days I'ma have to go."

"Sleep on it, baby. Stay the night with Fancy. See how she progresses tomorrow. Being on the court will be good for you but don't rush it. When you decide to leave, I'll keep an eye on Fancy while you're away. I promise."

I was supportive for Darius's sake but how was I going to keep watch over Fancy and DJ? I had to keep Darius in LA as long as I could. DJ hadn't stayed a day with nonfamily members. Maybe I could research preschools. I know, I'd tell Bambi to find DJ a day care center.

"Thanks, Ma. Let me say hello to my man."

DJ was partially wet so I put the phone on speaker, then held it for DJ.

"Hey, Daddy. Come get me. Where you at?"

"My man, I'm at the hospital with Fancy. I'll be home soon as I can. Right now I need you to take care of Grandma until I get there. Can you do that for me?"

"How come?"

"Because you're the man."

I raised a brow at that one.

"Does that mean she has to listen to me, Daddy?"

"Not at all. You're three."

"I'm almost four."

"I love you, my man. Give Daddy a kiss."

"Mmm, Daddy. I love you too. Bye!"

I took the phone off speaker. "Baby, you need to shower and eat. Why don't you come home later and stay with DJ and I'll sit with Fancy until you get back or until they kick me out."

"I'm not ready to leave, Ma. Her eyes are open. I'm fine and I promise to eat. Love, you. Bye."

I sighed. Part of my wanting to be at the hospital was selfish. I had to confront Grant about his e-mail. Convince him to take the test. Prove to him I was right.

"Grandma, can I talk to my mommy? I miss my mommy."

"Of course you can, sweetie." Why hadn't I thought of calling Ashlee? I dialed her number, then put my cell on speaker.

"Hello, Jada," she sleepily answered. D.C. was three hours ahead of LA. She should've been awake as it was almost noon her time. "Is it true? Bambi is your personal assistant?"

"Mommy! I miss you."

"Oh, baby. Mommy misses you too."

"Come get me!"

"Get you? Where are you? They're supposed to bring you to me today."

I answered Ashlee, "Yes, it is true. Isn't that great? You won't believe how much she's changed. I doubt you'll recognize her. I sure didn't."

Ashlee asked, "Did she ask you to call me?"

"No. Why?"

"Did you ask her to call me?"

"No. Why would I do that?" What was with all the questions?

DJ interrupted. "Mommy, we got into a big car crash. Bam! This car hit us from behind. Another car hit us from the side. I have bandages on my legs. And Fancy, she not doing too good, Mommy. Her head is wrapped up and she got a tube in her nose. All kinds of stuff. And she can't talk either. Daddy has to stay at the hospital with her all day and all night and I'm watching Grandma."

When did he notice all of that? I chimed in. "Ashlee, before you get upset, as you can tell, DJ is fine." Our not talking baby talk to him made DJ smarter than I'd realized. "Darius does have to watch Fancy and it wouldn't be a bad idea if you could come and help watch DJ for a week or two."

I didn't want to seem selfish but I had issues to deal with too.

"I'm on my way," Ashlee said. "Mommy will see you tomorrow, sweetie."

CHAPTER 18

Ashlee

Getting my son back was just the ticket I needed to get back at Darius and Fancy, and I knew Bambi was lying about Jada asking her to confirm my address. Bambi was up to something. If she wasn't careful, I'd tie her up, then beat her ass like I'd done to the guy at the W Hotel yesterday.

Literally jumping out of my bed, I scrambled for my cell, got my attorney on the phone. "Draw up my child support papers. I want full legal and physical custody of my son."

I went to my closet, dug out my pictures of Darius from the bottom of my keepsake box. I picked up the five-by-seven frame with Jay's picture, replaced Darius Senior's photo on top, then put the frame back on my nightstand.

"Whoa, Ashlee, slow down. Have you maintained your meds? Where is this custody issue coming from?" Baldwin asked. "What we need to discuss is what's really going on with Jay Crawford. Are you going to tell me everything that happened? I can't keep requesting a continuance for this trial if the man isn't guilty."

"What are you talking about? Jay who? Stay focused. I'm talking about Darius." I shut my eyes tight, then opened them.

Fuck Jay! He was guilty of quitting me for his baby mama.

"I don't give a fuck if he does twenty years up in that hellhole. He'll have plenty of time to think about dumping Ashlee Anderson. He got what he deserved! One down and one to go. And don't worry about me taking my meds. I'm not crazy. Those drugs make me sleep all damn day. I'm calling because Darius's wife was in a car accident. She's hospitalized. She can't take care of my baby. It's basketball season. Darius doesn't have time for DJ." *But he'll wish he'd made time for me.* "I'm the biological mother, not DJ's grandma! Get it! Got it! Now get my papers ready. I'm leaving in the morning on the first plane jettin'."

I went to my kitchen, placed my hand under the ice slot of the refrig, then pressed the lever. I filled my hand with cubes, then rubbed my face and neck. I slid an ice cube inside my pussy to cool me off more.

"Ashlee, slow down. DJ hasn't ever lived with you in D.C. You haven't had him since he was what? One year old or younger? You have every other weekend visitation. You can't demand custody—you have to establish cause to get your full rights back. With your mental instability, neither the judge or the law is going to be on your side."

Who was he working for? Baldwin was one more broke ass replaceable lawyer who had more bills than money. "Fine, if you can't handle the job, I'll find an attorney who understands that the law can be skewed."

Water ran down my thigh. I grabbed a handful of paper towels, dried my pussy, then trashed the napkins. DJ's picture was on my refrigerator. I kissed my baby. "Ha! I'm getting my baby back, baby back, baby back."

"Look, Ashlee. I'm sure we can work this out to your advantage," Baldwin said.

Baldwin was broke enough to be bought. I told him, "Well, Darius and Fancy moved from Los Angeles to Atlanta. The custody order is in Dallas. What if they didn't file their papers in Atlanta? I can establish jurisdiction in D.C. Right? Why hadn't I thought of this sooner?" I was too close to getting revenge. I was not giving in.

My attorney asked, "Does he still have his house in LA? When and where are you going to pick up your son?"

"Yes, Darius has his house in LA. And I just told you I'm going to LA to pick up DJ. What's your point?" I filled my hand with ice again. This time I massaged my arms and breasts.

"You probably thought it but no you didn't just tell me you were going to LA. Let me try to make sense of this. How do you know about this accident?" he questioned.

"My son told me."

"Great. A three-year-old told you and you believed him?"

"His grandmother confirmed it, okay? Call her yourself if you don't believe me. I'm on my way to your office to pick up my papers." I hung up, went online, and purchased a first-class round-trip ticket for myself, and a one-way ticket for my son from LAX to DCA. I knew my day would come. God didn't like ugly and Darius had been ugly to a whole lotta women. Fancy couldn't keep my baby from me forever. Finally, I get to see how they like every other weekend visitation. It was payback time for Darius Jones.

Only God will have mercy on his soul because I don't give a fuck about Darius.

CHAPTER 19

Bambi

What I was about to do would leave Darius with no support system other than me.

His soon to be deceased wife had one foot in the grave. His mother was outrageously obsessing over Grant. I planned to set up Jada with a tragic situation beyond her belief. She was on the edge. I might as well push her off the cliff. Give her a legitimate reason to be pissed off at Grant. Once I got rid of Fancy and Jada, I'd become Darius's newest best friend.

I sat at the computer desk in my hotel room at the Renaissance saturating my hair with glue release until I was able to peel off my blond front lace wig and brows. Showering, then shampooing my hair, I tried to plan what I'd do with DJ besides lock him in a closet like my parents had done to me. Working in leave-in conditioner, I finger-spiraled my curls into a dangling afro.

Checking myself out in the mirror, my size six pink designer suit, orange tapered button up, and stilettos were as fresh and natural looking as the day I'd interviewed with Jada. No wig, makeup, or body enhancements. I wasn't wired to entertain a kid. Babysitting wasn't on my "to do" list. I had to get to Jada's house to pick up the room key and hurry back to my hotel to meet Rita.

On my way out, I peeped in the tote bag I'd taken from Fancy's room last night. I saw Fancy's bloody clothes in a sealed plastic bag.

Pinching the tip of the bag, I temporarily tossed it in the trash. Those belongings were going back in this bag and back to the hospital. I shook the bag. Saw a dazzling sparkle.

No way. Couldn't be. I spread a towel on the bed, emptied the contents. "Well, I'll be damned." Fancy's purse, cell phone, credit cards, driver's license, cash, and rings were in the bag. I slipped my new engagement ring on my finger. Perfect fit. *Damn, I'm good.* The cell phone was useless, might have a tracking application. Didn't need her money or ID.

I parked in Jada's driveway, rang her bell. She opened the door. DJ stood behind her, clung to her leg. *Brat.*

"Come in. I tell you I don't know how I'm going to get through all of this," Jada said, handing me the key card.

I stood in the living room checking out the pictures of Darius on her mantel. I didn't care about the other people in the photos. "Your home is charming."

"Thanks." She told me the hotel and room number, then said, "It'll be obvious which things are mine and what belongs to Grant. Don't touch his stuff. DJ, say hi to Bambi."

"Nope," he said, running off.

Cool. The feeling was mutual. At least he only looked crippled with those bandages on his legs.

"DJ, get back here. You're going to spend the day with Bambi."

He stood beside Jada, stared at me, then asked, "How come?"

Yeah, how come? I whispered to Jada, "I don't think babysitting should be part of my duties. I'm really not good with kids and I think he knows it."

Jada said, "Use my company credit card. Take him to Disneyland or wherever he wants to go. Have him back in eight hours. DJ, don't you want to go to Disneyland?"

"My mommy can take me when she gets here."

Ashlee was coming to LA? "Let's go," I said, grabbing DJ's hand.

Shoving DJ in and dragging him out of the backseat of my convertible was a chore. The small space behind my passenger seat barely accommodated this kid. We went to Jada's hotel, then to mine.

"You're supposed to take me to Disneyland," he said, yanking his hand from mine.

I grabbed his hand, squeezed it tight. "You can make this easy or hard, kid. The choice is yours."

"Ow, that hurts."

"Not as much as it could, kid," I said, entering my hotel room.

"My name is DJ."

I did a quick change into my one-piece swimsuit, put on Fancy's ring. "Let's go, kid."

"My name is DJ. And that's Fancy's ring."

"When you're with me, your name is 'kid.' And it's my ring." I sashayed to the rooftop pool at the Renaissance with the kid trailing behind me. I lounged on a chair under the cabana, waited for my contact.

I told the kid, "Go play by the pool but don't get wet."

He frowned, stood at the edge of the pool staring at the other kids in the water. I told Jada I wasn't good with kids.

If he accidentally drowned or came up missing, it would be her fault.

CHAPTER 20

Bambi

Adjusting the volume on my Loud 'N Clear ear piece, I eased on my custom-fitted Chanel sunglasses and reclined. I couldn't relax. The thoughts inside my head competed for my attention. "This is the baddest ring." Finally, I was officially engaged to Darius Jones and had his ring and his kid to prove it.

The eleven o'clock sunshine warmed my body inside out. Seductively, I rubbed suntan oil all over myself to let my reality soak in. "Bartender, a bottle of Dom, a carafe of fresh orange juice, and a bowl of freshly sliced strawberries. Charge it to room 1806," I said. "A celebration is in order. I'm getting married." I flipped my wrist, showed him my bling.

"Damn. Well, all is right, Miss Diva Extraordinaire. Congratulations. That's quite an exhibit. I'll be right back with your order. With all that shine, keep your shades on."

He was the first to envy me. I was never taking off my ring. Never. I'd die first.

My contact headed in my direction, dragging her feet and looking an outright mess. Sliding her brown Birkenstocks, she adjusted her unkempt wig. Her floral print button-up dress was crinkled and her purse strap straddled her waist. Her fist was damned near wrapped twice around the strap. She hugged her purse to her hip as though all the money she owned was in it.

Flopping on the lawn chair beside mine, she said, "Hey, Miss Bambi," loud enough for the guests in the lobby to hear my name. Her country proper tone was at times adorable but more often annoying. Did all the people from Flagstaff along Route 66 speak this loud? Today I was happy so nothing could unnerve me.

I told Rita, "I've got to teach you how to chill LA style. Sit back. Relax and have a mimosa." I motioned for the bartender to pour two drinks.

He half filled the two champagne flutes on the tray, added a splash of orange juice to each, handed me my drink.

Rita picked up her drink before he touched it. She wrapped all four fingers and her thumb around the flute like it was a microphone. "Oh, chile. This is exactly what I need." Leaning her head back, she gulped the mimosa like it was straight OJ. She stared at my ring. "Bambi, where you get that from? You're getting married?"

"Yes, but I can't tell you to whom, so don't ask. He's famous and wealthy."

The best part about my contact was she was definitely unsuspecting. No one would deem Rita St. Thomas a hit and run driver. She was from that small town, Flagstaff, Arizona, where the attendant who checked your bags at the airport also loaded your bags on the plane and closed the door from the outside before takeoff. Hiring Rita, things had fallen into place for me in a weird kind of way.

I'd read all about Rita in the background check on Jada's computer. I knew that Honey was the name of Rita's daughter who died. Lace was her daughter who'd switched names with her deceased daughter, Honey. And Rita told me that she was so jealous of Honey she'd do the unspeakable to make Honey's life miserable.

Rita said, "Oh, chile. At first I thought I'd hurt Darius the way he was smashed up underneef that air bag. I had to pray on that cuz I know how important he is to you." This time she refilled her own glass with champagne only. "What do you do to look so good, Bambi? You on a diet? All these women in LA make me feel like I should go to the gym or at least watch what I eat."

"Sex," I answered. "I have lots of sex."

Rita frowned and nodded, at the same tightening her lips. "Hmm."

Not wanting to hear her response, I removed my sunglasses, stared in her eyes. I squinted, then hissed, "Let me make myself clear. If you hurt Darius, I will destroy you." She'd die if my thoughts could kill her. "Slow down on the alcohol. Here," I said, handing her a five-thousand-dollar bonus for a job well done.

She swished the champagne in her mouth, then swallowed. "Good. Now I can buy another truck. What's my next assignment? I need more money."

"I have to decide if you can handle another assignment." I already had one for her but didn't want her to make any assumptions. "Tell me about the accident." I scanned the pool area. That kid was still standing on the side. At least he listened. I still wasn't taking him to Disneyland.

Rita straightened her wig. Wiggled on the lawn chair. Scooted her chair closer to mine. Sat sideways facing me. Gapped her legs, then whispered, "Well, I followed them about ten blocks or so. When the light turned red I saw this here SUV flying downhill from a different direction. They had the right of way. I juiced my engine and slammed into the back of Darius's SUV and forced them into the middle of the street. I knew that other car wouldn't have time to stop so I juiced my engine again and hit Darius's car again to confuse them."

Rita damn near had me confused. "Next time I ask you to handle something, do not put Darius's health in jeopardy."

I didn't want to know what she'd done with the wrecked truck. It wasn't in my name. "Are you good with kids?" I asked her.

"I'm the best. Kinda," she said, frowning. "Didn't do such a great job with my own, but I can manage. Not like I don't know how to take care of kids, ya know. Honey's pregnant. But I'm already knowing she's not going to let me see my grandbaby. She's evil like that to me. If she'd given me some of that money she got, I wouldn't have to supplement my retirement by doing these here odd jobs for you." She downed another glass of champagne.

I didn't want to hear her life story. "Good enough." I yelled at DJ, "Hey, kid! Come here . . . Kid . . . Kid . . . DJ!"

He came running. "That's my name."

Sucking in my cheeks, I exhaled. "Rita, stay here and watch this kid until I get back."

I slid my half glass of champagne to her side of the table knowing she'd need that drink too. At least she was honest about not having been a good mother. "I have another appointment." I had to get away from her, get away from them.

I went to my room, showered off my suntan oil, then checked out of my room.

CHAPTER 21

Bambi

The thirty-mile drive to the uniform shop located in Bellflower took an hour and thirty minutes. I paid cash for three nursing uniforms and two pairs of shoes. I made sure one uniform was a white cotton short-sleeved V-collar pullover with pastel hearts and solid white pants like the one Anita Harris had worn. Both pairs of shoes were white leather.

Damn, almost forgot I was out of new lace wigs. I zoomed to Dream Girls Hair Imports on Sepulveda Boulevard in Culver City and snatched up twelve wigs from the owner, Tonya Thompson. "Hey, BC!" That was short for Brandon Charles, the finest and best stylist. If I weren't in love with my Darius, I'd make Brandon mine.

I bought the Brianna, Destiny, Loressa, Eboni, Thalia, Camilla, Tiffani, Blond Ambition, Aubrey, Caribbean Beauty, Samantha, and the Ivory. Each wig was a different color. Half were full lace that required gluing around my entire hairline. The other half were no-glue front laces that would allow me to apply the wig with tape and drastically change my look in ten minutes.

My next stop was the rental car agency. I traded my silver convertible for a black sedan, then headed to Walmart in Long Beach to purchase two infant car seats and a playpen.

On my way to my parents' home on East Seaside Walk in Long Beach to drop off the playpen, I made arrangements to meet Rita so I could pick up that brat DJ and drop him off at Jada's on my way back to the hospital.

CHAPTER 22

Darius

Almost forty-eight hours had passed since the accident. I hadn't left my wife's bedside except to use the restroom. The nurses brought me food, beverages, and my wife's teal bag was mysteriously returned to the room while I'd dozed off. When I saw the bloody halter-top dress on top, I stuffed the bag in the bottom of her closet.

Squatting in the chair, "Oh, wee," my body odor crept upon me. The home game was coming up in two days. I had to soak my nuts, go check on my son, in that order. Was worried about Mom. Hadn't spoken with her since yesterday morning.

My battery had gotten low so I borrowed Anita's charger. I posted on Facebook, Thanks for your prayers for my wife. We're not out of the woods yet. Going to shoot around in a few. Well wishes and more prayers poured in instantly. My fans did care.

How long would I have to wait before I could hold my wife in my arms again? I knew I shouldn't have those selfish thoughts but I was useless not being able to help her. Felt guiltier with each passing hour that she was the only one hurt. What was my lesson?

The little things I thought about were what would my life be like without her hugs, her kisses, her smiles, and her laughter. Her wisdom, her advice, and her loving touches kept me balanced. I missed those big brown eyes that spoke to me without her saying a word.

Her eyes stayed open a little longer today but she still hadn't spoken. The doctor said her progress was promising and my being here definitely helped. Doc's support was appreciated but I believed her condition would be the same if I weren't here. I sat beside her bed. "Baby, I'ma have to go home today to shower and change clothes. I'm going to shoot around for a few hours, get a decent hot meal, and I'll be back tonight."

Someone tapped on the door. I opened it, then stepped into the hallway. Couldn't lie. I was happy as hell to see my teammate and friend.

"K-9, man, what am I going to do?" I cried on his shoulder like a six-month-old, hungry, wet baby needing to be held. The tears surprised me. Thought I was all cried out.

"It's all good, man. We bleed too, nigga. We bleed too," he said. "Everyone on the team, the coaches, players, and their families, send their prayers."

"Yeah, I've spoken with Coach a few times. He wants me at the home game if I can make it. Says playing will help me take out my aggression in the right place. But he's leaving it up to me."

"Fam first, D."

"Yeah, problem is, I've got two. My wife and kid and you guys."

"Check it out like this. Say you go with us to Cleveland. You break the bank up in that Quicken Loans Arena. Then you get a call saying, 'I'm sorry, Mr. Jones, we did all we could.'"

That reality shit hit me hard. "If some crazy shit like that went down while I was away from my wife, I'd tear down the north and south towers of this hospital with my hands. I'd lose it, man."

There were no easy answers. Couldn't ignore my problems this time. I cried on his shoulder again. A couple of camera lights flashed. Paparazzi were lurking in the corners of the hallway taking pictures of my crying and hugging K-9. No telling where those photos would show up.

"Ain't that about a bitch," I said, shaking my head. "Guess he'll get his moment of fame for selling those pics to TMZ." I was too upset to give a damn.

K-9 yelled, "Get the fuck outta here before I beat your ass! Give me a sec, D. I'ma catch that punk ass before he have us on prime time looking like bitches." K-9 ran off behind the guy; they disappeared into the stairway.

I heard rumbling, went back into my wife's room. That was the reason I hadn't come out since I'd gotten here. Paparazzi came up here pretending to be visitors. Every network wanted an exclusive bedside interview with me holding my wife's hand. The police wanted more details about the hit and run. Far as I was concerned the police was another layer of paparazzi. The cops were the only ones who'd taken pictures of Rihanna but her photos were all over TMZ. The insurance company wanted a statement from me. Department of Motor Vehicles had forms hand delivered to the room. None of that shit would've gone down like this if I were an average Joe.

With all the drugs in her system, Fancy had fallen asleep, or maybe she was resting her eyes. I heard a tap on the door. Softly, I said, "Come in, man," trying not to wake up my baby. I was not prepared to see the face standing in the doorway looking back at me.

Why in the fuck are you here?

CHAPTER 23

Ashlee

A real woman's balls were always bigger than a man's.

I gloated as Darius's chocolate face turned two shades lighter. He was speechless when he saw me standing in the doorway. The fear in his eyes told me he wasn't that big bad shit talker who'd talked down to me in the past.

"What's up, Ash? Forgive me. Poor choice of words. I mean, how you doin', Ashlee?" K-9 said, ushering me inside the room.

Yeah, the three of us went back far enough for K-9 to remember my being trapped in the fire. Part of my face was burned but thanks to modern medical techniques my face was restored. The arsonist target was Darius but I was the one who suffered. I was in the building working late that night while Darius was fucking around.

Darius got out of his seat, stood in front of me. I put my left foot forward, hand on my right hip, tossed my head back, stared up at him. Had on my Nikes for traction, hair slicked back in a ponytail, no makeup, no jewelry. I came ready to kick Fancy's ass and outrun Darius. Assessing Fancy's condition, I was overprepared.

"I'ma pay for this one, D, but dude left me no choice," K-9 said, holding up a professional camera.

"Good to see you two haven't grown up," I commented. "That's not a good thing." I peeped around Darius's side. He moved, trying to block my view of Fancy. "Somebody needs to comb her hair. I already saw her. I'm trying to get a closer look to see if she's faking it." I pushed Darius. The strength of his body made me shove myself to the side.

"Like K-9 said, what's up, Ashlee?"

I stared at Fancy while answering Darius. "Your mom didn't tell you? She asked me to come help her watch DJ. Besides, it's my weekend to have him anyway. But I had to see for myself what condition she"—I nodded at Fancy—"was in. Pretty bad. Who was driving? You?"

Darius concealed his smile. No matter how serious the situation, I could always make him laugh before he got mad again. He shook his head. Shook off my comment. I wasn't giving him any relief. All the days of my life he'd fucked up, he deserved this shit.

He stood in front me. "Seriously, Ashlee. Don't you have any compassion for my wife? Can't you see I'm scared?"

"Where the fuck were you all the times I was scared?" I asked him.

"I can't change that, Ashlee. It's in the past. Right now, I don't know what I'd do without my wife." He walked me to the corner of the room, then whispered, "Ashlee, look. I'm sorry for all the fucked up shit I did to you. I wanna make it up to you, I swear. We were both young. After our son was born I didn't know how to love Fancy and emotionally be there for you at the same time. But this accident right here changed me for life. I'ma do whatever it takes to make you a part of our lives but you can't see DJ for more than two days."

What the fuck made him think I wanted to be a part of their lives? That sounded good (more so to him) but it came a lotta too late for me, and DJ was my damn son too.

Lunging toward him with my shoulders, I said, "Fuck you, Darius! You should've called me right away! That's your wife but DJ is my son, Darius. Mine. Not hers. You should've called and told me my baby was in a car accident. Your mother could've called me when it happened. Nobody called Ashlee until a day later! And even then your mother didn't tell me. Why did I have to hear it from my three-year-old?"

I saw Fancy's left leg move. *Yeah, twitch, bitch, you know I'm keeping it one hundred.* I got closer to Darius so he wouldn't look over his shoulder at her ass.

"Ashlee, please. Keep your voice down."

"Please my ass! Fuck you!" *Put one finger on me and your ass is going to jail.* Now both of her legs were moving. I wished K-9 wasn't standing there watching me—I'd do a Jay Crawford on Darius so fast.

"D, let it go," K-9 said. "She's not hearing you. You see where this is going." K-9 opened the door, leaned half his body into the hallway. "Nurse! We need a nurse!"

"Punk ass ballers." If K-9 knew what was best for him, he'd stay out of my warm-up with Darius and out of my lineup. I was just getting started. I could emasculate Darius and castrate K-9 at the same time.

Several nurses rushed into the room.

I didn't give a fuck about them. "We'll see how you feel when the shoe is on the other foot," I told Darius.

"Miss, you're going to have to leave the hospital," one of the nurses told me. "Or I'm going to have to call the police."

"Bitch, do what the fuck you gotta do." I looked at Darius squaring his shoulders. "If you keep fucking with me, I will kill you and her," I said, pointing at Fancy.

Another nurse said, "Oh, my gosh. Call the doctor. She's moving. Your wife is moving."

Darius rushed to Fancy's bedside. Guess that gave him a reason to keep standing tall. His day was coming.

I stared that bitch ass nurse Anita down, then told her, "I hadn't planned on staying." I handed Darius the envelope containing my custody papers, bypassed K-9, and left the building.

That bitch twitching was just the distraction I needed. I hurried to the lobby, picked up DJ from Jada, and kept it moving. By the time Darius called his trifling ass mother I'd be on the plane with DJ headed back to D.C.

CHAPTER 24

Darius

She moved. My wife moved.

I wasn't sure if I should thank Ashlee or curse her out. Ashlee could make a great situation bad or a bad situation worse without trying. Damn that girl was never happy. Never satisfied. Wasn't my fault she was passive-aggressive. She started out doing whatever it took to keep me happy. Then when I'd stopped making her happy, she'd done all she could to make my life a living hell. I know my mom wasn't bold enough to let Ashlee watch DJ for more than two days without consulting me first.

Nurse Anita said, "Everyone out, including you, Mr. Jones. Your wife's pressure is up. Out, Mr. Jones, leave now," she said, hissing between her teeth. "Your wife is fighting to recover and you're in here acting inhumane. I pray you haven't set her back. Leave, now."

Dr. Duke rushed into the room. K-9 grabbed my arm while holding on to the camera. We stood in the hallway. "Let's chill here for a minute. Give you and the staff time to calm down and Ashlee time to get out of your way."

"I messed up, huh?"

"D, females always trying to one-up on us. You good."

I posted on Facebook. Gotta go put up some shots before I lose it. Baby mama drama. Just sayin'.

Knowing Ashlee, if she was telling the truth about watching DJ, I might not see my son again. I sensed something bad was about to go down. I called my mom.

Mom answered all cheerful. "Hey, baby. How's Fancy?"

"Ma, where's DJ?"

"Ashlee just left with him."

"Just left with him? Where's she taking him? Where's she staying?"

"I don't know where she's staying. DJ wants his mom to take him to Disneyland," Mom said all nonchalant.

"She just left with my fucking son and you have no idea where she's staying. Where are you?"

"Darius, I need help and you can't help me. It's not my fault that DJ isn't used to staying with people he doesn't know. I tried letting Bambi watch him for a few hours yesterday and that didn't go too well. Ashlee will drop him off later. Darius, it's okay."

"Don't fucking 'Darius it's okay' me, Ma. Stop pawning off my son. I haven't even met this personal assistant of yours yet and you let her watch my son? Where were you that you didn't have time to keep him?" I already knew wherever Grant was my mom wasn't far from him.

"Check yourself. You're getting out of hand. I'm in the lobby at the hospital on my way up to visit Fancy. Where are you?"

"You know where the fuck I am. You can't see Fancy right now. Thanks to Ashlee coming to my wife's room causing commotion, Fancy's pressure is up. Stay there. I'm on my way down to see you."

"Here, man," I said, handing K-9 the envelope Ashlee gave me. "Open it for me."

K-9 laughed. "What if it's laced with anthrax? You know that female is certifiable. I think you'd better do the honors when you're by yourself," he said, handing the letter back. "For real though, D. You can't talk like that to your mom. The one thing I've learned is if a man doesn't respect his mother, his sisters, and females, a boomerang is gonna keep knocking him on his ass. I ain't saying you have to like them, but respect goes a long way. Give it five before you go to the lobby."

Fuck! I boxed with the air. Desperately wanted to punch the wall but I wasn't that stupid. My hands were worth millions. The tears running down my face were fueled with anger. My son was probably gone.

My wife, fighting for her life. My mother betrayed me. Me, I was a piece of shit waiting for someone to flush me down the toilet.

"D. Let's go shoot a few rounds. After you wash your ass."

He got no argument from me when I could smell my own funk. I smiled for the second time since the accident. I could continue soaking in shit but I had to regain control and shift my attitude. The choice was mine. Boxing with the wind wasn't resolving my problems.

"Fair, my nuts are starting to stick to my thighs," I said, getting on the elevator. "Man, she moved. That's great, right?"

"Fancy can kick your ass and mine. She's a fighter. She'll be fine. Let the nurses take care of her and I'll keep watch over you, dawg. After you handle that stench, we'll get something to eat, shoot around, and I'll bring you back here."

"Anita said don't come back."

"Man, you're hearing things. She never said that. That's your wife and you have a right to see her. They just need you to chill and not be upsetting Fancy. That's all."

Part of me was looking forward to coming back; the other part was ready to go to Cleveland. "Cool. That way I'll be refreshed and calm. But, dude, why my mom let Ashlee take DJ?" The elevator doors opened. I saw my mom in the lobby arguing with Grant.

"Guess you've got your answer, man. But I can't take cameras from all them." K-9 pointed at a group of reporters moving in my direction. "I'll be outside in my car."

Walking over to my mom, I said, "Ma, life is too short. He's not worth it. Let his ass go. Right now I need to know where my son is." I was so mad at my mom I didn't bother telling her Fancy's eyes were open and she'd moved.

Cameras flashed, making me angrier. Wish those sorry bastards would back off. "Leave me the fuck alone! Report that! Better yet, go find that trick that's responsible for my wife being in the hospital." With all the chaos, I hadn't had time to hire a detective to hunt down the bitch who was driving that white pickup truck.

Grant commented to my mom, "There, you heard it from your own son. I'm not worth it."

"Nigga, save your steps and your breath. I'm talking to my mother. You don't owe her but you do owe me. Don't make me beat your ass a million times to get my money back," I told him. I was on the verge of swinging at more than air.

Grant looked at my mom. "You want me to handle him? Because if I do, he's going to be on the third floor, in a room, in a bed, next to his wife!"

Mom pleaded, "Darius, don't." She placed her hand on my bicep. "I have to meet Bambi for lunch, then I'll come back and stay with Fancy until you get back."

"Get your hand off me, Ma. Don't pacify me."

She checked to make sure Grant wasn't leaving. "He's not worth it, son."

"Ma, forget lunch. Go find my son."

What the fuck was wrong with my mother? I moved my mom's hands. Didn't want her touching me in that way like she was protecting his ass from me. I looked down at her, then said, "Maybe you're the one who's not worth it."

CHAPTER 25

Jada

I let my son leave the hospital, thankful all the reporters had followed him. I didn't try stopping or calling Darius. I had to tend to my unfinished business with Grant and meet Bambi at CUT in Beverly Hills before visiting Fancy. For me, Ashlee's timing was perfect. For Darius too but he didn't realize it.

The lack of my ability to control Grant's actions and reactions made me lose self-control. Irrespective of my words, the outcome remained unchanged. I didn't get what I wanted. I got the truth. But I wasn't ready to deal with my truth. I expected Grant to tell me what I deserved to hear: "Baby, I love you. Regardless if Honey's babies are mine or not, nothing between us will change." That was my wishful thinking.

Telling my son, "Darius, don't," was my way of protecting Grant. Saying, "He's not worth it," was my way of degrading Grant. I had the right to humiliate Grant but didn't want my son or anyone else to do so.

I dismissed Darius's misdirected anger when he'd said, "Maybe you're the one who's not worth it," understanding my son was stressed and hadn't meant what he'd said.

DJ was fine with Ashlee. Ashlee being crazy didn't change that fact that she was DJ's mother. My son hadn't slept in two days. I accepted his aggression as the result of sleep deprivation. My son had good intentions but he was wrong to confront my man.

I turned to Grant. "You owe me closure. And if you're smart you won't end this relationship before finding out if those babies are not yours. 'Cause once I'm gone, don't expect me to come back."

Calmly, he said, "You're free to leave anytime you'd like. You've given me back my ring. There's nothing else you can give me. You're really too old to behave like your grandson."

Embarrassed, I scanned the lobby hoping no one had heard his insults. "So now you're talking down to me?"

"Can dish it but can't take it? I'm not worth it, remember? Why you wasting our time? If it'll end this nonsense, I apologize. I shouldn't have said that. Come to the nursery and see my boys. Maybe seeing them will convince you they're mine," he said.

My feet wanted to kick Grant, then walk out the hospital. My envy had to see the babies. I stood there like a damn fool but jealousy wouldn't let me move. What was wrong with me? I'd rather argue with a man who obviously doesn't want me than love myself and move on.

"Don't apologize. You said what you meant. Doesn't mean it's valid." I followed him to the ninth floor. The nurse told us the babies were with Honey in room 9109. "Now what?" I asked him.

"You'd better go check on Fancy. I don't think Honey would like having you in her room. I'll check on you in a minute."

"Are you insane? You asked me to come up, now you're telling me to leave?"

"I didn't think you'd come. Nor did I know they weren't in the nursery," Grant said, walking into the men's room.

I saw Valentino coming toward me with the twins in his arms. I moved in his direction to get a glimpse of those babies.

A nurse walked up between us and took the babies. "I'll take them, Mr. James," she politely said.

"Cool. I'll pick them up when I come back from grabbing a bite," Valentino said, getting on the elevator.

Intentionally I blocked her path. I stared into the infants cradled in her arms. It wasn't her face I had to see. I had to see Honey's babies' eyes. "Oh, they're so adorable," I said, staring at the boys. Their tiny pupils, little brown irises, button noses, and ruby red lips were too young to tell if they resembled Grant.

"Miss, please," she said in a muffled sweet soft voice. "I have to keep them away from strangers. H1N1 is everywhere. I have to go." The face mask covered her nose and mouth. Her fiery red hair was neatly spiraled into a bun. She had gray eyes. Cocoa brown skin with freckles. Wide hips. Flat ass. Her mauve scrubs didn't have a wrinkle. Her arms were covered with a white long-sleeve shirt that fit snug around her thick wrists. Her shoes were white. But that triple diamond pear-and-heart ring was amazing.

Go where? Something didn't seem right. One of the boys started crying. The woman rushed to the end of the hall and disappeared beyond the NURSERY sign.

I went to the nursery window waiting for her to put those boys in beds and roll them out alongside the other newborns. When no one was watching, I tiptoed inside the nursery, peeped around. I had to see them one more time before Grant came out of the restroom.

"Excuse, me. But you can't come in here," a nurse said.

"Oh, I'm from Child Protective Services." What in the world made me tell that lie? Maybe secretly I wished I were so I could legally take those innocent little creatures away from that whore. "I was checking to make sure the Hill twins were here. I'll go get my paperwork out of the car," I lied again, then left the nursery.

Grant hadn't come out of the men's restroom so I went in. I saw his shoes underneath the stall door. "Oh, wee! What you been eating?"

He flushed the toilet, opened the door, then washed his hands. "You." He laughed, then said, "Why are you still here?"

I didn't find humor in his response.

He kissed my cheek. "I'll call you later." Grant squared his shoulders. I watched my man swagger down the hallway to his Honey.

I wasn't releasing Grant without a fight. I had a few minutes to spare before meeting Bambi at CUT. I had to look into her eyes when I asked, "What happened to my grandson yesterday?"

I waited until the door to Honey's room closed, then followed Grant to 9109.

CHAPTER 26

Honey

Valentino was great with the boys.

I appreciated Valentino taking my boys back to the nursery so I could rest. A part of me hoped we'd occasionally get his twins and his older son, Anthony, together with my boys but his wife Summer had moved and no one knew where she was. The last time Valentino called her, the number belonged to someone else. He feared Summer had gone crazy after her twin sister, Sunny, was killed.

My best friend, Sapphire Bleu, who was an undercover cop, had Valentino's murder charges dropped but none of us knew for sure whether or not Valentino was responsible for Sunny's death. In my heart, I couldn't believe he killed Sunny.

I didn't judge Valentino. What drew us together was we were survivors. I knew firsthand what it was like to take a man's life. Would kill again if I had to. I closed my eyes. Before the upper lids touched the bottom, I heard, "Hey, Mommy. How are you?"

Grant stood beside my bed, held my hand. "I still wish you would've told me."

I shook my head. "Stop it. Please. I did what was best for me. You were the one who told me don't call you ever again. I honored your request."

I'd been a fool so deep in love with Grant I swam beyond the horizon and almost drowned. He was the first and only man I'd given my heart to. I was going under and he refused to toss me a life preserver. What hurt the most was he wasn't considerate enough to give me back my heart. He dropped my love, stepped on my emotions, walked away, then stole Jada's heart. I picked up my broken heart almost a year ago. Took me some time to heal but I'm good now. What I didn't understand was why, when our relationship was over, Grant treated me so heartlessly?

He nodded. "You have no idea how happy you've made me."

How happy I'd made him? Was I supposed to be happy now that I'd become a single mother? Was I supposed to be happy because Grant was happy?

"Maybe you can tell me," Jada said, standing in the doorway.

I'd seen Jada on television sitting in her plush box office suite at Darius's games. And I'd seen Grant strutting back and forth in Jada's suite like he owned the team. Jada was more beautiful in person. Her dark skin was flawless. She had beautiful hazel eyes and to say she was fifty, her body was banging, flat stomach, perky tits and all. I could put her on a stroll or two, make a quick five figures. She was that sexy. But I wasn't a madam any more. Got out of the business shortly before I'd gotten pregnant.

Grant released my hand. "Don't come in here like that. You know I love you."

I wouldn't readily believe that if I were her. I could tell by the tone of his voice he was lying. I smiled, recalling the times Grant and I shared those words. I also remembered telling him, "Sometimes love isn't enough." Like musical chairs, I'd gotten up, and Jada had sat in my seat. Better her than me. Grant taught me never to love a man who didn't love me first. It was hard for me not to call and tell him I was pregnant with his babies but in my former business, a person's word was bond.

"I guess her having your babies could be a good thing," Jada said, standing by the door, inside my room. "You have your sons, we don't have to adopt, and we'll have joint custody," Jada said, as if the decision was hers and as if her bitch ass could rightfully demand to see my boys. Now her ass wasn't so cute. She was about to get some Flagstaff whup ass. I might be from a small town in Arizona but I'd been around the world twice.

"You will not touch my boys unless I say so," I told her.

"You, my dear, are an unfit mother. You don't deserve those boys. Keep it up and I'll make sure they're taken away," she said, excusing herself from my room.

Jada had said some ignorant shit but the bitch wasn't crazy enough to keep standing in my doorway. Coward.

CHAPTER 27

Honey

I pointed at Grant. "You had better put that bitch in check. She does not know who she's fucking with. I don't give a fuck about your marrying her but if either of you touch my boys without my prior permission, I will kill you."

"Mommy, calm down. She's upset. She's not serious," Grant said, holding my hand again.

I told him, "Let me say, you've been put on notice."

"Honey, you and I were never right for one another but . . ." He paused, pressing his fingers into his tears, then continued. "Now that you've had my boys, I will always have a place in my heart for you. Honey, you have given me the greatest gift a woman can give a man."

"Yeah, and what if I slam your heart on the hot concrete, then stomp it into the ground? Huh? How would you like that? Don't try to play me again. Be glad I let you stay for the delivery."

Grant shook his head.

"Knock, knock," Sapphire said, walking in with Velvet and lots of flowers. "Grant, close your mouth. Only two things come out of a man's mouth and that's burps and lies."

"Well, I did not die. I had two babies," I said, laughing. "Y'all making me hurt my stomach." I loved my girlfriends. Their timing was perfect. Men were unpredictable. My girlfriends were loyal.

"That's why we brought you two bouquets," Velvet said. "We know Luke has to have his own everything."

"And six balloons," Sapphire said. "You should've named one of them Bleu. But I do like the names you picked."

I frowned, tilted my ear toward the door. "Do I hear Luke crying?"

"Girl, you need some rest. This is a maternity ward. All babies cry," Sapphire said, sitting on one side of my bed while Velvet sat on the other.

"No seriously. I know his cry. Grant, please. Go check on the boys," I said to his back. Grant was already on his way out the door. He needed something to do other than listen to my conversation with my girls.

My stomach contracted. "Let me see your ring, girl," I told Velvet, reaching for her hand. "You think it's big enough? Sorry about interrupting your proposal while you were onstage at your premiere. Damn! Congratulations are in order. You are one bad bitch."

Sapphire said, "I second that emotion. I've seen her make a full water bottle disappear in her pussy and come out empty."

Velvet's smile was wide and bright. "Yeah, I guess stripping had its benefits."

Sapphire said, "If anyone would've bet that the three of us . . . each of us, would be in happy meaningful relationships, I would have told them they were crazy. I'm married to a wonderful man and both of you are happy and engaged. Honey, when you get settled back in Atlanta, we have to celebrate."

My engagement to Valentino wasn't legit. But he was there for me throughout my pregnancy and sometimes that's all a woman needed from a man—for him to be there. I held their hands, smiled. "I want both of you to be godmothers to my boys."

"I've got Luke. He's a lot like you," Sapphire said.

Velvet smiled, then replied, "I guess that means I've got London. I'm going to teach him how to act."

Grant rushed into the room, interrupting our conversation. "Honey, did Valentino take the boys?"

"Yes, to the nursery." I sat up.

Sapphire and Velvet stood.

Grant shook his head. "The boys are not in the nursery."

"What! Oh, God. Don't tell me Jada took my babies for real." I placed my feet on the floor. The stitches in my uterus hurt so bad I had to sit down.

"Velvet, you stay here with Honey," Sapphire said. "I'll find whoever this Jada bitch is." Grant followed Sapphire.

Velvet held me. I cried until Grant and Sapphire came back to the room with the nurse, no babies. Valentino walked in behind the nurse. "What's going on?"

The nurse said, "A woman came into the nursery after you left." She pointed at Valentino. "Said she was with Child Protective Services. We were obligated to . . ."

Valentino and Sapphire ran out of the room. Grant rushed out too.

"Get out!" I yelled at the nurse.

Velvet sat on the side of my bed facing me. "Luke and London will be back shortly. I'm sure it was a simple mix-up. . . ."

As Velvet continued talking, I got up, gathered my open gown in the back. I held my stomach, dragged my feet two steps from my bed.

Valentino entered my room. "We're on it, baby."

A police officer opened the door, then asked, "Honey Thomas?"

"Yes, I'm Honey Thomas. Thank God you're here. Where are my boys?"

The officer asked, "Do you have knowledge of the whereabouts of Anthony Valentino James?"

My heart dropped to my stomach. My body tensed. I closed my eyes.

Valentino said, "I'm Anthony Valentino James."

I looked at him, at my BFF, and wanted to cry but I didn't.

The officer gripped his cuffs, locked Valentino's hands behind his back, and said, "You're under arrest for grand theft auto. Anything you say can and will be held against you."

"Velvet, go find Sapphire!" I cried. All of this was like a living nightmare. "Where are my babies?"

Velvet ran out the door.

I didn't shed a tear for Valentino. We both had jaded pasts. We knew the lives we'd lived could lead to imprisonment any given moment. I removed Valentino's ring from my finger. "I'll give this back to you when you get out. Don't worry. Sapphire will have you out in no time."

It was great having an undercover cop as my friend. Sapphire could get anybody out of jail. Grand theft auto was minor in comparison to Sapphire having Valentino's attempted murder charges dropped.

Valentino stared at the ring he'd given me, then asked, "Lace, why?"

Not responding, I watched the officer escort him out, praying Valentino hadn't betrayed me. Until they found my boys, everybody was suspect. He was the last one I saw with my babies. Did he know where my boys were? Was he plotting against me with Jada? Was everything Valentino had said and done for me during my pregnancy a damn lie? If he didn't know where my babies were, was Valentino the kind of man I wanted to raise Luke and London?

We knew Valentino had stolen that car. What I didn't know was how the police in Los Angeles knew about the car theft in Atlanta. Some hocus-pocus shit was going on. As upset as I was about Valentino, I was furious not knowing where my boys were. Alone in my room, I could not continue to lie in bed doing nothing but worry. I had to do something. I made it to my door, opened it.

Jada stood in front me, shrugged her shoulders.

The space in front of my eyes faded to black.

Silently I prayed. Brain? Courage? Heart?

I will strangle this bitch if she says one word.

CHAPTER 28

Bambi

*D*amn, I'm good.

D Jada saw me yesterday and didn't recognize me disguised as a nurse today. I'd pretended as though I was going into the nursery. Quickly, I detoured into the stairway.

Hurrying down the stairs, I stumbled. "Oh, shit." I fumbled one of the babies like a football, recovered him before his head hit the iron rail. What would I do if one of them were to get hurt or become sick? Well, the Pacific Ocean is part of my backyard. I had no intention of repeating a double homicide. Hopefully for all our sakes, I won't have them too long. If necessary, I'll sell them, two for the price of one. I could easily sell twin boys on the black market. Hell, they weren't my kids. I just wanted Jada's ass in the hot seat with Grant so she wouldn't have time to focus on Darius or Fancy.

I turned my back to the Exit door, pressed my butt against the bar, opened the door. The twins were each bundled in beautiful blue blankets. "How cute." With only their faces exposed, they looked like two pigs in a blanket. I prayed Darius didn't want any kids. That one he had was more than enough and exactly where he belonged, with his crazy ass mama. I had to make sure DJ stayed with Ashlee but I was positive that kid never wanted to be alone with me again.

One of the babies wailed. I prayed no one heard him. His golden complexion turned beet red. He was kicking and getting on my damn nerves already. "Shut up, you sissy. Toughen up like your brother and shut up all that goddamn crying," I yelled at him, rushing into the garage. My car was closest to the stairs. I turned my back and confirmed the duct tape I'd placed over the surveillance camera's dome a few minutes ago was still there.

There was no time to strap them in the two car seats in the back. I unlocked the passenger door, placed the twins on the floor in front of the seat.

"What are you doing?" a woman yelled, running toward me. "You can't put those babies there like that!"

Bitch should've minded her own business. I grabbed my ruby red lipstick, removed the top and pepper-sprayed her ass real good.

Screaming, she covered her face, fell to her knees. "I can't breathe. Help," she whimpered, falling to the ground.

She rolled on her back, kicked like DJ when he threw that temper tantrum. I beat his behind real good. That was probably his first real whipping. I'd stared that brat in his eyes, told him if he told anyone I beat him I was coming back in the middle of the night and I'd take him deep into the woods and feed him to the bears.

The bitch on the ground better be glad I didn't run over her ass. I inserted my prepaid parking ticket, zipped out the garage in my black sedan. I sped down South San Vincente Boulevard, hooked a right onto North La Cienega Boulevard. When the green light at Clifton Way turned yellow, I accelerated.

Whoop! Whoop!

"Fuck. Just my luck. Bambi, stay cool." I only had two miles to go and my mission was interrupted twice. How was I going to explain to the cop why I had the babies on the floor? I inched my way from the Japanese barbecue joint to LMG Studio to make certain I was the one he was pulling over.

CHAPTER 29

Bambi

Whoop!

Yep, it was definitely me. I grabbed a fresh vibrant blue lipstick from my Ho-on-the-Go bag, parked the car, turned up the radio to drown out that cry baby, and got out the car.

"Miss, get back in the car," he commanded.

Fuck that. I was not getting back in the car. Clenching my lipstick, I pleaded, "Officer, please don't take me to jail. I'm a nurse. I just worked twenty-four hours straight. I only have a few hours to go home and rest before I have to get back to work and help save some more lives. I was listening to 'Single Ladies' on the radio when Beyoncé said, 'Now put your hands up.' I accidentally accelerated to the beat. You know she won a Grammy for 'Single Ladies.' Of course you do. I promise I'll be careful. From now on I'll slow down at the yellow light. I promise. Please don't write me a ticket." I mimicked James Brown. "Please, please, please, please . . . please."

The officer started laughing, then threw his hands up. "Drive safe, miss," he said, heading back to his car. "And don't put on that lipstick while you're driving."

Soon as I got in the car, I started heaving, nearly vomiting in my lap. I'd done a lot of illegal things but I'd never been to jail. Prison terrified me. I would've uncapped my lipstick, pepper-sprayed him, and zapped his eyes out with my stun gun if I had to. I waited until he drove off, then continued driving along North La Cienega toward Interstate 10. I drove underneath the overpass, parked in the mini market lot next to Rita's car.

Rita opened her rear passenger door. I got out of my car, secured the infant car seats in the backseat of her new SUV, then strapped in the twins. Didn't want to take any chances with trusting Rita would secure them properly.

Handing Rita an envelope, I told her, "Here's five grand, the directions to my house on East Seaside Walk in Long Beach, the garage door opener, and a key. Drive safe. Do not run any lights or break any speed limits."

"These babies sure are beautiful. Their parents on vacation? Who they belong to? And how long do I have to babysit them? Hush, little baby," she said to that crying sissy, and for the first time his ass shut up. Rita closed her door, lowered her driver's window.

I stood outside her door. "You. For now, they belong to you," I told her.

"And how long do I have to watch them?"

"I'm not sure."

"Not sure like a week or not sure like a year?"

"Take them to the house. Make yourself at home but you are not allowed to leave the house with or without the boys. Not even for a second. Understood?"

Rita raised her brows. "What if the house is on fire or y'all have one of them things when the ground starts movin'?"

Shaking my head, I told her, "I'll be at the house shortly. I have to go buy diapers and milk. What kind of milk should I get?"

"Get some of that kind in the can, not that powdered stuff." She glanced over her shoulders, smiled at the babies. "I should've had boys. I would've been a better mother. Girls are complicated. What's their names?"

"Luke and London. Don't ask me which is which. Don't know. Don't care. I'll see you in a few. Don't stop on your way to the house, not even at a drive-thru. And don't open the door at my house for anyone. I'll bring you something to eat. Oh, and one more thing. Whatever you do, do *not* turn on any of the televisions."

"Would've been easier to give me one of them house arrest anklets like Madea."

"Don't tempt me." I got in my car, drove to the Beverly Wilshire on Wilshire Boulevard. I parked in the garage at the shopping center across the street. I grabbed my Ho-on-the-Go bag, went to the public restroom, and made a quick change in the handicapped stall. I removed my auburn lace wig, untangled my braids, dampened my hair and applied a small amount of conditioner. I finger styled my hair. Tossing the uniform and shoes in my bag, I squeezed into a pair of second skin black leather pants, snapped the four buttons above each ankle, put on a black satin top, and stepped into my open-toe stilettos.

I put my bag back in my car, headed across the street to CUT inside the Beverly Wilshire, and waited for Jada.

CHAPTER 30

Jada

"Let me go!" I gripped Honey's wrists trying to remove her hands from my throat. She had the strength of a mule. I wanted to knee her in her stomach but I couldn't breathe. She had my back against the wall. I muttered, "Let me go. I was kidding about calling . . ." I gasped, then continued, "Child Protective Services."

Was karma more of a bitch than Honey? Did people actually reap what they sowed?

"Lying bitch, you did call them. I should kill you. Where are my boys?"

I saw why Grant was attracted to her. She had long wavy golden hair and her skin was gold like honey. She was gorgeous. But she was also deranged.

I tried moving my leg back to give a good kick to her ankle, shin, anywhere. Grant came to my rescue, I thought, until he grabbed me from the side, and yelled, "Honey, stop it! Let her go!" Suddenly we were surrounded by security officers and nurses.

"Grant, you'd better get your hands off me, now!"

"Yeah, let her ass go," Honey said, shifting side to side with her fists in front her face.

"If you so ghetto bad, why you hiding behind your dead sister's identity? Your real name isn't Honey. It's Lace St. Thomas, you murderer!"

Grant said, "Jada, that's enough."

Why hadn't he grabbed his phony Honey? She was the one choking me. Security had to pry her fingers away from my neck. I bent over, started coughing. I prayed this hideous incident did not get to Darius.

"Come on, Ms. Thomas. Obviously this woman doesn't know you," the nurse said. "But you can't assault every person you think stole your babies. Keep this up and we'll have to admit you to the psychiatric ward. Let us handle finding the twins. You need to rest. And you"—the nurse looked at me—"are prohibited from coming to this hospital. Security, make sure her name is added to the Do Not Admit list."

I lamented, "You can't keep me from coming here. She started this. Plus my son is Darius Jones and his wife, my daughter-in-law, Fancy Taylor, is admitted here. She's on the third floor."

"Then you should've been on the third floor. You can't come back here. If you do, you're trespassing and security will detain you until the police arrive." The nurse escorted Honey inside 9109.

"This is all your damn fault! You taking up for her, take this." *Wham!* I slapped Grant's face as hard as I could.

"Miss, you have to leave," security said. "You've caused enough of a disturbance in this hospital. Please don't make me do my job."

"If you were doing your job, the babies wouldn't be missing. Touch me and you'll regret it," I said, squinting.

Grant grabbed my bicep. "I'll take care of her." He ushered me to the elevator, then to the lobby. "What did you do with my boys?"

Smack! I hit him again. "Get your hand off me and don't ever touch me again." Something came over me in that moment and I wanted to rip off Grant's clothes and have makeup sex in the lobby.

"Hit me again," he said angrily, then repeated, "Hit me again."

"Don't you ever hold me for her again." My pussy was getting hot. My whole body got hot. I started dripping with sweat.

"Here's a hot flash for you. I'll find my boys the legal way. And when I do, you're going to jail. I guarantee it." He got on the elevator.

I checked the time. I was twenty minutes late for lunch. I called Bambi.

"Hey, Jada. I got us a table. Are you here yet?"

"I have to take a rain check." I was on the verge of crying. I couldn't believe Grant would think I'd kidnap Honey's babies. What would I do with two newborns?

Bambi asked, "You okay?"

"No, I'm not. Honey's twins were kidnapped. The media is storming the hospital. I gotta go. I'll talk with you later."

A reporter shoved a microphone in my face. "Is it true, security said that you threatened to call Child Protective Services on Honey—or is her real name Lace St. Thomas?" he asked.

Security? Everybody wanted to be a superstar. My clothes stuck to my body, my hair to my head. "Honey Thomas can kiss my ass. Report that. All I know is she'd better not put her hands on me again or she'll be the one missing," I said, exiting the lobby.

CHAPTER 31

Honey

She'd be wise to return my sons before I was released from this hospital.

I choked Jada to let her know I was serious. She could have Grant. I wasn't competing with her. And she definitely was out of her league with me. The fact that Grant was standing in my room showed me he was done with Jada.

The nurse helped me into my bed. "Ms. Thomas, you have to rest. For the safety of our employees and other patients and their families, I have to place you on visitor restriction until you leave."

"And while I'm laying on my ass in this room by myself going crazy, are you going to find my babies?"

I was ready to rip off a head or two, hers included. Take out whoever had my babies, execution style if I had to. I wasn't scared of nothing and no one. My upbringing made me tough. My mother, Rita, was a tyrant. She hated me. Why? I still wasn't sure. Only reason I thought of was envy. It was a damn shame my mother believed I wanted to fuck her man. I was sixteen. I wasn't thinking about his old rusty ass. He was the one fondling me. Finally had my own kids and someone kidnapped them. Was this payback for my killing Reynolds? Hadn't I paid restitution by retiring my female escorts from the business and by giving them a million dollars each to start legitimate businesses?

"I'll find them," Grant said. "And I'll be here at the hospital for you."

I was too angry to cry. Tears of blood would stream down my face if I had. "You let all my people see me," I told the nurse.

"We'll see, Ms. Thomas," the nurse said, propping my pillow behind my back.

"See my ass. Let me find out you denied visitation and your ass is next."

Grant interrupted, "She didn't mean that. It's just that we have friends that have connections. We need to talk to them."

What was up with all the *we* stuff?

"I'm not going to accept threats from you, Ms. Thomas. Your friends and family can visit you at your house. You can go home now if you'd like," the nurse said. "I'll see if the doctor will approve an early discharge."

"Yes, please, and thank you," I told her. She wouldn't be so damn passive if it were her kids missing.

After she left my room, Grant said, "You sure you want to do that? I think you're better off here. You're over three thousand miles away from home and we have to find the boys. Where will we stay?"

"Stop, it, Grant. Just stop it. This is not about we, us, or what you think. What were you thinking when you ended our relationship over the phone? You weren't man enough to tell me face to face. Now you show up in my life thinking you're a part of it. Not."

He shook his head. "I was stupid. Forgive me."

"Well, I'm not stupid. Not anymore. Don't think you're back in my life because of the boys. Dear God, where are my babies? This is all your fault."

My purpose for staying at the hospital changed within minutes. I could recover after I found my boys. I didn't want to leave but I had to get out of this place. I went to the closet, saw my gown and two-inch heels from the premiere. The clothes I'd worn here were all I had at the hospital. Removing my hospital gown, replacing it with my other gown, I stepped into my shoes.

Grant laughed. "You can't be serious."

"Watch me." I picked up my purse, took several steps toward the door, then stumbled. My maternity clothes were at the Beverly Wilshire. Valentino and our room key were at lockup.

Grant's strong arms saved me from hitting the floor. In that moment, we connected. I felt his love, his energy. I became weak for him again. "Honey, our boys are safe," he said, trying to reassure me.

I had to hold on to hope, to Grant, praying he was right. "You sure?" I asked, removing my shoes, then my gown. I put on a fresh hospital gown, got back in bed. The soreness of my body sunk into the mattress. "Hand me my purse."

"Yes, I'm sure," he said, giving me my clutch. "Jada wouldn't harm them. When Sapphire gets back, I'll get you some regular clothes."

Hope turned to hate. "Are you saying you know for sure she has my babies? Are you involved in this?" I slammed my purse on the floor. The contents scattered at his feet, my lipstick and perfume slid across the floor. I'd forgotten I put an extra room key in my purse.

"Honey, no, baby." Grant stuffed my cash, credit cards, driver's license, and room key back in my purse, then cautiously put my clutch on the stand beside my bed. "That's not what I'm saying at all. Are you saying you're not going to let me be involved in their lives?"

"What I'm saying is I don't want you involved in my life." I detoured off my road back to vulnerability. Became cold and callous toward Grant. "You can have a relationship with . . . Dear God, where are my babies?"

Sapphire ran into the room. "Calm down. I heard you down the hall. Don't worry. I'll find them. There's an Amber Alert on the freeways showing twin boys were abducted from the hospital. Every news reporter in town is in the lobby. I've requested the surveillance tapes from the hospital and the nearby intersections, and I've instructed the staff not to allow the media access to you. You don't know anything so it's best not to talk to them. That goes for you too, Grant. What Jada said to you, my dear, wasn't nothing. The media will really portray you as unfit."

This time I had to cry. I started repenting for my sins and silently praying to God for His forgiveness.

"Focus. Stay with me," Sapphire said, sitting on the edge of my bed. "I had a chance to speak with Valentino before the cops put him in the car. He said he handed the babies to a redheaded nurse. And Jada was standing there when he did it."

Grant said, "Jada came into the men's restroom while I was in there. Maybe that was to keep me from witnessing the abduction. Then she followed me down here."

I added, "She came into my room, threatened me, then left abruptly."

"But she came back to your room," Sapphire commented. "So how could she have the babies, if you were strangling her?"

"Jada is brilliant and rich. She has an accomplice," Grant said. "She wouldn't do it. She'd have someone else do it."

Sapphire said, "Well, Child Protective Services knows nothing about this situation. Let's see. I wouldn't rule out Valentino. Who else would have a motive? Aw, shit!" Sapphire leapt from my bedside.

"What?" I asked. "What?"

"I'm with you," Grant said. "It could be an inside job."

"Exactly. I have to request the police and border patrol set up a checkpoint into Mexico."

"And LAX," I said. "Grant, take this key, go to my room at the Beverly Wilshire, get all of our things, check out, then come back and get me. I'll be ready by then. I have to be."

Grant took the room key, hurried out of the room.

"I've already got LAX covered," Sapphire said, standing in the door. "If the boys are taken out of the country, you may never see them again. Gotta go."

CHAPTER 32

Rita

"Geeze!" The house was the biggest I'd ever seen my whole life. I took one baby inside. I left him in the car seat, sat the seat in the middle of the living room floor, then went and got his brother. I sat them facing one another. Had to make my acquaintance with the house before Bambi got here.

"She said this here was her dead parents' house. The way it's decorated and all, looks like they still live here."

There were pictures on the living room wall of two people who looked like they could be her parents. I needed eyeglasses but refused to get them. I could see the things I wanted if I got close enough. I squinted. Didn't understand why narrowing my eyes made me see a bit better but it did. They seemed happy. The man looked white. The woman, she looked light-skinned like Bambi. I got real close. Stared at the woman's face.

"Yep, she Bambi's mama all right. They got them same pushed back in the forehead dark eyes."

In search of the bathroom, I passed through a kitchen with a big white island that had a bar overhang with pots and pans dangling in the air. There were two stools on one side underneath the counter-top. "Wow." All of that was in the middle of the kitchen floor. "That's pretty fancy."

Still hadn't made it to the bathroom. I opened a door to my left. "Wow, sure hope this is my and the boys' room." The bedroom was laid out for a princess. A high white canopy bed with a pink and white lace bedspread. A real bench was at the foot of the bed. I could sit there and stare out at the ocean. One of them fancy things where folk hide the TV was in there too. I closed the door. Saw two more doors down the way. I'd get to them later, already picked out my room. I headed back toward the boys.

They were fine. They'd fallen asleep. This time I noticed a patio off the kitchen. So busy admiring that island, hadn't looked any farther. There was a table for six inside the nook area. Outdoors on the patio there was another table for six with one of them huge umbrellas covering it.

I opened the glass double doors. "Oh, my. Bambi is rich."

Round the corner of that patio table was the longest wraparound porch I'd seen in my life. 'Bout a quarter of a block long. "Where the neighbors at?" The porch was surrounded by beautiful white wooden rails, and had a few white posts on the corners and in the middle that went all the way up to the roof. I walked down five stairs and white sand was beneath my feet. I was really on the beach. The blue waves rolled toward me. Thank goodness they were too far out to wet my feet or drag me into the ocean.

I sat on the porch, brushed the sand from between my toes, knocked my Birkenstocks together, put my shoes on and went to check on the boys. They were fine. One was asleep. The other one watched him.

The dining room had its own setup and a separate bar with high stools. Not the bar that was connected to the island. This here was a different area. I pulled back the curtains and saw the ocean again. "It's pretty at sunset but I bet it's scary at nighttime. That Bambi could throw me in them waters, the sharks would smell my blood, eat me up, and no one would know I'm missing. I better not make her mad. She ain't wrapped too tight. Long as she keeps giving me money, Rita stays until Rita wants to go."

There was one door at the end of the opposite hall. I stared down that long hallway. Took a few steps in that direction. No escape doors to the left or right. Just that one door at the end, facing me. I took a few more steps in that direction. I was halfway there. Might as well keep going. If Rita's gon' be up in here, I need to see what was up in there. I took a few more steps. I gripped the door lever. My legs got weak. Slowly I pushed down on the lever, pushed the door open a little bit.

"What on God's earth is that?" I almost peed on myself.

Maybe my mind was playing games with me. I stepped inside the bedroom. Sho nuff these old eyes weren't deceiving me. There were two closed coffins. I felt my pee trickling out but I had to know if dead people were in there.

These were beautiful bronze coffins with them fancy golden long handles. There was no bed in the big ole room. Them coffins sat high like the funeral was over, they'd removed the folding chairs, and everybody had left and forgotten the bodies. I tiptoed, stood between the coffins. "Which one should I open? Hmm. Eeny, meeny, miny, mo. Catch a fella by his toe, if he hollas let him go. Eeny, meeny, miny, mo." The one to my right.

I placed my hand on the bottom half of the casket. Didn't want to see no dead person looking at me. Slowly, I tried to lift the bottom. "Oh, Jesus!" The coffin slid, almost fell on top of me. I straightened it out, then shut the door closed. My heart raced faster than my feet back down that hallway.

I had to catch my breath. I went to the living room, brought the twins in the family room, put them where they could see me, then sat in one of dem upholstered chairs in front of the fireplace panting like a fit to be tired dog. If the bathroom was in that bedroom, I'd pee in a pot on the porch, then throw it in the sand if I couldn't hold it.

Took me a few minutes but I got myself together. I was pretty sure there was a bathroom close to my room but no more opening doors for Rita until Bambi got here. Didn't know what to call this room here for sure. Could be a family room? Entertainment? Sitting? I believe them sitting rooms don't have no TV.

Who would report Rita St. Thomas missing if someone came out of that room and ran after me? Didn't care 'bout that Bambi's two bits change, I had sense enough to leave this house if need be. I'd been gone from Flagstaff for over a month. Talked to one of my friends once a week. She might miss me or think I'm busy but she wouldn't call no police. Told her I got this here secret assignment in Los Angeles that's paying me thousands of dollars. She didn't believe me. Only person that checked on me on the regular was my daughter who died.

Shoulda been Lace that died. Lace sho was a pretty baby. The older Lace got, the more prettier she got. She was a good girl. Smart. Never gave me much trouble. Didn't smoke weed and stay out all night like her sister. But her sister wasn't pretty. I saw the way my man Don used to lust after Lace whenever she wore them short shorts. Somebody had to go. I wasn't no spring chicken or a cougar so I wasn't kicking my old man out of the house for nobody.

I rocked them baby seats with my feet. "I wonder what Lace would've done with her life if I hadn't put her out. I know my baby wouldn't have been no prostitute and madam, that's for sho. Wouldn't been no millionaire either. Maybe I'd done her a favor. Oh, well. I can't undo the past. I can't blame Lace for stealing her sister Honey's identity." Honey was mischievous but she ain't do half the thangs I heard Lace was out there doing. That was why Lace moved to Atlanta and disowned me.

She had millions of dollars, minks, and them fancy cars with that Jaguar symbol on the hoods. Told me to my face I'd never be in her will. Well, I'm supposed to die first anyway. She could've let her daddy and me hold a few hundred thousand while we're still kickin'. I was still her mother no matter what.

I picked up the remote from the coffee table, turned on the television and heard, "Breaking news!" I saw all them news reporters around the hospital with microphones in this dark-skinned woman's face. She sho was pretty. Wet, but pretty. "Oh, I forgot. Bambi said don't turn on the television." I hurried and turned it off. Didn't want no mess from her.

Taking the babies out of the car seats, I lay them on the love seat side by side. I unwrapped their blankets, stretched their arms, rubbed their stomachs.

"You two are too cute. I ain't never seen no babies this beautiful. Not even my own," I said. I stretched their little legs straight, then bent their knees and stretched their legs again. They had cute blue ankle bands around their left feet.

I held up their left legs and almost died.

Luke Hill was on one. London Hill was the other. Mother, Honey Thomas, was on both. "Well, Rita will be damned. These here are my grandbabies?"

CHAPTER 33

Bambi

After Jada cancelled lunch, I sat at the bar inside CUT, at the Beverly Wilshire, ordered another dirty Goose martini, then clicked on Darius's Facebook page. His last posting, Gotta go put up some shots before I lose it. Baby mama drama. Just sayin', was hours ago. "It's okay, my Darius," I whispered. "Mama's gonna make it all good for us."

Admiring my engagement ring, I switched to the ABC News highlights of the day on my iPhone. I loved the pureness of the all-white decor of the restaurant. The ambiance was serene. Soft instrumental jazz resonated throughout the place. I saw the media practically shoving microphones in Jada's mouth as she parted the crowd. Her hair and clothes were soaked. It wasn't raining. She was the only one dripping wet. At her age, had to be a hot flash. Better her than me.

I called Jada. Was about to hang up until I faintly heard her say, "Hi, Bambi."

"I saw the news. I'm still at CUT. I've got an idea to minimize your media attention. If you still want to meet, I'll wait as long as you'd like."

"No, it's okay. I need to be alone." Her sadness sounded like the onset of depression.

I offered, "Need help with DJ?" hoping she didn't. I hadn't called Ashlee today but hopefully that kid was with her by now.

"That's a good idea. What am I thinking? That's a horrible idea. DJ isn't used to being with nonfamily members. I've got to get some rest before Ashlee drops him off. I'll call you tomorrow."

"I'm here anytime, day or night, you can depend on me." *And if you believe that, bitch, you're too damn trusting.*

Jada whispered, "Thanks," then ended our call.

A toast. I held my glass in the air. "Another job well done, Bambi. Cheers, bitch." I tossed back the vodka, swallowed an olive, almost choked. "Damn, this is my lucky day." I started to close my tab when I saw Grant Hill walk in. Waving as though I knew him, I stood, then motioned for him to come in my direction.

"Hey, I saw your story on the news. I'm so sorry to hear about your twins. Sit. You look like you could use a drink." I didn't wait for him to answer. "Bartender, two more of the same, both with two large olives. Make that three olives."

I had his attention the second I mentioned his boys. Grant sat on the edge of his stool, placed one foot on the foot bar, the other on the floor. The imprint of his big dick made my pussy twitch.

Grant's eyes focused on mine. His navel pointed in the opposite direction of the bar. His body language said he didn't want to be rude but he had to go soon. "Thanks, I could use a drink. But just one. I have to get my sons' mother's things from her room upstairs." He stared at his feet. Blinked several times. Became silent.

I loved it when men volunteered too much information. I gave him a moment, touched his thigh, then let him know, "I can't disclose what I know but I can help you get your boys back."

Grant eyes widened, then narrowed. He stared at me. "Are you serious? Or are you bullshitting me?" His navel faced me. Desperation kept him on the edge of his stool. "Why should I believe you? I don't even know you."

Hunching my left shoulder, I said, "You're right. You don't have to believe anything. But I guarantee you I know more than you about where your boys are." I motioned to the bartender. "Close me out."

Darius should be done shooting around and Fancy should be dead. Shit was constipated, backing me up. The bartender placed our drinks on the bar, along with my bill. Grant was fine. I wanted to fuck his brains out but I didn't have all day to seduce him. I had to go check on Rita and the twins.

Grant said, "Please don't leave. Give me a moment," then headed toward the men's restroom.

Damn, he had a sexy ass stride. I had to accelerate my mission to fuck that man. I put my hands inside my purse, opened my bottle of Cialis, shook two five-milligram tablets in my hand, placed them on my tongue. I picked up the green plastic toothpick holding his olives, inserted them in my mouth. Pretending I was sucking, I pushed those tablets inside the olives with my tongue. I put the olives back inside Grant's martini.

Before he sat on the stool, I handed him his drink. Surprisingly he slid all three olives off the toothpick into his mouth. "A little unusually crunchy but good. When you're starving, everything tastes good."

Well, I sure hoped he was starving for this good pussy between my legs. Swallowing my olive whole, I said, "I totally agree."

In fifteen minutes Grant's dick would be rock hard and deep inside my pussy. "What you think about those New Orleans Saints going to the Super Bowl?" I asked, trying to keep his mind off the boys.

He chuckled. Damn, he had the sexiest smirk and perfect white teeth. "Well deserved and long overdue. I hope they win. I bought tickets but I'm not going. You can have them," he said, downing his drink.

"Really?" I touched his thigh above his knee, slowly slid my hand toward his dick, then back to his knee.

"Hey, that ain't cool right now," he commented, scooting back on the stool.

My touch gave his dick a wake-up call. I arched my back, to give him a full view of my cleavage. "I'd love to have them." I handed him my card. "Bartender, one more round."

"I can't. I have to go. I'll send you the tickets to"—he looked at the card, then said—"this PO Box. Bartender, charge the last round to room 1221." Grant adjusted his dick. It got bigger each time he touched it while looking at me.

Seductively, I said, "No, I want to thank you. Why don't we take these drinks up to your room and I can explain to you in private how I can help you find your boys."

CHAPTER 34

Bambi

We made our way to room 1221. He sat the tray on the coffee table.

"You don't have to drink the martini if you don't want to," I said, sitting on the edge of the bed. I patted the space beside me. "Come. Relax for a moment."

He hesitated to sit next to me. Fully clothed down to his shoes, he stretched out on the bed, rolled onto his stomach. I rubbed his shoulders. "Wow, you're tensed."

I hadn't met a man that didn't enjoy my massages. Alternating between soft and firm, I massaged Grant's shoulders and the nape of his neck. His firm body felt so amazing my eyes scrolled upward. I felt his body gradually sinking into the mattress. I straddled him, stroked lower, kneading his shoulder blades. Then I pressed my pussy into his lower back.

"I don't know what's happening. I feel strange and embarrassed." He squirmed on the comforter.

"Turn over for me." I slid my pussy over his ass and down his thighs before standing.

He hunched his shoulders, rolled over. His dick imprint was huge.

I unbuttoned, then removed his shirt. Sat beside him, then massaged from his biceps down to his thick fingers. I could ride that middle one and squirt all over him. "Let me massage the edge off," I said, unzipping his pants. *Yeah, with this good pussy.*

I slid his pants under his ass, down his thighs, and over his feet, then removed my clothes. I grabbed a wet towel, freshened him up, placed my sunglasses on the desk facing us, opened the gold packet and slid the condom on with my mouth. Slowly, I mounted his big beautiful dick.

I was ready to get the orgasm that I needed. I prayed when I was done cumming, his erection would subside in less than thirty-six hours. And he'd have to pray that the incriminating video I was recording didn't ruin his chances with Honey.

Grant was speechless when I eased down on him. In slow motion, I slid up and down his dick. My pussy danced on his pole. We both needed this outlet. I placed his thumb on my clit, then moaned softly.

He stroked my clit while staring at me. "You're so beautiful. What did I do to deserve this? You feel so good, I can't hold back."

I rode him a little harder, a lot deeper, constantly hitting my spot. He was not cumming without me. The sex was better than I'd imagined but not better than the days I'd dreamt about fucking Darius.

Grant's body shivered. I waited until he stopped moving, then I dismounted him and removed the condom. Grant stroked his dick. Not in a sexual way. He looked confused. Probably trying to figure out who I really was. Why he'd fucked me. How he would explain to Honey what took him so long. And when in the hell his erection was going to subside. He looked pitiful, like a dog that was stuck and didn't know what to do. His problems, not mine. Men were so easy. Too easy.

"Maybe if you take a shower," I suggested while putting on my pants. "I'll see what I can find out today. Call me tomorrow."

CHAPTER 35

Bambi

Soon as Grant closed the bathroom door, I was outta there and headed to the Safeway in Long Beach to buy stuff for his boys. I browsed the aisles for baby formula. I stood there in a quandary reading. Soy. Lactose-free. Isomil DF. Similac with Iron.

"Damn. Another reason not to have kids. Rita said no powder. Or was it get powder?" I tossed one of each in the basket and added a gallon of 2% milk just in case. I chose the Pampers Swaddlers for newborns, pacifiers, bottles, baby wash, baby powder, and four newborn outfits because I was leaving Rita with the twins for the next two days. I picked up a dozen frozen meals for Rita's breakfast, lunch, and dinner.

"Wow, you look good, mama, to say you just had a baby," the clerk said as she scanned my groceries.

I checked Darius's Facebook page. Still no update. "Come, on, baby. I need to know where you are."

"That'll be one hundred thirty-seven dollars and fifty-two cents."

That bitch scanned me harder than the groceries. "I'm straight." I slid my Visa.

"You trippin', Mommie? I was simply giving you a compliment. Don't get me confused. Here's your receipt."

I left her holding the receipt in the air, pushed my shopping cart to my car. An hour later I parked in the garage at my house, unloaded the groceries. Rita was on a down comforter asleep on the floor with the boys beside her.

"Hey, Rita." I nudged her.

Yawning, she stretched her arms above her head. "Hey, Bambi." One of the babies started crying.

I grunted, "Shut him up quick." Did she always have to call my name so loud? I placed my purse on the island. "Here, organize this stuff. I have to get ready for my trip."

"Trip? Where you going now? How long am I watching my, I mean these boys?" Rita said, getting off the floor.

I didn't miss the "my" part. "Not long. I brought you some frozen dinners. This should hold you until I get back in a couple of days. Oh, and I forgot to tell you. Never ever under any circumstances go in the room at the end of the long hall. That's sacred. That was my parents' room."

Rita's brows damn near touched the ceiling. She started trembling. She couldn't speak. I ran to the room, opened the door. Everything was the way I'd left it. My mother's coffin was to the left of my dad's. After their double ceremony, instead of burying my parents at a cemetery, I had the funeral director deliver the coffins to my house at midnight.

I shut the bedroom door, asked Rita, "Why are you shaking?"

She shook her arms and legs. Jerked her neck. "A little stiff from falling asleep on the floor, I suppose."

"Shut him up! I can't take all that whining." I didn't care if he was two days old.

Rita sung softly. "Hush, little baby, don't you cry. Please, don't cry, little baby." Rita sounded like she was about to cry. I had zero tolerance for that kid.

"I don't want you sleeping on my floor. Sleep in the first bedroom on the right or the other bedroom directly across the hall from the one on the right," I said, pointing down the opposite hallway away from my parents' bedroom. "The boys can sleep with you. But don't open the other bedroom door that's straight ahead. That's my room."

"What am I going to do all day without watching television?"

"There's hundreds of DVDs. Watch movies." I went into my bedroom, closed the door, braided my hair. I attached my brown shoulder-length lace wig, changed into my black Baby Phat sweats, and black tennis shoes. I dropped Darius's loc in a plastic bag, then zipped it tight. I locked my parents' bedroom and mine with a key.

"You sure do change your look a lot," Rita said. "How come?"

"Because I entertain for a living."

"Entertain? Oh, you one of them girls. These babies for your boss?"

Don't play dumb with me. I left Rita talking to herself while rocking that crybaby in her arms. The other one seemed content lying on the sofa beside her. Tonight, I'd sleep at the Marriott near LAX.

I had to stay on top of things. My two choices were: Kill Fancy. Or follow through with having an unbreakable love spell cast upon Darius. The two-headed lady said not to call her. She'd know when I was in the French Quarter. I hoped she was telling the truth.

My flight to New Orleans was departing in the morning.

CHAPTER 36

Jada

I'd become a prisoner in my home.

Grant called every ten minutes. I wanted to turn my phone off but was afraid to miss a call from Darius. First Grant didn't want me around. All of a sudden he's leaving demanding voice mail messages that are filling up my mailbox. I'd grown tired of checking and erasing each message.

"Jada, I know you have my boys. Return them to me immediately or I'm coming to your house to get them."

"Jada, I know you know where Luke and London are. I won't have you arrested if you tell me where my boys are."

"Jada, you haven't witnessed my bad side. I will do whatever it takes to get my boys back."

"Jada, I'm on my way to your house," was the last message I'd received, fifteen minutes ago.

I wish he would. Getting out of bed, I opened my blinds, stood on my balcony in my cream camisole and satin baby doll shorts. I exhaled fresh air, thanking God for the sunshine. California was breathtaking. Admiring the peaks of mountains—some covered with snow, others with trees—I felt in love again with myself. I wasn't reluctant to deal with Grant. I feared the next conversation with my son.

Darius, at times, had said words that could stop my heartbeat for the three seconds that could've killed me. When I should've been there for him, I was selfish and foolishly chasing Grant. If I'd been there for my child, Ashlee wouldn't still have DJ and I wouldn't have been banned from the hospital.

"Lord, where is my child? Please keep my grandbaby safe. What a mess I've gotten myself into this time." Ashlee hadn't returned DJ. Nor had she responded to any of my calls. *Maybe I'm overreacting. Maybe Ashlee is keeping him for her two days.*

I stared at the entrance gates. *I can't believe this.* A black Town Car with tinted windows entered my driveway. I hurried into my bedroom, slipped on my sheer robe, then opened my front door.

The driver opened the back door. A pair of brown square-toed men's shoes planted on my cobblestone. His beige slacks and button-up collared shirt loosely hugged his body. His broad shoulders squared, chest protruded.

I stood in the doorway as Grant casually approached me saying, "You left me no choice."

"You've always got a choice. You made yours. I did the same. Please leave my house now."

He bypassed me, entered my house. "I'm not leaving until you tell me. I can be here five minutes or forever."

Once upon a time I wanted him forever. Now five minutes was too long. "Who in hell do you think you are! You are a heartless selfish son of a bitch! You deserve whatever happens to you."

He shook his head, sat on my sofa. "And you are old and desperate."

"I'll tell you what's old. Your calling me 'old.' " I sat beside him. "I wasn't so old and desperate when you proposed to me on Fisher Island. Or when you had the violinist play what used to be our song. Or when we used to finish each other's sentences."

Softly he said, " 'The First Time Ever I Saw Your Face.' " He nodded like his memory had returned. "I'd forgotten about that."

Selective memory is what I'd call it. I stood in front him. Tied my belt in a double knot. "Grant, do you remember telling me, 'Jada Diamond Tanner, I, Grant Hill, promise to be your faithful husband. To forsake all others, to make love only to you, and to never have sex with another woman as long as we are one. I promise to never sweat the small stuff. I want to share my dreams, my goals, my life with you, never taking you for granted. And I promise you that divorce is not an option . . . if you, will you, Jada Diamond Tanner, marry me?' Do you remember those words, Grant? I certainly do."

He laughed. His laughing was getting old too. His finding humor in what's important to me was no joke. I'd give him a moment to erase that stupid smile. When the time was right, I got one for him.

"Damn, what did you do, record it?"

"No, I listened and I believed you were telling me the truth."

"I was. But things changed unexpectedly."

I pulled his arm trying to make him stand up. He pulled back. Kept sitting on my sofa like he was the man of my house.

"So, how in the hell did Honey end up pregnant supposedly by you?"

"Look, I didn't come here to relive my proposal or to explain why I never stopped loving Honey."

Smack! "Get the fuck out of my house. Now!"

Grant leapt from the sofa, started roaming my house. "Not until I'm sure my boys aren't here. I've got people helping me. You will not get away with this."

Stomping on his heels, I followed him into my entertainment room. "You don't know what love is, Grant! You don't know how to love! You're heartless. And you're careless with your words." I picked up my cordless phone. Was this thing still working? When was the last time I'd used my home phone? I pressed the talk button, got a dial tone.

"You've got one minute to get out or I'm calling the police. Speaking of police, where was your Honey when you went to jail? She probably set you up! But you're so dumb, you think that's love. Or maybe you're feeling guilty, huh? For all the wrong things you've done to her."

Grant roamed though my bedrooms, then back to the living room. "You don't want me to leave you. You say all these bad things about Honey hoping it'll make me love you and not her. I can't change my heart. I tried with you. But I never stopped loving Honey. Never. And you're right. She didn't bail me out. But you know what? I can't blame her for that. When I broke her heart, I didn't bail her out of the pain I caused her. If she'll let me make it up to her, I'ma do right by Honey this time. And like it or not, those are my boys and I'm going to find them. Just pray I don't find out you had anything to do with their kidnapping. I know a man is not supposed to hit a woman. I won't make you that promise," he said, walking toward the front door.

"Ha, ha, ha, ha, ha." I laughed at his back. "Poor little Grant, living in a shoe, screwed so many women, you don't know what to do. Well, let me help you out. Go fuck yourself!" I yelled, then slammed my door.

He'd made me numb. I was done with him.

CHAPTER 37

Honey

The wheelchair the nurse rolled into my room was supposed to signal happiness. My boys should be in my arms. Grant should be pushing the chair. Joy should have filled my broken heart.

I asked the nurse, "Give me a minute alone in my room before I leave."

I sat in my wheelchair and wept. "Dear God, keep my babies safe. Please don't let anyone hurt them. Please don't let them be dead, or cold, or hungry, or sick, or in pain. Give me their pain. Let me suffer, not them." My throat ached. I felt like I was gonna die. But I had to live for my babies. I, Honey Thomas, had a reason to live. I'd never felt this way before. "Momma's gonna find you, Luke and London. I promise."

"Knock. Knock." Sapphire opened the door. "You ready . . . ? Oh, mama you're crying. I understand. I promise you I'm going to find your babies." She leaned over the chair and hugged me. "I'm on it. Trust me. Grant is downstairs with Valentino. They're going to take you to Velvet's house. You need to dry those tears and put on your thinking cap, you hear me? I need your head clear. And start thinking about your sleeping arrangements."

I sniffled. Smiled a half smile. "You're right. I do have to keep a clear head. You got Valentino off?"

"Actually, Grant posted his bail. Said he owed Valentino one. Don't

ask me. Men. But my people will have Valentino's charges dropped."
Sapphire sat at the foot of the bed. "Which one of them you want,
Honey?"

That was a question I hadn't thought about much. I actually had a
choice between two men. "I'm not sure I want either of them."
Valentino and Grant entered the room. They deserved to hear what I
had to say so I kept talking to Sapphire.

"I love Valentino. In a brotherly way. Kind of like we're cut from the
same cloth. Sexing Valentino when I was his madam felt good but I
felt bad afterward. But now that I've witnessed his good side, I'd do
anything for him. We both hustled our way to multimillionaire status.
We don't look for trouble but if trouble finds us, we have no problem
doing whatever we have to do to survive. His parents are deceased
and mine might as well be dead. We're two people who need one another but I'm not in love with Valentino."

Valentino said, "A nigga can accept you keeping it one hundred.
But I still want to help raise the boys."

See, "nigga" was in every other sentence for him. Pimpin' was in his
blood. Valentino wouldn't be content for long, living the family life. If
that was what he truly wanted, he'd be with his wife and kids, not here
with me.

"Come here," I said, extending my hand to Valentino. I picked up
my purse from the bed, removed the ring he'd given me, then said, "I
want you to take all that love that you have in your heart for me and
my babies."

Grant interrupted. "Our babies."

"Nigga, she ain't talking to you. Put a lid on it before I put a cap in
it." His threat was filled with sadness.

I patted Valentino's hand. "You're right. I'm not talking to Grant so
look at me, not him. I want you to take all your love and give it to your
twins, your son Anthony, and even if you don't want to be with Summer, you owe her an apology."

"A nigga don't owe her no apology. She left me hangin' with the
kind of change that left a hole in a nigga's pocket. She don't need
me. And a nigga don't need her."

This conversation was taxing on me. Weighing down my spirit. Why
were men, no matter how strong, weak underneath their armor?

"That's where you're wrong. You were her first. Do you remember telling me that? She loved you before you ever met her twin sister. And if Summer's father hadn't banned you from seeing your first-born, we wouldn't be having this conversation. Don't do the right thing for me. Do the right thing for your wife and kids. Pride don't love nobody. Love don't love nobody. People love people. Try loving your wife again. You have nothing to lose but much to gain. I'm gonna be just fine," I told him. I gave Valentino a hug, then gave him back his ring. He slammed the ring to the floor, left the room with tears in his eyes.

"What about this one?" Sapphire asked, nodding toward Grant.

Grant stood tall like he was the defendant and I was his jury.

"Grant, he's different. His parents are upstanding." I thought about but wasn't going to mention Grant's brother, Benito. Don't know how I dated him for three years. "The most trouble Grant has been in is a result of his being associated with me. He wouldn't shoot a person if you paid him."

Grant asked, "But do you still love me?"

Why did he pose that question as opposed to confessing his feelings? Grant always wanted to make sure he wasn't the one taking a chance on loving me unless he was positive beyond the shadow of a doubt that I loved him first.

I looked at him and said, "Yes, I do still love you. I will always love you." He smiled. "But I'm not in love with you." His smile slowly faded. "Like I've said before, sometimes love isn't enough. You crushed my heart, then stomped on it by throwing Jada in my face like she was better than me. I don't compete with no bitch. I don't have to. She's not better. She's different. And if she's had anything to do with my boys being missing, I'ma kick her ass first." I stared into Grant's eyes, then continued. "Then yours, and I'm dead serious. If you think you can ease your way back into my life because of the boys, you're wrong. You have no idea what love is."

Sapphire stood. "Well, there we have our sleeping arrangements—separate rooms for everybody," she said. "And I, my dear, have to get back to finding our babies. You guys can continue this conversation without me. I'm going to pay Jada's son, Darius, an unexpected visit." Sapphire left.

Grant sat on the edge of the hospital bed, rolled my wheelchair in front of him. "Honey, can't you see I love you?"

He didn't get it. He kept making himself the victim. "No. Love is action supported by words. It's not something I can see. Valentino was with me every day of my pregnancy. He went with me for my check-ups. Took me to the doctor when I wasn't feeling well. He knew the babies weren't his and he still cared for me. That's love. And maybe he loved me because he needed someone to love him. Whatever his reasons, that was okay with me because his heart was in it. You on the other hand told me not to call you again ever. What had I done so wrong that you never wanted to hear my voice again?"

I held my hand up to him. I wasn't finished. "It takes two people to love unconditionally. When you love someone, as you claimed you loved me, you don't intentionally hurt them. You fucked me one day, then the next day you told me you were marrying Jada. You're a fuck-ing user. You coaxed me into loving you, then you find a reason to end our relationship. You didn't want to talk about it. Fuck what Honey thinks. Fuck how Honey feels. I had to pick myself up. . . . You're scared. You're afraid to let yourself truly love someone. Dump them before they dump you. Hurt them before they hurt you. That's the spirit, G. You used me and now you're using Jada. You haven't apologized to me, not once."

He shrugged his shoulders. "Don't forget, Valentino kidnapped and tried to kill you. But I guess that's okay with you too?"

I stared at Grant. What was wrong with him? I turned my wheel-chair toward the door. He swiveled my chair facing him.

"Honey, I'm so sorry," he said with tears streaming down his face.

"Save it. I didn't say those words for an apology. You need to think about what you're doing to women. Keep it one hundred with your-self. I have more important people to worry about. Get me out of here."

CHAPTER 38

Darius

The envelope Ashlee handed me at the hospital haunted me.
Hadn't heard from her since she'd left. I didn't want to open the envelope, but I had to. I held the white letter-size in my sweaty palms. I was home. Alone. Sitting in my family room with no family. No DJ. I missed my lil' man. I missed my wife terribly. I hated not being at the hospital with her. My mom had made things worse for me by involving Ashlee. Wasn't sure if I was glad or not that my mom wasn't around.

My cell phone rang. It was someone calling from the hospital. My heart thumped in my chest. Glad or not, I wished my mom was here with me right now because I needed her. . . . But she wasn't here to make me feel better. K-9 was a true friend but he had to be in Cleveland for our game tomorrow. I wanted to be there too. But I stayed in LA, for my wife.

For the first time in years, since that day I'd tried to commit suicide, I felt alone. Back then I had no one depending on me. Now I have my son, my wife, my teammates, and I'm man enough to understand I have to look out for my mom no matter what I think about what she'd done. She was an only child and my family was all the family she had.

I knew I was learning what unconditional love meant when I opted to stay in LA. The game would go on without me. I couldn't go on without my wife. I placed the envelope on the end table.

"Hello."

"Mr. Darius Jones, is he available?"

I recognized the voice. "Yeah, it's me, Doc."

"I have good news," he said. "Hold on."

The softest voice, barely above a whisper, said, "Hey, you."

All I could do was cry her name. "Ladycat?"

"Yeah," she said.

Then I heard, "I told you I had great news. But we have to keep her here a little longer. She should be home in a week or so. Therapy could take weeks or months before she's back to normal but I expect your wife to make a full recovery. I want you to come see your wife this afternoon."

Weeks? Months? "Thanks, Doc." I held the phone to my ear a minute after the call ended. "Yes!" I thrust my fist in the air, jumped up and down in one spot, and said, "A full recovery. Thank You. Thank You."

I glanced at the letter, ripped the seal. "What the fuck?" Felt like the wind was knocked out of me. My joy faded to anger. A court hearing? In D.C.? For full custody of DJ? Was Ashlee for real? What's next?

The doorbell interrupted my decision to call Ashlee. I didn't recognize the curvaceous woman standing outside. She appeared harmless. Didn't have any *Awake!* magazines in her hands or another person behind her.

I greeted her, "What's up?"

"Hi, Darius. I know you don't know me," she said. "I'm Sapphire Bleu, a retired private investigator and a personal friend of Honey Thomas. I just want to ask you a few questions about your mother and the kidnapping of Honey and Grant Hill's twin boys."

I glanced over her head, scanned my driveway. "So Grant married Honey?"

"No, no. Sorry for the confusion."

I had my own issues with the media showing up at my door questioning me about my wife. I didn't need my name or my mother's name attached to no kidnapping. "Lady, you crazy. I can guarantee you my mother had nothing to do with that kidnapping. From what I hear, that chick Honey has crossed a lot of people. Never know who was waiting for revenge."

Had to take my words into consideration. What if Ciara, Maxine, and Ashlee were all waiting for the perfect opportunity to bring me down? What would I do?

"I wouldn't be so sure your mother isn't involved on some level."

"Well, I'm sure the department wouldn't appreciate your knocking on my door being that you're retired."

My mom's drama was involving me? How did this woman get my address?

"You can report whatever you'd like to the department. They're not going to side with you. I disclosed that information to let you know that I am helping and will continue to help Honey find her babies."

So she unofficially showed up at my house? Why not my mother's house? "What are your questions," I asked, still standing in the doorway. She was not coming inside.

"Was your mother with you yesterday?"

"No."

"Did you speak with your mother yesterday?"

Had to think about that for a sec. "Can't remember. The days are rolling together."

"Can't remember or won't say?" she asked. "Your mother will be arrested when the truth comes out. You don't need the bad press. If you cooperate, you can help save your mother. I reassure you she's wanted for kidnapping."

Now, either this woman thought I was really dumb or super clever. Didn't matter. "I don't know where you're going with all of this but obviously you don't have any evidence or you'd be at my mother's house, not mine. You want me to help you? Find the owner of that white pickup truck that rammed the back of my SUV three times." I needed solutions to my own damn problems.

Sapphire said, "Consider it done. But when I come back with your information, I want you to tell me everything you know about your mom's involvement with the kidnapping."

I watched her walk away, get in a car, then drive off my property. Her response fucked me up for a second. Would she really find the person responsible or was she baiting me?

I closed the door, picked up my phone, and called my crazy ass baby's mama.

CHAPTER 39

Bambi

I was in the City that Care Forgot strolling down Bourbon Street after dark.

The sidewalk was grimy beneath my black and blue Nikes. Moisture and grit crunched underneath my soles. I loved the glove-tight fit of my Lunarglide+ running shoes and how they molded to my feet. The traction would keep me from slipping on the slimy sidewalks that were filthier than the streets. The light weight would excel my sprints if I had to make a mad dash. I had grip to maintain my balance if I had to escape the unknown.

On television I'd seen the sea of natives and tourists covering every inch of Bourbon Street after the Saints won the NFC Championship. People huddled together like the team, interlocking their arms in an attempt not to be separated from family and friends. Some appeared successful. I was glad tonight wasn't one of those nights. The crowd, like my shoes, was lightweight.

I opened my purse, retrieved my cell phone, then answered the "unknown" call. "Hello."

"I see you made it." I recognized the two-headed lady's voice. "Take your time. Turn left on Bienville. I'll call you back." She ended the call.

This was some eerie shit. Thought she was lying about knowing when I'd made it to the French Quarter. She must be Jamaican or from the Bahamas. Every time I went to the Caribbean, the natives could find me any time of the day or night.

I looked up at the balconies above my head, saw a few normal-looking intoxicated people. Was that two-headed lady's lookout standing up there dressed in a black feather mask wearing a black gown? Or was she the woman on the other balcony with no shoes and a miniskirt barely covering her ass?

I took my time strolling along Bourbon. The sound of blues blared in my right ear, jazz in my left. From one block to the next there were small clusters of people partying. Some staggered from Iberville toward Bienville. Three young male tap dancers performed on the sidewalk soliciting tips. If I didn't have to open my purse, I would've gladly given them five dollars.

"Hey, Red. What cha know dat dere?" a man shouted.

I looked behind my back, to my left, to my right, then back at him.

Dragging his words, he said, "Don't be lookin' round, Red. I'm talkin' to you."

I slid my engagement ring all the way up my finger, unsnapped the side pocket of my Louis Vuitton Petit Noe drawstring purse, put my cell phone stun gun in my hand hoping I wouldn't have to jolt him with 950,000 volts.

"Don't be cheeky like dat, Red," he said, walking toward me. "Oh, you gon' give me your number? That's what I'm talkin' 'bout." As he got closer I saw a mouth full of gold teeth.

Bypassing him, I kept walking. He followed me. I took a left on Bienville, walked a half block. He was on my heels. I stopped. Warned him. "Stop following me. Leave me alone."

"Just give me your numba and . . . aw, damn, Red," he said, falling to the ground.

I leaned over, gave him another 950,000 volts to let him know I was serious, then walked away. I opened my bag, pulled out my real cell phone again to answer the call. It was the two-headed lady. Damn, she was serious about knowing I was here.

"Meet me at the cemetery outside the French Quarter at midnight," she said, then howled like a wolf. "Not the one-square block graveyard on Conti and Treme near the Municipal Auditorium. That's the St. Louis Cemetery number one. Meet me at the St. Louis

Cemetery number two. You can't miss it. It's three blocks long and one block wide. It is where the overpass meets the underpass but do not pass either."

"Three blocks? How will I know if I'm in the right block?" More and more, casting this love spell on Darius seemed like a bad idea. What if it backfired?

"Go to the open tomb. It is raised exactly three feet from the ground. It is surrounded with cement. Look inside. You will see a dark hole. Climb into the hole. I will be there waiting for you exactly at midnight. Don't go to the wrong location," she warned. "And whatever you do, don't get inside the wrong tomb. There are demons and angels who refuse to cross over to the other side, lurking in every cemetery. Mortals have disappeared in this cemetery never to be seen again. I'm sure you've heard about the girl who was on her way to her prom and detoured through that very same cemetery."

I wasn't about to ask what happened to that chick.

"Demons are like drug lords. They rule their territory. If you cross into their territory, they will bury you alive. Do not be one second late." Her voice trailed off into another howl.

"Hello. Hello." No answer. It was almost midnight. Bravely, cowardly, or stupidly, I continued my journey. Bienville Street grew darker. With the exception of the drunks passed out on the sidewalk, there weren't many people in view. I didn't hear any jazz or blues.

Couldn't see behind the wooden gates to my left. I'd heard there were beautiful courtyards with water fountains and gardens, and condos and houses behind the French Quarter gates I'd passed but I couldn't confirm.

The Quarter was a unique kind of place where pagans enthusiastically came to sin. Those who considered themselves Christians, once in the belly of the French Quarter, bartered their religion for good times. Maybe the French Quarter slave trade stirred the energy of sinners. *God only knew how many slaves died here,* I thought as I quickened my pace.

All in the name of love, I was doing this for Darius's uncontrollable attraction to me. I saw a shadow as I approached the corner of Burgundy. I put my lipstick pepper spray in one hand, had my stun gun in the other. When I got to the corner, the shadow disappeared. If I hurried, I'd be on time to meet the two-headed lady by midnight. A little relief came as I reached Rampart. It was a well-lighted main street. My cell phone dinged twice indicating I had a text message.

"Please don't let this be Rita."

It was a detailed text from the two-headed lady reiterating the instructions on where to meet her. Technology was in her hands too. I kept going. Once I crossed Elk Place I could barely see my hand in front my face.

Bienville came to an end and there was only one way out.

CHAPTER 40

Darius

It was nine o'clock at night.

I'd sat next to my wife for six straight hours holding her hand off and on. God had answered my prayers. He'd given me a chance to re-marry my wife. After my next commitment at the altar before God, I was never going to let another woman suck my dick.

I whispered to my wife, "Ladycat?"

"Yes."

"I would die for you." I meant that. Her accident was my fault. We should've eaten our food at the restaurant. I shouldn't have let the conversation with my mom interrupt our dinner that evening at BOA's. Or I could've reproposed to my wife at home, had our chef prepare an intimate dinner for us on my lawn under the moonlight. Or we could've gone out on our yacht for a sunset cruise. Or I could've driven that day.

She shook her head. "No. Don't say that."

She couldn't speak too many words at once but I was serious and had to let her know. "I love you so much. I want you to plan the biggest wedding in America's history."

"My ring," she whispered. "I want my ring."

I had taken the teal bag with all of my wife's belongings home. I was concerned with her health. I hadn't checked for the rings but was sure they were in the bag. "Your rings are at home."

She smiled softly. "I can't wait to put them back on. I feel naked without . . ." Her words trailed off.

The time had come to let my wife know. "Now that you're doing better, I'm going to head out in the morning and catch the game in Cleveland, then I'll be back when they discharge you."

Her eyes drooped. I could tell she didn't want me to go as she said, "I understand."

Damn, Darius, you forgot again. Ashlee cursing me for not telling her DJ was in an accident reminded me I hadn't called Fancy's mother Caroline. I didn't think my mother had contacted Caroline either. Caroline had to have seen the news or heard from her friends but I hadn't heard from her. *Lord, please don't let anything have happened to my wife's mom. I'd die for sure.*

I pulled out my iPhone. "Baby, forgive me. I need to call Caroline."

Fancy smiled. "Put that thing away. My mom called the hospital. She'll be here in the morning. Where's Jada?" Ladycat asked.

I shook my head, tucked my phone in its holder. In addition to being banned from the hospital, my mom had too much madness in her life. I didn't tell my wife about the custody hearing but that was the real reason I had to go. Otherwise, I would've stayed with her.

"And how's DJ?"

"Get some rest. I love you, Ladycat." I kissed my wife.

Her hair was slightly tangled from moving about on the cotton pillowcase. She was beautiful with no makeup. The bandage was gone. The oxygen machine, gone. The IV was still taped to her arm.

She whispered, "Love you too. Kiss DJ for me. Can't wait to see him."

It was hard walking out of the room but I had to stretch my legs. I left Cedars. Had to have a drink. Didn't want to drink alone. En route to my house, I decided to see what was up at the Playhouse on Hollywood Boulevard. That was my kind of upscale place. Never know, might run into Kobe or B. Shaw. Damn, I wasn't even sure who they were playing tomorrow night. I'd better not have too many drinks. I sure knew who I was facing off with tomorrow if I decided to go to Cleveland. The one player trying to snatch my MVP. I was torn. Wanted to say, "Fuck Ashlee," not worry about the custody hearing in

D.C. and go to Cleveland. Ashlee might be playing games. There might not be a hearing at all. I'd call the courthouse in the morning.

I stepped in the spot. The music was thumpin'. An exotic dancer was suspended above the dance floor wrapping and winding her scantily dressed body with pink ribbons. She spread her legs east and west. When I tilted my head backward, her pussy was damn near in my mouth. Would've stuck out my tongue for fun but I'd never tasted another woman's pussy since I'd married Fancy.

Two females danced inside the oval-shaped cage elevated above the bar. I wasn't going to be here long, didn't bother jogging upstairs to see what was jumping off in VIP. Chick dipped another full split on me.

Shake that shit off, man. Too late.

Slugger protested. There was an uprising in my slacks. Damn. Didn't help that bangin' bodies with bodacious booties were jam-packed wall to wall. "Welcome to Hollywood. Where fantasies become reality." I knew all too well about these buxom beauties.

A shortie with breast implants that would shame Wendy Williams, a waist the size of Kim Kardashian's, and butt that would make the women in Brazil say, "Damn!" thrust her tits into my dick, then greeted my dick.

"Hi, Darius. What are you doing here all alone? Aren't you supposed to be in Cleveland? Oh, what do you feed this thing?" she asked, brushing her breasts back and forth over my rock hard shaft.

I had to break a smile when she finally looked up at me. Found space in the crowd to step back. Turned away. Made my way to the bar. Almost forgot how bold these LA women were. "I'll have a double Herradura Suprema."

"Ah, yes." The bartender kissed his fingertips. "The best."

"Make that two doubles, on me," Shortie said.

I handed the bartender my credit card. She knew I'd pay for the drinks. I doubted she knew the cost for the two doubles was $200.00. Looking at her titties bouncing to the music, she was the perfect height for a standing ovation.

I signed the tab, included a forty-dollar tip, tapped my glass to hers, then said, "Enjoy." I turned away, decided to check out the VIP section. Security let me in right away.

"Hey, Darius. Shouldn't you be in Cleveland? Can I get an auto-graph?" He was a big dude up top with stunt legs.

Didn't anybody in LA watch the news? Didn't they know my wife was in an accident? Or did they not care? "No problem," I said, head-ing for the seat in the corner. Giving him an autograph led to signing ten more before I could chill away from the VIP crowd.

I sniffed my tequila. Inhaled the agave, dry wood, vanilla, cinna-mon, rose petal aroma. "Ahh." Amazing how the scents didn't over-lap. I closed my eyes, swirled the vanilla, citrus, rose petal, rich amber, sweet cocoa in my mouth, then swallowed. "Um, um, um. This is the best."

"I'm the best too. Mind if I join you?"

Damn, who was that? I opened my eyes and saw the most amazing set of brown sugar legs standing before me. I mean she was so tall I could clearly see her waxed pussy and protruding clit. I wanted to finger fuck her and see if her juices smelled better than my drink. I hate to rush a great drink.

I downed my Suprema, placed my glass on the table, and got the fuck up outta the Playhouse.

CHAPTER 41

Bambi

I had to go left onto Saratoga.

I took the first right on Iberville. My steps converted into a light jog. It was 11:51 P.M. I'd made it to what she called the underpass. Interstate 10 was above my head. Below the freeway were parked cars. I'd heard the Indians gathered here during Mardi Gras for their own festive historical celebration. I heard voices resonating from across the street, sounded like men having conversations, but I couldn't see faces.

I mumbled as I reread my text message. The northeast corner of cemetery block number two. Walk three raised graves to the west, face southeast, then look down into the grave that is three feet high. I'll be waiting.

What kind of madness was this? I paced back and forth in darkness using my cell phone for light. I wasn't sure if I'd found the right open grave. Process of elimination, I waited beside the grave that appeared three feet high but I wasn't about to get in unless I was positive this was the right grave.

A woman's voice said, "Bambi, get in. I don't have all night."

My legs trembled as I sat on the edge. I swung my legs over, put my feet in, kept my purse strapped to my shoulder. The tomb reminded me of the California mud baths except there was no mud and I was not here to get pampered. I felt dry dirt beneath my soles. That was good. I prayed I wasn't going to sink below the earth. Facing her, I squatted inside the open grave. My ass touched the ground, my back leaned against the cement wall.

"That's fine. Do you have the bag with Darius's loc?" she asked, opening her palms. She lit several candles.

Her face was smeared with a black shiny paste. Eyes, dark and deep like mine. Lips, painted white and wide like the warriors that paraded in Zulu. Locs, down to her waist. Cowrie shells dangled from her ears, hung around her neck, and decorated her wrists and ankles.

"Yeah, I have it." My voice was faint and I was on the verge of fainting.

"Give it to me." She sounded exactly like and reminded me of Diahann Carroll when she played Elzora in *Eve's Bayou.* She was quiet for a moment. She opened the bag, then said, "Ah, I see you have one loc. Very good. And you're sure it's his?"

"Positive."

"We're safe here. No demons will bother us," she said, lighting a large white candle. "Sit facing me. Fold your legs like a chicken wing."

I prayed she wasn't going to pull out a dead chicken, reenact Lisa Bonet's scene in *Angel Heart,* and splatter chicken blood on me. I'd pepper-spray, then zap any live or dead sacrificial animal with my Taser.

"That won't be necessary," she said. "Place the back of your hands on your thighs, open your palms, and close your eyes. Now, take three deep breaths with me."

With the first breath, I began to relax. The second one, I went into a meditative state. By the third breath, the background noise faded. I only heard her voice.

She chanted, "Goddess Aphrodite. I summon you on this full moon. Please, come." She was quiet for a moment.

"Thank you, oh goddess, for coming. Bambi is in need of your loving favor. She comes today in search of love. Not just any love. Bambi has brought the loc of her desired lover, Darius Jones. I ask your special favor that you bond Darius Jones with Bambi in a way that he will only have eyes for her."

My left eye opened. I didn't see any goddess. Was this chick scamming me?

"Your energy is interrupting my connection. Be quiet." She became quiet again. She picked up a scalpel. "Lean your head forward, my child."

Oh, hell, no.

"I cannot continue if you refuse to cooperate."

Reluctantly, I leaned my head toward her. She massaged her fingers below my net stocking cap down to my scalp. "What on earth is all of this? I need a few strands of your hair. Yours."

Didn't trust her precision by candlelight. I took the scalpel, made a slit at the base of my full lace stocking cap, sliced the tip of a braid from the middle cornrow, handed it to her.

She sprinkled our hair with dust, then rolled our hair together beneath her palm like she was shaping a breadstick. "I sure hope that's not ashes from a dead person," I whispered. She dug a hole between us and buried our hair in the grave's dirt. She dipped her fingers into a bowl, sprinkled liquid on top. Smelled like charcoal. "Please don't set me on fire," I pleaded.

She hissed, "Will you be quiet? I can't hear myself think." She breathed in and out. "From this day forth, your love for Darius will grow."

I interrupted her. "Hold up. Wait. Wait. What do you mean my love for Darius will grow? I need for him to love me."

She hissed again, "You are too impatient. You are selfish. And you have a very dark side. You should be grateful I'm doing this. Do not think I do not see what you did to your parents. In order for Darius's love to flourish for you, you must first pray for their forgiveness, then you must do something nice for someone. Your parents do not know it was you who killed them but I do."

I thought, after what they'd done to me, my parents deserved to die. I had not come here for this bullshit.

The two-headed lady stared into my eyes. The candlelight illuminated her face. "Then you can leave now."

Damn, how did she do that shit and who did she think she was?

She stared at me. Her silence penetrated me. "Stop wasting my time." She motioned to blow out the candle.

"I'm sorry. I will do a good deed."

"You must do a good deed or your love spell will not work." She paused, then continued, "Maintain focus. Meditate. Every day you must think good thoughts of Darius. When the time is right, he'll come to you."

"What if I have bad thoughts about his wife?"

"You must be careful," she warned. "For the mind, at times, resides in another world. When you dream, you're having an outer body experience. You're in the afterlife with angels and demons. That's how you have nightmares and sometimes can't move or feel like you are suffocating. When you dream you attach the faces of the living to humans and animals that are dead. That is why you cannot kill a person in your dreams and they cannot kill you."

The candle flickered. She was right. I was impatient. Was she alive or dead? All I knew was that I was anxious to be with Darius. I wondered what he was doing. Wondered how much longer I had to sit here. Wondered how I could speed up the process.

She paused. When I stopped thinking, she continued talking. "And sometimes you have dreams with happy endings, if you know what I mean. Daydreams are not in the afterlife. However, depending on how deep you go into a dream, you may," she clapped, then said, "not come out. You'll become schizophrenic. I have granted you your desire. You are now connected to Darius. To answer your earlier question, both."

"What question?"

She shook her head. "If you have problems remembering, you are going to have a hard time being with Darius."

"Can the spell be broken? Can anyone keep me from my Darius?"

"Those are two separate but very good questions, my dear. Yes, the spell can be broken but I cannot break it," she warned.

This situation had become more complicated than I'd envisioned. "Then who can?"

"He can. You must never let him cut off his locs. Your spell is controlled by his hair." She patted the spot where she'd buried our hair.

"Anything else?"

"There is one woman standing in your way. She can block your connection. Even I cannot remove her. She has spiritual powers. She can't control your mind but she can read you. Your advantage is, she doesn't know she possesses the gift. Stay away from her. If you get too close to her, you will encounter major problems."

Great, another layer of complication. "Who is she? What does she look like?"

"That I cannot tell you."

"I thought you were supposed to know all the answers."

"I said I cannot tell you. I did not say I do not know. Your time is up and I must go tend to the leftover sinners on Bourbon Street," she said.

As the sunshine cloaked the graveyard's ground, I tried but could no longer see the two-headed lady's black smeared face or wide white lips. "Please, don't go. I've changed my—"

Before I could ask her to cancel my love spell, she vanished. Her voice echoed, "Remember everything I've told you. Be mindful of your thoughts, Bambi Bartholomew."

"Oh, my God! Come back!" I yelled. "Come back!" Frantically, I felt my hands, my finger.

My engagement ring was gone.

CHAPTER 42

Ashlee

It felt good to be back in D.C. in my bed. The sheet was too restraining. The ends wrapped around my body. I kicked, tugged, then snatched the cover over my head. I wasn't ready to get up.

DJ covered his head too. "Mommy, I'm hungry."

"Not now, DJ. Go back to sleep."

He cried. "But I'm not sleepy."

"Then just lay there and be quiet before I spank you." I wrestled with Darius's energy. This was no dream.

Lowering the sheet below my eyes, I peeped over the edge. I saw an image of Darius sitting at the foot of my bed. "Ashlee, please forgive me. I never meant to hurt you."

I didn't believe him. He spoke those words to manipulate me. To convince me not to fight for my parental rights. Now that I had my son, I didn't want DJ. If only to prove to Fancy that I was the better woman, I had to have Darius. I wanted to curse the image of him sitting on my bed like I'd done when I was in LA at the hospital.

Darius's mouth, eyes, and shoulders. Drooped. His spine curved toward his feet.

Ashlee, don't fall for it. You're daydreaming. I sat up.

DJ sat up too. "Mommy, please."

"Get out the bed and go stand in the corner until your grandmother gets here. And shut up all that crying for nothing. I'll feed you when I'm ready."

The streetlight shining through a crack in my blinds let me see DJ's upside down smile. I loved my son. I was afraid not to have him close to me. I needed DJ more than he needed me. I went to the corner where he stood, gave him a hug. "Mommy loves you."

I gripped the sides of my head. "Darius, I can't take anymore. If you lie to me or hurt me again, I will kill you."

"I'm sorry, Mommy," DJ said. "I didn't mean to hurt you. Please don't kill me."

I sighed. "DJ, be quiet." I sat on the floor beside my son. I replayed memories of Darius in my mind.

"I know, Ashlee. I don't blame you. I deserve to die."

"Darius, do you remember when we were twelve and we'd plan on running away from home? You'd told me, 'Make sure you pack a toothbrush, and lots of clean underwear and socks.'

"I'd asked you, 'Is that all? What about food?'

"Then you told me, 'I don't know. My mom always says, "Darius, you got your toothbrush? And extra underwear and socks?" so I guess that stuff must be pretty important.'"

I was the one with Darius, holding his hand, when he'd gotten his HIV test results. Darius was so scared that he might have it too. When he found out he was negative, I was the one he twirled around like a ballerina. I was always there for him.

The room became cold. DJ hugged my neck.

"You cold, baby?"

He said, "Hungry."

I changed the thermostat from seventy-two to eighty. I peeped out the blinds across the street at Jay's house. The only lights were the streetlights. My God, had I slept all day? Had I fed my son since we'd gotten off the plane? Where was my mother? She was supposed to be at my house when I got here. She was probably at some man's house.

"DJ, honey. Just stand in the corner until Mommy gets it together." My thoughts went from my mom, to DJ, back to Darius.

I remembered the first time Darius made love to me. His strong hands covered mine on the exercise bar above our heads. He eased the spaghetti strap of my gown over my breast and caressed my nipple. We straddled the exercise bench. He leaned me over, entered me from behind. Everything felt so right. So wonderful.

I thought with Maxine being out of the picture, Darius and I would get married. Along came Ciara and she stood at the altar beside him. When things didn't work out with Ciara I thought, here's my second chance. Darius threw me a curveball and Fancy slid into home plate.

I heard a car engine. I raced to the window. My mom parked her rental car in front my house. She had on a waist-length off-white coat with a plush black collar, black tapered pants, knee-high boots. An oversized shiny black purse hung on her shoulder.

Beep. Beep. She remotely locked the car, headed to my door.

"DJ, it's your grandma," I said. Didn't want my mother to see him standing facing the corner.

"Yay! Grandma came to get me!" He ran to the door. His smile vanished when he looked up at my mom. He went back to the corner.

"Well, that's no way to greet your grandmother. Come here and give me hug," my mom told him.

Somberly, DJ went to my mother. His arms hung beside his thighs as my mom hugged him. "I'm hungry, Grandma."

"Ashlee, this isn't going to work out. Maybe you should send him back to his father," she said, removing her coat. "You look a mess. When was the last time you and this child ate?"

I'd almost forgotten how distant my mom and I were. She didn't want me when I was a kid, insisted I stay with my father. "I was just getting ready to feed him. Are you hungry too?"

"You learn how to cook yet?" she asked, following me into the kitchen. "Go put on some clothes. I'll fix us something to eat."

I hated when my mother referred to my son as "this child" or "him." Didn't know who treated me worse, Darius or my mother.

I hated Darius because I loved him. I didn't want Fancy to die but wished she'd go away. My having DJ meant seeing more of Darius. I had to find a way to make him mine again. As long as Fancy didn't give him a child, I had a chance. Not sure how but I sensed Darius was coming back to me.

Would he love me the way he loved Fancy? Or would he end up hating me more than ever?

CHAPTER 43

Darius

The head doing the most thinking was below my waist. I hadn't had Slugger polished since my wife was in the accident. It was cool to get sidetracked once in while when she was healthy. But sliding to the left on her under the circumstances didn't seem right.

This actually might be the best time to relieve my stress. What she didn't know wouldn't hurt us. A lil' head was on my big head's brain tonight. Tomorrow I'd be in Cleveland, maybe. Maybe not. I hadn't had a real workout in a few days. Releasing myself tonight, putting in OT in practice tomorrow, I should be ready to match up with LJ provided Ashlee was bluffing about the custody hearing.

I stepped out of the Playhouse and stepped on Alfred Hitchcock's star. Hope that wasn't a sign of what was to come. Strolling down Hollywood Boulevard, I left my car parked around the corner from the Playhouse. The fresh air helped my dick cool off. One step at a time, I was clearing my other head. I walked on Count Basie, Dr. Seuss, Fats Domino. That shit was close. Shortie at the club could've caused a volcanic eruption in my pants. That's how close I was to cumming when she rubbed her torpedo tits on my dick.

Women had no clue how tempting other women were. That "Just Say No" shit didn't apply to our dicks. Wasn't that fucking simple. If it were, we'd decline new pussy every time. I stood on Diana Ross, looked up at the Hollywood Guinness Museum wondering what man held the world record for receiving "the longest blow job." If she fell asleep with his dick in her mouth, would that time count in her favor?

Continuing my stroll, sometimes I prided myself in doing the right thing. And I wanted credit for that shit if I ever got caught. What the hell was I saying? I'd never been caught. If it should happen, I'd deny that shit until I was six feet under and they threw dirt in my face.

A few steps later, I'd trampled on Marilyn Monroe, Jay Leno, Little Richard, Vanessa Williams, Angela Bassett, and Michael Jackson. I was almost at my destination. One more hour before last call for alcohol. California's two A.M. cutoff for serving adults liquor was dumb. "Let's put all the party people who are totally fucked up out of the clubs at that same time. Let all the intoxicated morons who get behind the wheels of their cars try not to kill anyone before they reach their destination."

I loved that New Orleans didn't have a last call for alcohol. I'd partied there several times until the sun came up. I wasn't a heavy drinker but I could have my first or last adult beverage in the Big Easy whatever time I chose. New Orleans was a strange animal. My chances of getting shot by a nigga who had been drinking were higher than my odds of getting hit by a drunk driver.

New Orleans. Yeah. I was wrong for fucking that white girl Heather like she had four legs. I was angry with Maxine, glad I hadn't tested HIV positive, and all I remembered that night was somebody's daughter had to pay for my frustrations. Too bad it was one of my mom's top executives. I didn't give a fuck about Heather or the fact that I left the hotel from being with her and ended up at the Intercontinental on St. Charles Avenue fucking Ginger. New Orleans was like that. That place made me want to sin the second I got off the plane. The longer I stayed, the more voodoo pussy I'd gotten into. Those New Orleans women knew how to pop that pussy, and oh, my God—Slugger was on swole—thinking about that project chick sucking my dick on Tchoupitoulas. She was so bad, I had to pay her ass for an encore.

On my way back to Heather's room, I'd stumbled upon Colette's around the corner at 822 Gravier Street. Now that three-story sex club was a beast. Chicks and chicks, chicks on dicks, private rooms with chicks, orgy beds stacked with chicks, and they had a damn eight-room bed and breakfast on the third floor with eight different themes. I could've stayed in the dungeon or slept in a low to the floor oriental bed and I could've brought more chicks from the club to a private room. Only in New Orleans.

Bill Cosby was beneath my feet. Then there was Etta James, Stevie Wonder, Sophia Loren, and Earvin Magic Johnson. By the time I stood on the the Dead End Kids' star, I was at My House.

The bouncer opened the gigantic double oak doors. I knew the routine so I waited until the oak doors closed. When they opened the double glass doors inside, I entered the club. The owner was clever for building the best soundproof club in Hollywood. People on the street never heard a beat. They'd just walk on by.

I loved the lay and the layout of My House. I went upstairs, sat on the king-sized bed facing the Jacuzzi and chilled.

"What would you like to drink?" the waitress asked.

I ordered another double Suprema.

"Hey, Darius. Shouldn't you be in—"

"Yes, Cleveland. Yes, I should."

"I take it everyone's asking you that same question. I can't wait to see you match up with LJ," she said. She had the most amazing mouth. Juicy lips. Long legs. Big breasts. And a nice ass.

Damn! How much of that was an illusion? With all the butt pads, push-up bras, body magic, lip plumpers, instant weaves and wigs, my eyes could be playing tricks on me.

"Mind if I join you for a cocktail?" she said.

"Only if everything I see is real and you don't have the same shit under your skirt that I have in my pants."

She laughed, tossed her head back. She straddled me, put my hands on her breasts. "Squeeze hard. These are all mine." Then she put my hands on top her head. "You can pull, run your fingers through my hair, whatever you'd like. This is all me." She did an about face, sat her ass in my lap, grabbed my hand, and stuck my finger in her pussy. Her pussy quivered. My dick damn near busted my zipper. She stood. "I'm one hundred percent one hundred," she said. "Now may I join you?"

I scratched the back of my neck. The waitress handed me my drink. "Give her whatever she's having." I patted the space next to me. "On second thought, let's take this downstairs to the sectional." I had to get off that bed or she was going down on me in the club.

"I'll have what he's having," she said, following me to the first floor.

I wasn't interested in conversation, didn't hear what she was saying. She was drinking and talking and I was drinking and fantasizing. Watching her lips, all I knew was, "Hey, let's get out of here."

"Ready when you are."

Standing on the Dead End Kids, I looked across the street at the Church of Christ Scientist. Better not go that way. I remembered, "Damn, my car is at the Playhouse."

"Don't think you'll fit in my little two-seater Corvette in the garage across the street. I'll walk with you."

The mile walk back to my black whip with tinted windows took forever. The Playhouse was closed. Hollywood Boulevard was busy with tricks on the stroll. We turned on Wilcox, got in my car. I wasn't taking her to my house or to a hotel.

"We can do whatever you'd like," she said.

Those amazing lips came toward me. I hadn't kissed another woman in a sexual way since I'd married Ladycat. Kissing was too personal. I didn't know her name. Didn't want to. I unzipped my pants, reclined in the driver's seat, and pulled out Slugger. Even I had to admit Slugger was a handsome dude. Perfect circumcision. Smooth head. Wide body. Long shaft. Big nuts.

She smiled at him. I closed my eyes as she eased her mouth over my head. Her hot wet mouth and tongue swirled around my head. She took her time suctioning the underside of my giant mushroom head in and out her mouth.

I exhaled, savoring the moment. This shit here was the ultimate stress reliever. Felt like my dick was going to explode. Slugger couldn't get any bigger.

She made me a liar. She gripped my dick at the base, tightened her fingers, then pushed down into my nuts as she kept sucking my head. She wasn't trying to deep throat but I wanted her to go deeper so I grabbed a handful of her hair and pushed her head down. She gagged but didn't resist. Ready to blast off down her throat, I pushed a little harder.

"Aw, damn. You ready? Here it . . . aw, shit." The waves kept hitting the back of her throat. She kept gagging. I couldn't stop cumming. I had to make her swallow it all. When I was done, I let go of her hair. "I'm sorry but you were so amazing."

I slid my wallet from my pocket and handed her a grand. "If I had more cash on me, I'd give it to you."

Bright lights beamed through my window. Cameras flashed. "Stop right there. Get out the car."

"Aw, fuck! Bitch, you set me up?" Instantly my dick slumped to my nuts.

"Who you calling a bitch?" she said, throwing the ten hundred-dollar bills in my face.

"You too, miss. Step out of the vehicle," a woman said.

I zipped my pants. "Get out," I told the chick in the passenger seat.

I didn't know what to think or do when I saw standing in front of me that bitch ass retired cop Sapphire who had showed up at my house unannounced questioning me about Grant and Honey's twins. No police. No police cars. Just a fucking cameraman snapping pictures of me and the trifling ass female who'd just sucked my dick. Glad I made her swallow.

"Come here," Sapphire said, walking to the trunk of my car. "I told you, Honey is my friend. I need you to step up your game. I do believe your mother either has the twins or she's responsible for the twins' abduction. The pictures he took, ah, consider them collateral. You tell me what I need to know. I'll give you all the digitals as opposed to giving them to the media. Plus I'll tell you who the owner of that white pickup truck is.

"Deal?" she asked, extending her hand.

Sapphire was low down. I'd heard how cops pressured innocent people to confess to shit they didn't do. I wasn't doing that to my mom. And if Sapphire could find the owner of that white pickup in a day, might take me longer but I could find the owner too.

"No deal."

CHAPTER 44

Honey

The police had cause to arrest me when they'd handcuffed Valentino.

I struggled internally to find the true Lace St. Thomas. Spooning with Grant, I wondered what Valentino thought as he slept alone in the adjacent bedroom. "Grant?" I glanced over my shoulder, looked in his eyes.

"Yes?" he said, easing his hand under my waist.

I faced him. Lay my head on the pillow. We were eye to eye. "Do you believe I'm attractive on the inside? Be honest."

He smoothed back my hair. "Yes. I wouldn't be here if I didn't think you were attractive."

Hmm. He'd said think. That meant he was unsure. "What could I have done differently to protect Luke and London?"

"I wondered the same."

We became quiet. I blamed myself. Found fault in Grant. Was angry at Jada. Hated the people at the hospital. Maybe I was . . . "You think I deserve this?"

"Not this," Grant said.

"But you believe I deserve to have something bad happen to me?"

I was abusive to my prostitutes, not to mention having killed Reynolds. But I wasn't a bad person. What about my ex-husbands who abused me? What about my mother? Had bad things happened to Rita?

Grant looked at me, then answered, "If you believe in karma, yes."

Drug dealers expected to but never wanted to be killed. Politicians illegally spent taxpayers' money but they never expected a payback. Husbands cheated on their wives but felt cheated when they had to give up more than half of their assets in the divorce. Guess my selfish ways weren't much different.

I turned my back to Grant; we spooned again. The human touch was amazingly healing. Lying in the spoon position with Grant's arm around my stomach gave me some comfort. I still worried about my sons, about Valentino.

Valentino had asked to stay a few days with me at Velvet's. Said he needed time to find Summer and his boys before he could attempt to go back to his family. He said her parents probably lived in the same house or town. Sapphire agreed to help Valentino find his wife but somehow I doubted he honestly wanted to go back to Summer or Nevada.

"You awake?"

Grant kissed the nape of my neck. "Yeah, I can't sleep either. I was hoping you were asleep. That's why I hadn't said anything."

"Do you think they're safe? Or hungry? My breasts are about to pop like a balloon with all this milk. They hurt. Not as much as my heart though." I sniffled, letting my tears soak into my pillowcase.

"Let's stay positive. You know you hear about other people's kids missing all the time. But it doesn't hit you how much they're suffering until it's your own," Grant said.

"You tell your mom and dad about the boys?"

"Nah, not yet. My mom would go insane. My dad would go insane because of Mom. Whenever she worries, he worries more. I'm not sure how to break this news to my parents. They didn't want us together."

"Say what you mean, Grant. They didn't want you with me."

I'd met Grant's parents one time. What should've been a happy Thanksgiving was a man-made disaster. I learned a valuable lesson that day. I'd lived three years with Grant's adopted brother and never once asked to meet his adoptive family. Benito disowned them so I disowned them too. The disconnect was easy because I disowned my family. But when I arrived at Grant's parents' house with Grant and saw Benito at the table, my relationship with Grant changed instantly and I could've killed Benito on the spot for not introducing me to his family.

Benito was the type of man that nothing fazed him. He pissed away the money he'd made in the NFL. His parents paid his child support and helped raise his son. I was shocked when Benito's son's mother took him back. He had no job, no income, and she took him back. Well, they say money can't buy love. With all my millions, I did love Grant, but I wasn't in love with him anymore. Someone had to protect my heart.

"Honey?"

"Yes."

"I'm truly sorry for all I've put you through. I was an idiot. You're right. Jada's right. I don't know how to love. It's scary, you know. Opening up, being vulnerable. What you made me realize is I have to take ownership and responsibility for your feelings and be considerate of you no matter what. Can I ask you a question?"

"I'm listening."

"Did you have sex with Valentino?"

"Did you have sex with Jada or anyone else since you've been here in LA?"

Did he forget he was lying next to an ex-prostitute and madam? Real women never tell. Once a man gets a picture in his mind of his woman fucking a man who he knows, every time he sees that man that's all he's going to think of and the first time things go wrong, he'll throw it in her face.

"You're right. I shouldn't have asked that question. Here's another one. Can you forgive me for all I've done, let me start over, and teach me how to love you?"

It was easy to forgive that which you didn't know, until the shit hit you in the face. I wasn't giving up freebies for free.

"You might want me to answer that later. I'm going to press charges against Jada. I believe she had something to do with our missing boys. And I want you to tell the police she was the last one seen with the twins and that you were the one who saw her."

CHAPTER 45

Bambi

Had to try one more time to find the two-headed lady. Fuck breaking the love spell, she was gon' give me back my engagement ring or I was going to second-line all over that bitch.

Her ass claimed she was headed to Bourbon Street to save leftover sinners. She'd best be worried about saving her own ass. I was headed back to the French Quarter. I checked out of the Windsor Court Hotel on Gravier across the street from Harrah's Casino. I handed the valet attendant my ticket, got in my National Car Rental SUV. Once I crossed Canal Street, S. Peters changed to Decatur. Made a quick stop at the twenty-four-hour Café Du Monde, ordered three beignets and a café au lait to go.

Opening my car door, I stopped, stared at the statue of Andrew Jackson across the street at Jackson Square. "Yeah, you may be a hero for the Battle of New Orleans but I'm about to replace your ass for whuppin' the Voodoo Queen," wherever her ass was.

I closed the door, made a U-turn on Decatur, right on St. Peters. These Peters—South and Saint—were starting to confuse me. I parked between Pat O'Brien's Bar and Preservation Park. I grabbed my bag of beignets and my purse, made my way to Bourbon Street.

There was no place in the world like this joint. I described the two-headed lady to a few people and asked if they'd seen her. A man said, "Ba-ba, I ain't afraid of no two-headed nothing, no. They best be 'fraid of me, yeah. You must be from Californya talkin' all proper and thangs." He mimicked me. Wasn't in the mood to give him 950,000 volts this early but I did. Kept it moving.

All the natives talked different. Rolled their words together. Separated syllables that should've been connected. Some spoke what they called Cajun, a combination of French and English. A few more blocks up Bourbon toward Canal I ran into a street party. "This early? Do they ever sleep?"

Rebirth Brass Band played that zydeco music that I'd heard on Spike Lee's documentary of Katrina. Everyone danced as though they were having a séance. At the sound of the first note heads bobbed, bodies jerked, legs wobbled side to side, people closed their eyes, dropped toward the ground, sprung back up but they never touched the ground and their feet never stopped wobbling. Umbrellas popped open like popcorn, then twirled in the sunshine. White handkerchiefs waved above their heads but no one was crying.

"I've never witnessed anything like this. The whole parish is possessed. If I never come back here, it'd be too soon."

Forget the two-headed lady, I had to get back to LA. Hadn't seen my Darius in two days. Still no Facebook postings from him. I stepped over the guy I'd tased a few minutes ago, made my way back to my car.

An hour later I was at my gate at MSY airport wanting to hop a flight to Cleveland but in order for my love spell to work I had to do something good for someone first. What if my good wasn't good enough? The only thing I could think of was to return the twins. I didn't need them anymore, especially that crybaby.

Waiting to board my plane, I checked in with Rita.

"Hey, Bambi. I need a break. I need my money. You gotta come back here."

"I'm boarding my plane. I'll be there in eight hours tops."

"I got a question for you," Rita said in a matter of fact tone.

"Okay."

"Are these my grandbabies?"

She'd caught me off guard with that one. "Why?"

"I can call my daughter and find out for sho."

"No, don't do that. Honey asked me to keep the boys," I lied.

"You lying. I can tell. You trying to set me up? 'Cause Rita will tear you a new asshole if you tryin' to come between me and my daughter. And who you got in them coffins up in that bedroom?"

I held my forehead. This bitch better be lucky I can't do some *Matrix* shit and transport myself through this phone. "You've messed up, Rita. You don't give a damn about your daughter. You cross me again and I'll frame you for kidnapping."

"Rita ain't afraid of nothing living with two legs but a grizzly bear. Double my money and I'll keep my mouth shut or Rita gon' sang like a canary."

Double? Was that all? "Sit tight until I get there. I'll double your money and I'll explain the whole thing," I lied. I didn't owe Rita or anybody an explanation. "Rita?"

"Yes, Bambi," she said the loudest I'd ever heard.

"If you call your daughter or the police, that will be your last call."

I powered off my cell and got on board.

CHAPTER 46

Jada

Thankful for a new day, I rolled over, picked up my cell from my nightstand, and phoned Ashlee. I hadn't heard from her since she'd left the hospital with DJ. I missed my grandbaby.

"Hey, Jada."

"Oh, hey, Ashlee, hi. Where are you? Where is my grandson?" I asked, ready to go pick him up if I had to.

"We're good."

I waited for her to keep talking but she didn't. "Oh, okay then. Great. Let me say hi to DJ?" He'd tell me where he was.

"That's not a good idea, Jada. How's Fancy?"

What the hell? My eyebrows raised at her response and question. "Are you okay?"

"Are you okay?" she snapped.

"I can come get DJ if you'd like. Your weekend visitation is over."

"Darius didn't tell you? And you haven't seen the news? What's wrong with you? Depressed? The only way you'll see DJ is if you show up at the custody hearing."

"Hello? Hello?" Ashlee was gone.

Custody what? Hearing? Was this the same sweet little Ashlee I'd helped raise? I picked up my remote, turned on the television. The remote slipped between my fingers, my mouth opened. I picked up the remote again, turned up the volume, changed the channel. My son's picture was on every station.

"Darius Jones was caught in his car with an alleged prostitute last night near the sixty-five hundred block of Hollywood Boulevard. The prostitute refuses to speak with the press but here are pictures of her getting out of Darius's car."

I was stunned. She looked more like a supermodel than a prostitute but why would Darius do this to Fancy now? Guess he really is like his biological father, wherever Darryl was. Hadn't heard from Darryl since Darius went pro and refused to let his dad be his agent.

"His solicitation for sex comes at a time when Darius's wife is hospitalized and fighting for her life. This is worse than the O'Neal, Woods, and Phillips cases shaken together. No warrant has been issued for the arrest of Darius Jones at this time. Reportedly Darius is on a plane headed to D.C. for a custody hearing tomorrow. I guess he can kiss his son and that MVP award good-bye."

I dialed my son's number. It went to voice mail. "Oh, my God. Baby, I just saw the news. Call me as soon as your plane lands. We're going to make it through this. I'm going to have Bambi flood the media with positive information about you. I love you. Call me immediately."

Prostitute? I called Bambi, got her voice mail. "Call me as soon as you get this message."

Custody? Over DJ? Custody made me think of Grant. I prayed they'd find his babies but was glad he had stopped bothering me. Was that nurse serious? I couldn't go to the hospital. I had to see Fancy. I prayed she wasn't coherent enough to understand what the reporters were announcing. Maybe she wasn't watching the news. This news might send her into shock. Dear God, why was the news always negative?

I called the hospital. Asked them to transfer me to the nurses' station on the third floor. "Yes, I'm calling to inquire about the status of my daughter-in-law."

"Sorry, we're not allowed to give patient information over the phone," she said.

"Well, how am I supposed to find out if I've been told not to come see her?"

"What's your name?"

"Jada Diamond Tanner."

"Darius Jones's mother?" She snickered.

"Yes, and it's not what it appears. My son is innocent."

"Hold on just a moment, Ms. Tanner."

I overheard her talking to someone. "No, she can't come to this hospital period. I told her that."

Whosoever that was in the background, who in hell put her ass in charge? Making up her own rules. I wish she would try to stop me from seeing Fancy. Why hadn't Darius called me before he left?

Someone said, "But."

But what? What are they talking about? I increased the volume on my cell phone but couldn't make out what they were saying. Then I heard, "Oh, yeah. That's right. Tell her she can come."

The woman told me, "Ms. Tanner, you can come."

"Great, I'm on my way." I ended the call, turned off my television, showered, and left.

When I arrived at the hospital, several news vans were parked out front. I prayed they weren't questioning Fancy. I stopped at the registration desk. I didn't want no mess from these people. The same security guard who escorted me out stood in the lobby watching me. I flashed my visitor's badge in his face, attached it to my blouse, and waited for the elevator.

The doors opened to the third floor. I stepped into a crowd of reporters. A police officer approached me. Video cameras rolled. Digital cameras' lights flashed. I covered my face, stepped backward to get back on the elevator. The doors closed before I could leave.

"Are you Jada Diamond Tanner?" the officer asked.

"What's this all about?"

"Just answer the question, ma'am."

"I have the right not to talk to you. I don't have to tell you who I am until you tell me why you're asking."

The nurse who'd told me not to come back to the hospital walked up to the officer. "That's her. She's trespassing."

Before I responded, Grant came from the back of the crowd. "Yes, that's her, officer. She's the one who kidnapped my twin boys."

The ordeal was surreal. I was speechless. I wanted to kill Grant as the officer tightened handcuffs to my wrists, then said, "Jada Diamond Tanner, you're charged with trespassing and kidnapping. You have the right to remain silent. Anything you say can and will be used against you. . . ."

"Where's the warrant?" I demanded.

"Right here," the officer said, waving a piece of paper in my face.

I was no criminal. Had never been behind bars. Darius was on a plane. Hadn't spoken with Bambi all day.

Who would bail me out?

CHAPTER 47

Bambi

The media had better get their stories about Darius straight. And they'd better do it pronto! I wasn't marrying a male whore.

How was I going to get my Darius out of this horrible mess? I sat in first class reading the front page of the *Times-Picayune*. Opening the barf bag, I heaved my undigested beignets. I wasn't sure which situation made me more upset. That two-headed lady stealing my engagement ring or the media lying on my Darius.

"Miss, here," the attendant said, handing me a trash bag. "Let me get you some water."

I shoved that trash bag in her direction. What the hell did she think I was? Trash? "Ginger ale, with ice." I spread the paper wide. Who was the tramp in the picture in the paper with my Darius? I read the article twice. There was no mention of her name.

The man next to me moved my arm. "Miss, please. I don't want to read your paper. I've got my own."

Darius was complicating our lives. I'd come too far to give up. But was he worth it? Vacillating the remainder of the flight, I was the first one to deplane at LAX. I stopped at the shop next to McDonald's, bought the *LA Times*. My heart raced. Think, Bambi, think. The twins weren't going anywhere. I had too much happening at once. Darius. The twins. And I hadn't forgotten about Fancy. But I'd almost forgotten about Grant. He was a great fuck. I went to the Red Carpet Lounge for a drink and to hear the news.

When I entered, the news reporter announced, "Remarkable. First, Darius Jones is allegedly caught with a prostitute; now his mother is arrested for kidnapping. Jada Diamond Tanner is being held on a million-dollar bond for the kidnapping of her ex-fiancé's twin boys, Luke Hill and London Hill. The boys are still missing but Mr. Grant Hill told reporters that Jada knows where the boys are. Police have searched her primary residence and reportedly there are no signs that the twins were ever there. We'll keep you up to date on both situations throughout the day."

They say it comes in threes. I had three brilliant ideas.

I retrieved my bags, hopped the shuttle to National Car Rental on Aviation Boulevard, took the escalator to the upper level, picked up a blue Dodge Charger from the Executive section, and phoned another one of my contacts. "Can you get me eight ounces of potassium chloride packaged in an IV bag?"

"Damn! I don't wanna know. You know the deal. I can get whatever you want for the right price. It's gon' cost ya one grand. How soon do you need it?" he asked.

"Meet me outside at the Coffee Bean and Tea Leaf on Beverly in exactly three hours."

"No prob. You need any more Cialis?" he asked, laughing.

"Sure, just in case," I said, smiling.

"I'll toss those in for free. Peace."

Didn't bother calling my parents' law firm. Didn't want to use my pro bono services to bail out Jada or have the attorneys questioning my motive. I tossed my phone on the passenger seat beside my purse, headed to Aladdin Bail Bonds on Avila. Taking the 405 would've doubled my drive time for the same thirty mile trip so I took 105 East to 110 North.

Jada and I hadn't had our lunch date yet. Definitely couldn't do so if she was locked up. I posted the ten percent of her bond, told the bondsman, "Make sure she knows Bambi bailed her out."

My next stop was the Coffee Bean. That ten-mile trip from Aladdin took thirty minutes. I parked in one of two spaces adjacent to the bus stop, went inside, requested a brown pastry bag from the cashier, then posted up at an outdoor table under the red canopy and waited. I neatly folded the cash, then stuffed it inside the small paper bag.

He arrived on time, parked in the vacant space beside my rental. He got out of the car holding a Tiffany & Company bag in his hand. "Let's do this," he said, sitting across from me. He sat the bag on the black circular iron table. "How long you gon' live this incognito lifestyle?"

Ignoring his question, I said, "Thanks." I gave him his package, took my package. I went inside the coffee shop, bought a Red Bull, went back out. I sat outside the coffee shop people-watching and thinking. Staring across the street, I saw Cedars Max Factor Family Tower was to my left, Starbucks to my right.

Fancy was obviously the one woman standing in my way. She was the only one in love with Darius. Ashlee was too crazy to care. And Jada, she had motherly love, but she wasn't one of those crazy mothers who treated her son like he was her man. But I wasn't quite through with Jada yet.

I couldn't bring my parents back, nor did I have any remorse for injecting them with a lethal dose of potassium chloride. Didn't care that they were dead. Didn't owe them an apology. I had business to take care of.

It was time to permanently silence my next victim.

CHAPTER 48

Bambi

I got my Ho-on-the-Go bag out of the trunk, walked straight to the back, went inside the unisex restroom at the coffee shop. I changed my lace wig to another glue-on platinum blond lace front. I brushed the hair in a circular motion, then let it fall naturally. The right side was layered above my ear, the left side curled under my chin. I switched my contacts to lavender. To make my lips look thinner, I outlined my lips halfway from the top and the same from the bottom, then filled in with a brilliant red Taylor Swift lipstick. Now it looked like I barely had lips. My eyeliner and eyelashes were dark. My foundation was ghost white. I had to admit I looked a mess. I eased my white collarless v-neck scrub over my head, put on my matching white drawstring pants and shoes. I was on my way to Cedars.

I parked at a meter on Beverly Boulevard near Emergency but I knew an alternate escape route out of the building. My stun gun was secured in my girdle and my pepper spray was tucked in my bra with my car key. Picking up the light blue bag with the IV, I quickly entered the hospital lobby. With thousands of nurses on staff, getting past registration was easy. I made it to the third floor. All I had to do was get inside Fancy's room, switch the IV bags and leave.

Quietly and quickly, I opened the door to room 3117. Hanging my head, I walked to her bedside. Turned my back to her. I successfully gave her the bag of potassium. It only took a minute.

I heard voices growing closer. I had to hurry. After I switched the bag, I stood with my back to Fancy for fifteen seconds. I wanted to watch her die like I'd done with my parents. I had to see her exhale her last breath. Afraid Fancy was the one the two-headed lady was referring to when she'd said the woman could read me, I couldn't let Fancy see my face.

There was something fascinating about watching a person die. The fight. The struggle. The surrender. I preferred their eyes remained open. That way I could tell for sure. Closed eyes were deceiving. Thirty seconds had passed. The voices grew closer.

I glanced over my shoulder. She stared into my eyes and screamed, "Ahhhhh!"

Fuck! I didn't know the bitch could speak. Why the fuck didn't the media cover that shit? I snatched the pillow from beneath her head, covered her face. I knew I should've run out the door. I stood over her holding the pillow. Anxious to watch Fancy take her last breath, I hadn't noticed the slow drip of the IV. At this rate the potassium chloride would take too long for her to go into cardiac arrest. I tried to adjust the drip. She snatched the pillow. I snatched it back, pressed the pillow harder against her face.

She grabbed my hair, pulled my wig off my head. "Ahhhh!" I screamed. That shit hurt. The hair from my front hairline ripped from my head and stuck to the wig glue. "You bitch. I'ma kill your ass for sure now."

The door flung open. "What the hell are you doing?" one of the nurses yelled.

The other nurse grabbed me. I refused to let go of the pillow. I back-kicked the nurse in her shin. She screamed, then let me go. The other nurse opened the door, then screamed, "Get security up here now!"

I slammed the pillow against Fancy's face, held it with determination.

The time for this bitch to die was now.

CHAPTER 49

Darius

Thanks to Moms, my life was fucked up again. In a monumental way this time.

I was my mother's son and her keeper, not her damn baby and babysitter. I knew my mom. She was many things; a kidnapper wasn't one of them. Yet, there was no way I knew for certain if she had information on the whereabouts of Grant's twins. The likelihood was slim but with her obsessive behavior I'd begun to have doubts. Tried to tell her leave the dude's ass alone. I knew he was still fiendin' for that Honey chick. What the fuck was my mom trying to prove? She couldn't make him love her.

If Mom hadn't been involved with dude, that underhanded (no longer undercover) bitch wouldn't have set me up. I owed that female who'd sucked my dick an apology. She was just kickin' it with me but I was so busy treating her like a whore, I blamed her for the situation when I should've blamed my mother.

That woman, whoever she was, her refusal to grant media interviews let me know she was legit. I'd never been caught cheating on my wife. This was the first time. I prayed my wife hadn't found out. I had to get back to LA. I had to tell Ladycat my version face to face. Let her look into my eyes. See how much I loved her. How I never meant to hurt her. I was just giving that woman a ride to her car. That was my truth.

Normally I'd travel with the team on our private jet. Being I was a straggler, I'd copped a seat in first class to D.C. Would've bought all the first-class seats if they'd let me. The guy next to me kept looking at the front page of the *LA Times,* then at me. Good for him he'd kept his mouth shut or my size eighteen shoe would've went up his ass and came out his fuckin' mouth.

I exited the plane at Dulles International. I decided to do the right thing and sit this game out. It was still preseason. My team could do without me. Didn't want the media embarrassing my teammates, plus I'd confirmed I had an official custody hearing this morning. If the judge honored my custody order in Dallas and allowed me to keep DJ, the media would see the softer side of me.

Waiting for my driver to get my bags, I powered on my iPhone. I'd missed one, two, three, four . . . ten calls from Mom. Probably calling to apologize for letting Ashlee take DJ. No missed calls or messages from Ashlee. Ashlee could've let DJ give me a shout. She was probably gallivanting over my bad press. Camera crews surrounded me at the baggage carousel snapping photos. At this point all I cared about was my son, my mom, and my wife.

I kept scrolling. *Fuck!* Fifty missed calls, from the hospital. *Boom!* My heart exploded harder than that truck that had slammed into the back of my SUV. Damn shame how that hit and run driver almost killed us. Who was looking for them? After I got DJ situated with Fancy, I was going to personally find the owner of that white pickup truck. They were going to feel my pain.

Before I could return the calls, my phone rang. It was a call from the hospital.

Following the driver who'd collected my bags, I answered, "Don't tell me any bad news. Please, I can't take any more."

"Oh, so you can dish it out but you can't take it? Mr. Jones, I don't know how to say this any other way. Thanks to you, your wife almost died a few hours ago. This is nurse Anita Harris."

"Almost?" Ladycat must've heard about the woman in my car. My wife wasn't dead. I didn't have to make funeral arrangements or prepare for the worst. But I held my breath, pressed the phone closer to my ear, and listened.

"Thank God we got to her in time. If you were here, where you should've stayed, with your wife, instead of running all over Holly-wood sticking your dick in a prostitute, this wouldn't have happened."

She's not a prostitute.

"The person who tried to kill your wife, she got away. I stood be-tween her and your wife and I was hit in the side with a stun gun. She pepper-sprayed the other nurse, then ran out the room. Security couldn't find her. Listen. As soon as your wife is better, we're dis-charging her. And, yes, I am suing you. If my counterpart is wise, she'll sue you too. We're not operating a patient protection program here. Mr. Jones, this is a hospital. I hope busting a nut was worth it. I hope you can live with yourself, Mr. Jones."

A woman tried to kill my wife? Who? Why? Was it the same person from the accident? I'd reserve those questions for the police. "I'm sorry for all of this. My wife. What's her condition?"

"Thankfully the slow drip IV we had in her arm saved her life. God showed her favor today. She's stable. At least one of you are."

I exhaled. "What happened with her IV?"

"The woman switched her IV bag to a bag filled with potassium."

"Potassium. That's good for you. Right?"

"Just like your fucking a stranger, Mr. Jones, too much of a good thing can kill you. For your wife's sake, I hope you used protection. The amount of potassium chloride that entered your wife's blood-stream wasn't lethal. The amount in the IV bag could've killed three people, three times. We gave her oxygen. She's breathing on her own again. Her verbal and motor responses are good. You must've done a lot of cruel things to a lot of people to have this kind of karma. Bad luck comes in threes, Mr. Jones. In your case it might be to the tenth power."

I'd begun to feel this woman had had a distorted crush on me, per-ceived me to be a failed role model, or she felt I'd let her down. I asked, "Is my wife's mother there?"

"No, Mr. Jones. She never made it. You might want to check on her."

Whoa. I hoped Caroline and her daughter were okay. "What about my mom? Is she there?"

"Kind of hard to be in two places at the same time. Your mother was arrested from this hospital earlier today for kidnapping and trespassing. I told you, in your case, Mr. Jones, your bad luck is shooting through the roof. You're already at three. I have two words for you, Mr. Jones. Prayer and restitution. Bye."

Four, if I counted Ashlee taking DJ. The three most important persons in my life needed me and I wasn't doing all I could to ensure their safety. This wasn't a good time to call Ladycat. I felt alone. My mom? In jail? I called her cell phone anyway.

"Hi, Darius," she answered.

"Hi, Mom. Thank God. You're not in jail?"

"Not in jail anymore. I'm suing the hospital, that nurse Harris, and Grant. When I'm done with him, he'll wish he'd never met me."

"Who bailed you out?" I asked her.

"My personal assistant is heaven sent. Bambi bailed me out."

"Can't wait to shake her hand."

"Son, you're adding more drama to my task list than Grant. But the good news is Bambi is working on generating good press for you. You know it's harder than I realized to make you likable. You haven't contributed much to your community. After the season is over, we're starting a nonprofit organization in your name. I owe Bambi. That was considerate of her to post a hundred thousand dollars. We can exchange stories when I see you. Where are you?"

"No thanks to you, I'm in D.C. for my custody hearing tomorrow. I have to go."

What the fuck did she mean, I added more drama to her fucking task list than Grant? He had her arrested for kidnapping. Was she pissed because I wasn't there to bail her out? I ended the call with my mom so I wouldn't regret telling her what I really wanted to say.

And who in the fuck was this Bambi chick scoring Brownie points with my mom?

CHAPTER 50

Bambi

She wasn't a Siamese cat descended from the sacred temple of Siam. She didn't have nine lives. The bitch was lucky. Landed on her feet, back to back. The good thing about luck was, at some point it had to end.

Security tried outsmarting me. Blocked the stairway exit on the first floor. Out of shape amateurs. I'd gone to the opposite end of the hall, darted into a vacant room, crawled out the window onto the fire escape, and trotted to the second floor. I jumped from the second floor onto the top of a SUV, slid down the windshield onto the hood, then to the ground. I hurried to my car, then cruised past the Beverly Center. I'd have to find another way to terminate Fancy.

Hated my parents' house but I was happy to get to the place I legally called home. I opened the door. Every light in the kitchen, living room, and family room was on. Rita was in the family room watching a movie. The boys were in their playpen beside the love seat.

She sat up. "You a nurse too, Bambi?" Rita asked. "Your clothes, they all dirty. Oh, you must've had one of them fantasy jobs. You into mud wrestling? Anyways, I'm sho glad to see you. What we gon' do with my grandbabies? Where's my money?"

Not answering any of her questions, I went to my parents' old bedroom, opened the dresser drawer, counted twenty grand, went back to the living room. "Here's your money. You can leave in the morning." Rita opened the envelope. Counted every C-note.

One more night and I was done with Rita. If she left tonight, the twins might not make it through the night, especially if that crying one aggravated the hell out of me.

"You overpaid me," Rita said, handing me a stack of hundreds.

"No, I didn't. This is your last assignment. Plus, you can't talk to Honey about anything that you've done or you're going to jail. Not one word." That was true. Her daughter could press charges for the kidnapping and Fancy could press charges for the hit and run.

"Jail? I thought you said we were babysitting. That's not a crime."

"But what you did to Fancy and Darius is. Pack your things and everything for the twins and set it by the garage door. Good night."

I walked down the long hallway to my room, opened the door, then locked it from the inside. I turned off all the lights, sat in my old wooden rocking chair. The same purple cushion from when I was a child was tied to the back posts. I stared out the window. The ocean view was beautiful during the day. The waves I heard weren't visible in the dark.

The memories weren't pleasant. My childhood scars were permanent lacerations. I wasn't molested. Molestation would've been a welcomed tragedy. My parents had me when they were in their midforties. My mom was a successful lawyer but after she had me she became a stay-at-home wife. My father wasn't as successful as my mom but he refused to be a househusband.

"Bambi, I wish you were never born," my mother would say. "You've ruined my figure, my career, my life. Look at me. I'm fat because of you." I heard that almost every day as a child. It wasn't my fault she got toxemia when she was pregnant with me. She went from a size two to a size twenty-two in nine months.

My father would say to me, "You're fat just like your mother. No man wants either of you. Your mother is right. We shouldn't have had you. You ruined our lives."

As a kid, my mom fed me all day. The more my parents told me, "I hate you," the more I hated them. I didn't like but understood the kids at school calling me fat and not playing with me. But my parents were supposed to love me no matter what. Darius was the only one who never teased me. Since I was six years old, I'd given all the love I had to him. Darius was the only reason I didn't want to die.

One day I'd seen an episode on television where this male nurse was killing elderly patients with an overdose of potassium chloride. I'd heard about how mixing finely crushed glass in a person's food daily could cause unstoppable internal bleeding. I'd researched assisted suicide, death with dignity, and aid with dying. In the United States it was legal in Oregon, Washington, and Montana but not in California. Suicide in California was illegal but whom would the law hold accountable?

Potassium chloride was perfect. It was odorless and colorless. My parents were aging but growing old didn't make them compassionate. I'd become their caretaker. At sixty-two years of age they still degraded me daily. Over the years I'd become immune to their decades of emotional abuse.

One day I snapped. I'd decided it was time for them to go. That night I added a lethal dose of liquid potassium to their nighttime beverage. I watched them drink their last drink, packed up all the evidence, and left this house. That was the last time I saw my parents alive.

I couldn't sleep. I rocked in the chair until sunrise came at 5:20 A.M. I showered, glued on my long chestnut lace wig. Thanks to Fancy, for the first time, it hurt me to put on my wig. I attached my brown lashes and put on a black sweat suit. Rita had fallen asleep on the love seat. The boys were asleep in the playpen.

"Rita, wake up. It's time to go."

"Bambi, what time is it?" she asked, pulling the comforter over her shoulders.

I snatched the cover. "Let's go, now!"

Her eyes widened. She hurried to the bathroom, returned to the family room, changed the boys' diapers, wiped them clean all over, then changed their clothes. "Let's go," she said.

"Help me put the boys in my car and you can go home or wherever you'd like but don't tell anyone you've been here and don't ever come back here."

I drove off with the twins in their car seats. They were in the back.

Fortunately neither of them were crying. In transit, I retrieved my iPhone from my purse, called Jada.

"Hey, Bambi. You okay? It's seven in the morning."

Like I didn't know what time it was. "I'm good. Calling to see if you can meet me for breakfast. I need a favor."

"Of course. I owe you. I cannot thank you enough for bailing me out. I'll have a reimbursement check for you for the full amount. Where would you like me to meet you?"

"Roscoe's Chicken 'n Waffles on Manchester at eight-thirty. Is that good?"

"I'll be there. Bye."

I made my way through the LA traffic. Where were all these people going this early? I arrived at Jada's house at eight-fifteen. Unlocking the car doors, I left the twins in their car seats. The playpen and all the boys' food and clothes I'd bought were in the trunk. I'd dump that stuff later.

I prayed Jada didn't end up back behind bars but that wasn't my concern. Just in case one of my good deeds backfired, I'd done two. Now I was on my way to Roscoe's to have breakfast with my new mother-in-law.

CHAPTER 51

Darius

Hadn't been to D.C. since our last game. I sat in the corner at Wilson's, a hole-in-the-wall spot on V Street Northwest, famous for its country-style breakfast. My court appearance was in an hour. I was less than ten minutes from Moultrie Courthouse at 500 Indiana Avenue Northwest. Didn't want to arrive one minute early. Didn't want to go anywhere upscale to eat. Wasn't hungry. Stomach was in knots. Head throbbing. Had to keep things in motion, which was why I'd left my hotel. I wanted to walk into court, give my spill, let the judge do his or her thing, and keep it moving.

Hopefully Ashlee would bring DJ to court. That way if she was awarded custody, I could hug and kiss my lil' man good-bye. I had two one-way tickets to Los Angeles. Someone had to keep DJ. Didn't trust Mom to do the right thing with my son. I had to see my wife, ask her to keep DJ, then get back on a plane to catch up with my team in Miami.

"I'd like to have a large orange juice," I told the waitress.

"The restaurant is starting to fill up. Don't know how long I can avoid seating folks over here."

I handed her a fifty. "I'll be outta here in fifteen minutes."

"You got it," she said, stuffing the money in her front pocket.

Quarter to nine. Time to face the music. A patron mumbled as I exited the restaurant. "Is that Darius Jones? What's he doing here?"

"About to lose the shirt off his back," were the last words I heard as the door closed.

Never that, I thought, getting in the back of the Town Car. With five minutes to spare, I entered the courtroom. Ashlee was seated alone up front. "Fuck you, Darius," resounded in my ears as the judge called my name. All eyes were on me.

"Here," I said. I hadn't bothered hiring a D.C. attorney who knew nothing about me except what he may have heard in the media. I could handle this.

Ashlee looked fucking fantastic and quite fuckable. Her hair was slicked back into a neat ponytail that highlighted her facial features. Makeup neutral with cotton candy lips. Her blue and black dress was tailored to her breasts, flat stomach, and bangin' booty. The dark stockings worked the outfit.

After roll call, the judge announced the court protocol, then said, "Case of Anderson versus Jones."

I was relieved we were first. I stood on the left side of the courtroom. Ashlee and her attorney were to the right.

"Mr. Baldwin, I'll hear from you first," the judge said to Ashlee's attorney.

He squared his shoulders. "Your Honor, my client is petitioning for full legal and physical custody on the basis of Mr. Jones's inability to provide a safe and stable environment for Darius Henry Jones Junior."

Adamantly, I said, "I object."

"You'll have your chance to speak, Mr. Jones. Mr. Baldwin, please explain."

"I'm sure you've seen the paper. I have a copy here in case you haven't. Mr. Jones was caught on Hollywood Boulevard soliciting sex. He's a big—"

The judge interrupted. "I know who he is. Are there any pending charges?"

Mr. Baldwin cleared his throat. "No, but."

I was glad she'd asked that question before I'd have to sue him for defamation of character. No one had proof of my having been with a prostitute yet they all wanted to label me.

"Any other reasons why Mr. Jones shouldn't have shared custody?"

"Yes, your honor. His wife was in an automobile accident. She was in a coma."

The judge interrupted. "Was or is?"

"I'm not sure," the attorney answered.

"Mr. Jones?"

"My wife is no longer in a coma. We're scheduled for release from the hospital any day now. Our doctor is keeping her for observation." Selectively I chose words like "my wife," "we," and "our," hoping the judge would be lenient.

"Anything else, Mr. Baldwin?"

"That's all for now."

"Mr. Jones, you don't have representation?"

"No, Your Honor, I don't." This case should be decided in my favor once I explained my position.

"I can order a continuance to allow you to secure representation."

"Your Honor. There's a custody order in Dallas giving me and my wife full legal and physical custody because"—I hated saying this but had to—"my son's mother is mentally unstable. She left our son in her car alone to stalk me at my house in LA. And after we broke up, she entered my house with the extra set of keys she had made and replaced my wife's aspirin with abortion pills. Then she harassed my wife to the point where my wife ended up taking what she thought was aspirin."

"Where do you live, Mr. Jones?"

What the hell? All the testimony I'd given her and she wants to know where I live? "I moved to Atlanta."

"Where did you live when the custody order was issued?" the judge asked.

Was that a trick question? Best to answer truthfully. Didn't want to get locked up for perjury. "I was in Los Angeles at the time, Your Honor, but then I was drafted."

She interrupted. "Based on your residence, jurisdiction must be reestablished. Based on Ms. Anderson's filing, this court will make the final ruling. Would you like a continuance? I can grant temporary shared custody. I'll order legal custody remains with you until I make a final decision."

That seemed reasonable. By the time I'd have to return, Fancy would be with me. I opened my mouth to agree to come back when Ashlee cut me off.

"Your Honor, I don't want my son around him, his wife, or his mother. The press is following him everywhere. The majority of the people in here are media."

The judge said, "Everyone with the press stand up."

I glanced over my shoulder. Three fourths of the room stood.

"Get out of my courtroom now," the judge ordered.

Ashlee continued. "This is what my son will be subjected to when he's with his father. Plus, yesterday someone attempted to kill his wife while she was at the hospital."

The judge looked at me. "Is this true, Mr. Jones?"

I nodded.

Ashlee was on a roll. "And to top it off, his mother has trespassing and kidnapping charges against her right now. I don't want any of them near my son."

"Mr. Jones?" the judge said.

I nodded again.

"The court will make its final ruling today. Full physical and legal custody is granted to the mother with supervised visitation to the father every other weekend and alternating holidays. The court will take a fifteen-minute recess."

CHAPTER 52

Rita

I needed a break from all the madness. For the first time in months, I was anxious to get back to Flagstaff. First, I had to find out where Bambi was taking my grandbabies.

Trailing her to a big ole house, I kept driving when she pulled in the driveway. I wondered why Bambi went there. I parked three cars back on the side street. Being I'd just turned off a one-way street, eventually Bambi would have to come this way.

Before my engine was cool, there she was driving by. I took my chances driving a half block in the wrong direction back to the house. I started to leave my car at the gate and walk but my old legs wouldn't carry me fast enough if a loose dog got behind me.

I drove close as I could. Couldn't believe my eyes. No way in heaven. I got out my car, tiptoed to the front door. Sho nuff she'd left my grandbabies. I started to call the police but remembered what Bambi had told me. I couldn't leave them there. They so tiny and all, a raccoon might eat 'em alive. I had no clue who lived in this fancy house. My daughter lived in Atlanta.

Maybe there was a reward for the person who'd give information leading to finding the babies. "Nah, I couldn't do that. That wouldn't be right, Rita. I know. That's why I'm not going to call no police."

I picked up one car seat. Put it in my car. Went back for the other one.

"Stop, put your hands up! Don't move!"

Suddenly, I had to pee again. My hearing must be failing me 'cause I didn't hear none of them police cars drive up. One, two, three, four, I lost count. "I'm innocent," I said, straightening my wig.

The officer said, "You're under arrest for kidnapping. Put your hands behind your back. You have the right to remain silent . . ."

I folded my arms underneath my breasts. I wasn't letting him put them things on my wrists. "Do I have the right to pee?" I asked him. Before he answered, we were standing in a puddle of my urine.

Two other officers picked up the babies in their car seats. Then they put the car seats in the back of one of them police cars.

"Lord, they can't even crawl and already going to jail." Bambi would kill me when she found out I sang like a canary. Oh, yeah. Rita St. Thomas could blow louder than one of them train whistles. My daughter would chew me up, spit me out, then shoot me. I had to do something 'cause I wasn't going with them policemen.

When the officer touched my arm, I fell in my puddle of pee and lay there like a possum.

CHAPTER 53

Honey

Happy not to have two babies pressing against my bladder, I enjoyed urinating like a normal person. I sat on the toilet peeing, praying, and crying at the same time. I wiped myself, washed my hands and face, then joined Grant, Valentino, Sapphire, Velvet, Velvet's son Ronnie and her mother, Ms. Waters, at the table for breakfast.

"Sorry, for holding everyone up," I said, sitting beside Grant. "Ms. Waters, you keep feeding us like this three times a day and I'm going to look pregnant again."

"I'll still love you, baby," Grant said, kissing me on the lips.

Men. Was his PDA intended to impress Ms. Waters? Was Grant trying to prove his love to me? Was he attempting to make Valentino jealous? Or all of the above?

We held hands, bowed our heads. Ms. Waters's grace was always a welcoming prayer. She said, "Dear Lord Jesus, as we collectively humble ourselves before You, we ask that You watch over Luke and London. Yea, though we walk through the valley of the shadow of death, let us fear no evil for we know that Thou art with us. Let not Honey's and Grant's hearts be troubled. Let Thy rod and Thy staff comfort them, Lord Jesus. You gave them two beautiful sons. We know You see

Luke and London right now. We ask that You prepare a table before them in the presence of their enemies. We know with You all things are possible. Please, Lord, make it possible for Honey and Grant to have their babies back safe and sound. In Jesus' name."

Everyone said, "Amen," in unison.

Sapphire's iPhone rang. "Excuse me. I have to take this call."

Grant said, "Ms. Waters, I know you told me not to but I have to thank you and Velvet for welcoming us into your home. Hopefully we won't be here much longer."

Sapphire stuck her head into the room, then said, "Ms. Waters, let's pray all your prayers worked. Honey and Grant, come with me."

Ms. Waters lifted her hands, palms facing up, and said, "Thank you, Jesus."

Grant and I stumbled over one another worse than Mister and Celie chasing after Shug in *The Color Purple*. He handed me my jacket, I tossed him his shoes, he grabbed my purse. Outside, Grant held Sapphire's car door open for me. Waited until I was safely in the front passenger seat, then closed the door behind me.

"Let's hope this is what we've prayed for," Sapphire said, speeding out the driveway. Clouds of smoke trailed the car.

I told Sapphire, "Well, tell us something. Where are we going?"

"Did they find our boys?" Grant asked, leaning between the front seats.

Sapphire didn't respond. She whipped onto the 405. Grant fell back into the seat. I became quiet. I stared out the window. Traffic was horrendous. My stomach ached. Tears streamed down my cheeks onto my maternity blouse. Hadn't wanted to go shopping for post-pregnancy clothes. I thought about Ms. Waters's prayer, wondering if the Lord had indeed prepared a table for us. Any table would be good as long as our babies were at the table with us.

An hour later, Sapphire pulled into a long driveway, parked behind several police cars. There were vans from all the major news stations. Cameras flashed like we were about to attend another premiere but the only red carpet was the trail from my bleeding heart. "Let's pray this is it."

Oh, my God. I got weak. *Please, let them have my babies.*

Grant yelled, "I knew it. Baby, I was right!"

"Right about what?" I asked. "What? Tell me."

Sapphire got out the car, rang the doorbell. A policeman stood in the doorway. "Come in, everybody, and have a seat."

CHAPTER 54

Honey

There were two police officers standing on opposite sides of the doorway outside this huge mansion with skyscraping spiraling white pillars.

I whispered to Grant, "Baby, where are we?"

"You'll see in a minute," he replied, as if he had a secret and a surprise.

Sapphire entered first, Grant next. I scanned the police officers head to toe, then went inside. *Now I see.* Jada's house was immaculately gorgeous. She was seated in a chair across the room. Her arms were folded under her breasts. There was an empty chair centered in front of the mantel.

"You two, sit here," the officer said.

There were police officers standing at every possible exit of the room. Twelve officers, to be exact. Their hands were on their guns. I stared at Jada. She was too calm. That bitch better not have set me up.

I sat on the sofa, whispered to Grant, "I told you she did it. I hope they give her," not me, "life."

One of the policemen said, "My name is Officer Austin. Lawrence Austin. I need everyone to remain quiet. Do not speak unless I ask you a question. I'll be back in five minutes. No talking."

We sat there looking at one another. Five minutes seemed like fifty.

Grant kissed me, hugged me. His hug was reassuring. I was scared. Sapphire stood by the fireplace between Jada and the empty chair. Good. Make sure she doesn't try to do anything crazy. I hope she burns in hell for putting me through my own hell.

Officer Austin entered the room escorting a short person. A sheet was draped over the person's head; all I could see was from the knees down. The person wore black Birkenstocks and a black skirt. Austin sat the shrouded figure in the chair. Slowly he slid back the sheet. My chin dropped toward my chest when I saw my mother dressed like she was going to a funeral.

"Rita? You? You took my babies!" I rushed toward her with my arms stretched forward and my hands parted just enough to strangle her evil ass.

"Let go, Ms. Thomas. Let her go," Officer Austin said.

My fingers locked around her neck. "Haven't you done enough to hurt me? You stole my babies! I will kill you!"

Surprisingly none of the other officers in the room moved. I wasn't sure if they had specific orders not to move unless instructed, if they felt my mother deserved an ass whipping, or if they enjoyed watching two women catfight.

Rita couldn't speak. She couldn't breathe. I didn't care. I was serious. I had no intentions of letting go until she'd exhaled her last breath.

Grant grabbed my waist. Pulled me in the opposite direction of Rita. The policeman pried my fingers away from Rita's neck. Rita rushed me. Punched me in the jaw. Loosened one of my back teeth. She lost her balance, fell to the floor.

"Let me go, Grant. We need to have this out! Mama, you think you can still beat my ass! Let me go, Grant." I stomped Rita the same way she'd done me when she kicked me out of her house when I was sixteen. If I could get closer, I'd stomp up and down her ass ten times.

Grant said, "Honey, stop it! That's your mother?"

"No, she's not. That bitch is a surrogate. I don't know her and she damn sure don't know me." I kicked Rita in her ass.

"Break this up right now," Officer Austin yelled. "Everybody sit down."

Jada never left her seat. She stared at Grant, tilted her head side to side while pressing her lips together. She raised her eyebrows, smirked at me.

I told her, "Bitch, I'll knock your teeth down your throat."

Jada calmly said, "You've got one more time to call me a bitch up in my house."

"Bitch." What was she going to do?

Next thing I knew, a crystal paperweight was flying at my head. "Ow!" Grant yelled as he blocked the weight with his hand. Blood dripped from his fingers.

Rita laughed. "Shoulda hit her in the head. Knock some sense into her."

Officer Austin spoke at room tone. "Does anyone here care about Luke and London Hill?"

I started crying. I got so caught up with Rita, I hadn't listened to the officer until now. Grant hugged me. All of us were quiet.

Officer Austin looked at Rita and said, "Ms. St. Thomas, you want to tell your daughter what you told me?"

Rita shook her head.

"I'm not asking you this time," Officer Austin said.

Rita took a deep breath. "Bambi Bartholomew paid me to watch the boys and I ain't giving nobody my money. I swear on a stack of Bibles and a pig's foot that's all I did was watch them babies."

Jada stood. "Bambi who? Bartholomew? As in my personal assistant? She's lying. I just had breakfast at Roscoe's with Bambi. She's working on a media campaign for me."

Rita frowned. "Might be two peoples with the same name. I don't know."

I'd forgotten how country Rita was. I noticed Jada sat, scooted to the edge of her seat, arched her back, stared at us. I looked at Grant. His face froze, his body tensed. "You okay?" I asked. He didn't respond.

Rita continued, "I told the policeman everything. Bambi paid me to take care of Fancy. But that wasn't me at the hospital trying to kill Fancy. No, siree, not Rita. Don't know nothin' about that 'cept what the officer told me. But I do know that Luke doesn't share very well and London never liked that Bambi girl around us. I promise you, Lace, I did nothing but love them boys."

Why'd she have to call me by my real name?

Jada leapt from her seat this time. "She did what?" Jada picked up her cell phone.

Office Austin took the phone from Jada. "Let us handle contacting this Bambi woman. We'll get the truth out of her."

Jada sat in her chair, tilted her head to the side, kept staring at us. Grant was still speechless.

Rita continued, "Bambi told me she'd kill me if I ever told. Well, if I end up dead like her parents that's in those coffins in their bedroom in her house, you know who done it."

Dead people. In coffins? In a house? Rita had lost it. But for the first time in years, I felt compassion for my mother. Still had no regrets for beating her ass. She deserved that. But I believed she took good care of my babies.

Officer Austin left and returned with Luke and London. He gave Luke to me and Grant took London. I told Grant, "Put him on the floor." I did the same with Luke. I unwrapped their blankets, inspected every hair on their heads and counted every toe on their feet. I didn't need to see the hospital ankle tags to tell them apart but I was glad the tags were still on. I kissed my babies' feet. I cried. Bundled them back up, hugged them so tight. Luke cried. I handed London to Grant. Rocked Luke.

"He likes for you to sing to him," Rita said. "Can I? Please."

I handed Luke to Rita. Couldn't believe she started singing, "Hush, little baby, don't you cry," and Luke stopped crying.

I walked over to Jada. "I'm sorry for putting you through all of this." I was horrible at giving apologies, hated apologizing to her, but it was the right thing to do.

Jada stood, bypassed me, walked up to Grant, then said, "She's not the one who owes me an apology."

CHAPTER 55

Darius

The time for me to apologize to Ashlee face to face was right now. I followed her outside the courtroom. The press was waiting for me. Camera lights flashed in our faces. "Mr. Jones. What was the outcome? Did the judge deny you custody of your son based on your encounter with the alleged prostitute? Is your wife still in a coma? Will you lose your wife and son in the same week?"

Sorry ass relentless motherfuckers asked one question after another. Several reporters asked questions at the same time. I didn't respond to those bastards' questions but I did ask, "What, y'all want a fucking press conference?" Didn't shield my face from them either. I knew I was famous when professionals spent their lives getting paid to shadow mine.

I pleaded, "Ashlee, wait. Let me talk to you."

She kept walking. I kept following her.

"Ashlee, please. Give me a minute." I knew to keep my hands to myself when it came to dealing with Ashlee. Didn't need the media adding woman beater to my list of hiccups.

Ashlee stood on the steps of the courthouse. Looked up at me. Put one foot forward, her hand on her hip. "What is there to say, Darius?"

Damn, she was ravishing. Suddenly my appetite kicked in. "Can we get in my car? My driver is right there." I pointed at the tinted-window Town Car parked in front the courthouse.

Thankfully she got in. I sat beside her. Reporters took pictures until the driver closed the door.

"Ashlee, I apologize. I'm sorry I treated you horribly. I was wrong. Please say you forgive me."

"Oh, so now Darius Jones is sorry. Now you're sorry. Why? Because"—she extended her arms, east and west, then continued—"the media is all over your ass with bad press. Huh?"

I wouldn't admit she was right. Had none of this happened, I wouldn't have apologized to her. "Ashlee, please, don't do this." My head hung low. I tried to hide my tears. Whenever my life was fucked the hell up, Ashlee made it better.

"I don't care anymore, Darius. You need to cry. You know how many times I've cried over you? When have you ever stood up for me? Every since we were kids, I always had your back. Always. I was there for you before Maxine, Ciara, Ginger, Heather, Miranda, Zen, and Fancy. We were supposed to get married after you divorced Ciara. I watched you get married twice. You knew I loved you. What? You thought I was happy when you proposed to Maxine? All the days I listened to you brag about fucking your mom's executives, you thought I wanted to hear that shit? Even when you weren't positive that you were HIV negative, you still fucked around. And let's not mention Fancy raising my son. You're so busy ballin' out of control you don't have time for DJ." Ashlee screamed in my face, "Have your own baby because you won't see mine again ever!"

That was a long list of things but I had a list too. Ashlee wasn't Rihanna but she was close to making me Chris Brown. I could deal with all she'd said because it was in the past and I couldn't change any of those things, except the part about my never seeing my lil' man ever again.

"He's our child, Ashlee. I am his father. And how can you say I never stood up for you?"

"Never, Darius. When? Tell me."

"What about that day in court when I lied to the judge? Told him I erased your voice mail confessing you'd killed the baby inside Fancy. You killed our child. If I had told the truth, there would've been no custody hearing today. You'd be in jail. I guess that doesn't count."

"That was three years ago. You brought that shit up again today in court and now because that shit didn't work for you today, you're try-ing to make me feel like you did me a fucking favor?" I didn't mean to make Ashlee cry. "Darius, can't you see? I never stopped loving you. I hate that I still love you. You have no idea how it feels when the per-son you love abandons you. It hurts me that we're not a family. And that you do all the things for Fancy that I wished you'd do for me." Ashlee held her stomach.

I wiped her tears with my thumbs. "I do love you, Ashlee. I'm just not in love with you. I'm in love with my wife." No woman could re-place Ladycat. When I fell in love with Fancy, I knew she was the one because I no longer wanted to stick my dick inside another pussy. "Please forgive me for all the pain I've caused you. I never meant to hurt you."

"But you did," she cried, then opened her door.

I leaned over her lap, closed the door. "Let me drop you off at your car."

"I took Metro," she said.

"Then let me drop you off at home on my way to the airport. Please." I was hoping to see DJ for a few minutes. Give my man a hug. Tell him I love him.

"How do two innocent six-year-olds go from being friends, to step-siblings, to lovers, to hating one another?" she asked.

I shook my head. "I don't hate you. But speaking of being six, do you remember someone in our class named Bambi?" I had to find out who she was and why she'd bailed my mom out.

Ashlee stared me down with squinted eyes. "Don't tell me you're fucking her too? Is that why she's working for your mom as Jada's per-sonal assistant? Is she your personal assistant too?"

"Is she legit? Tell me the truth."

"This isn't about her. You've made me learn to hate you. You used to be my best friend. My daddy told me you were like your mama. He was right. Your mom married my dad because she didn't want to raise you alone. And as soon as Wellington came back to her, she dumped my dad. Guess you get your ugly ways from your mama. Y'all screwed up our lives. The only reason she asked me to come help out with DJ was so she could chase behind Grant."

So Mom only asked Ashlee to help out, huh? That was pertinent.

Ashlee technically kidnapped DJ. Oh, there would be another hearing sooner than she expected. Hadn't thought about my parallels to my mom's life until now. I wasn't winning that argument.

"Can I ask you a question?"

Ashlee hunched her shoulders.

"What man do you love? And please don't say me."

CHAPTER 56

Ashlee

How was Darius going to ask me that question?
I told him, "You're the only man I've ever loved."

This conversation was pointless. Part of me was glad I was home. The other part didn't want to leave Darius. Still couldn't figure out how we got to this point in our lives.

"Ashlee, please. Can I see DJ before I leave?"

Finally, Darius's ways had beaten him into submission. Never seen him humble a day in his life. "DJ isn't here. He's with my mom." *In Dallas.*

My mom took DJ so I wouldn't have to take him to court or continue to subject my baby to my alternating personalities. I wasn't emotionally stable enough to care for DJ on a full-time basis. I had to make sure Darius never found out that my mother agreed to raise DJ until I got better.

"Can I meet up with her so I can see him for a few minutes?"

"They should be back soon. You can come in and wait if you'd like." I was ovulating and if I could get pregnant with Darius's second child, then Fancy would leave him and I'd have no other woman in my way. Bambi was obsessed with Darius but she was no competition. Without Fancy in his life, and our new baby on the way, Darius would have to love me.

I saw through Bambi Bartholomew. She was up to something. But that bitch would have to go through me to get Darius. Ashlee Anderson was on the pitcher's mound. Bambi was on third trying to score a run. Fancy was up to bat. It was time for me to do a double-play and take both of those bitches out at the same time.

Darius got out of the car, held the door for me. We went inside my place. I slid the dimmer halfway up, shading just enough light to almost see the entire room.

"Make yourself comfortable. I'll be right back."

"You know approximately what time they'll get here?"

"I'll call my mom and check." I went into my bedroom, slipped into a pair of short shorts, a tank top, and let down my hair. I pinched my nipples hard so they'd show through my clothes. I lightly sprayed perfume in my hair, behind my ears, and behind my neck, then brushed on a soft cherry-flavored lip gloss.

I prayed my chances of getting Darius to fuck me were good. I went into my kitchen. I didn't cook much so I didn't have a turkey baster. I searched my utensils drawer. Nothing I had would work.

"You want something to drink?" I shouted from the kitchen.

He shouted back, "No, thanks. I'm good. If they're not here in fifteen, I gotta go catch my flight."

Bingo! I had an unopened box of Monistat with the applicator. That would have to do. I joined Darius in the living room. Sat beside him, gently touched his thigh. "I want things between us to be amicable for DJ's sake. I won't hold you to supervised visitation. You're right, he's your son. You can see him whenever you want. All I ask is that you respect me as his mother."

Darius's eyes lit up like when we were kids. He hugged me. "Ashlee, you don't know how happy this makes me. Thank you."

I rubbed my hand up and down his back. "We can be friends again." I kissed his ear. Kissed his cheek. Held my lips to his cheek hoping he'd smell the sweetness of my perfume and the cherry scent of my gloss. I prayed he'd kiss my lips.

"I'd like that." Darius pressed his lips to mine. He hadn't kissed me in years.

I rubbed my nipples against his chest. Slid my hand up his thigh to the base of his hard dick. I held my hand there.

His hips moved in my direction. I removed my top. Placed his hands on my breasts. "Just this one time," I whispered, removing my shorts. "Please don't deny me." I straddled him. Smeared my pussy juices on the crotch of his pants. I ground my pussy against his erection until I came. Then I spread more juices on his pants.

I unzipped his pants, released his dick into my palms. There he was. Slugger. He used to be my best friend too.

Darius leaned back on the sofa. "Ashlee, stop. What are we doing? I can't do this," he protested.

Ignoring him, I went down on him. I knew Darius couldn't resist having his trophy waxed. I started sucking his bulging head into my warm wet mouth. I stroked his dick at the same time. All I needed was for Darius to give me enough semen to fill my applicator so I could have his second child.

His head leaned back. He grunted, "Ashlee, please, stop. I'm about to . . . I can't. Please, stop it." He pleaded.

I was determined to prove to Jay Crawford that I could get a man other than him. That I could get married before him. That I wasn't crazy like him. I sucked Darius's dick with determination as I stroked him faster.

His body trembled. He grabbed the back of my head. "Aw, fuck!" he yelled. He shoved his dick to the back of my throat.

I tried to lift my head but I couldn't. I grabbed his wrists. I needed his semen in my mouth not my stomach. I wiggled my head but couldn't lift it. I had no choice. I swallowed all of his cum.

"Ashlee, you shouldn't have," Darius said, zipping his pants. "I've got to go. I hope you were sincere when you said we could be friends. I'll call you when I get to Los Angeles. I have to go check on my wife." He let himself out, left me sitting on the floor naked.

I could do nothing, I could throw up, or I could dial 9-1-1 and say, "I've been raped."

CHAPTER 57

Darius

One step forward, two back.

Again, I'd fucked up. I asked my dick, "Man, what's wrong with you? You've gotta cut this shit out."

"Excuse me, sir."

"Nah, man, I'm not talking to you," I told my driver. "Put up the divider."

My life had to get better. I'd wronged so many people, maybe I shouldn't search for the hit-and-run driver. What was I going to prove? That I could bring another person to their knees? With so much shit happening at once, my life couldn't possibly get any worse. I stared out the window, reflected on the way I'd treated women. Was I really that big of a whore? Women, like the one I'd picked up at My House, shouldn't mistake my confidence and arrogance for rudeness. She wanted to suck my dick. I hadn't forced her. I wasn't to blame, women personalized shit too much.

I had to do a one-eighty. Get back on track. En route to Dulles, I phoned Ciara. Since I'd started apologizing, might as well keep it moving in that direction. Maybe an apology would make her feel better.

"Thank you for calling Ciara Monroe Casting Agency. How may I be of service?"

I cleared my throat. "Is Ciara available?"

"Mrs. Monroe is on the other line. Would you like to leave a message?"

Mrs.? How long did she take to remarry after our divorce? Probably married that dude she'd fucked when I was her husband. Or was he the one killed in the car accident? No, that was her son's father, Solomon. Better avoid mixing the two of them up. Screwing up would defeat my purpose of calling.

What was my true reason for calling Ciara? "Tell her it's an emergency. It's Darius Jones."

The woman laughed out loud, then tried to cover it up like she was coughing. Hope her ass choked for real. "Excuse me. Hold on." Before she muted the call, I heard her mumble, "Ciara is going to love this."

Love what? The chick on the opposite end of the phone didn't know me. Why were strangers analyzing my life? She needs to look in the mirror and question her life. Bet she'd done some fucked up shit too.

"Well, well, well. I see you finally landed on your ass," Ciara said.

No hello? Suppose I deserved that. She could've said, "Hey, Darius, looking great. I see you've been hanging out above the rim."

"I called to apologize for all the wrong things I've done to you."

"Oh, this should be real good. Let me have my receptionist make me some popcorn and bring me a drink," she said, then laughed. "I'm listening."

Displaying my feelings was no fucking sideshow. I started to hang up on her ass. I do hang-time above the rim, guess I could hang in there for this apology. "Listen, I'm sorry for trying to manipulate you. I wasn't in love with you. I shouldn't have married you. Please forgive me." That was all I recalled.

"You're not close to being finished, Mr. Wannabe MVP. Keep going. Get to the part about how you're sorry for recommending I hire your jump off Kimberly. And how you're sorry for lying to me about not fucking Ashlee. Or how you made this big huge announcement on the plane about how you love and respect me and how you wanted to spend the rest of your life with me. And you shed those fake ass tears when you proposed to me. Or be honest. The only reason you proposed was to take over my company. Or how you didn't want us to have a child. Actually, I should thank you for not being my baby's daddy. Oh, you'll get a kick out of not apologizing for this one. Remember when you shoved me when I nine months pregnant? You made me hit the back of my head on the sharp edge of the coffee table. Left me for dead. Unconscious on the floor in my office. You lied and said I'd slipped. Well, looks like you've already slipped and I hope your ass slides right into a one-way jail cell and I'll gladly swallow the key, shit it out, and swallow the key again if that means you'll stay incarcerated the rest of my life. And don't call me back to clear your damn conscience because that's all you're doing. You don't even sound sincere. Whatever you get, you deserve." Ciara ended the call.

That shit was deep. I guess women do have memories like elephants because I'd forgotten all of that. I wish my MaDear were alive. She'd tell me how to handle all this. I was on a roll, needed some positive reinforcement, might as well call Maxine. I knew she'd forgive me. Had a few more minutes before we arrived at Dulles. Maxine's call shouldn't take that long.

A person answered, "Hello," but she didn't sound like Maxine. Maybe her voice had changed.

"Maxine?"

"This is Maxine's mother. Who's calling?"

"Darius."

"Jones?" she asked.

Hesitantly, I said, "Yes, Darius Jones."

Her voice was pleasant. "I'm glad you called. I've been wanting to thank you," she said.

I exhaled. Tapped my forehead, chest, left, then right shoulder. "Thank me for what?" I smiled. Maxine must've been doing well. The last time I ran into her she was working for the Centers for Disease Control.

"I'd like to thank you, Mr. Jones, for killing my daughter. She died one year ago today. If Maxine had never met you she'd still be alive and I wouldn't be struggling to raise my grandchildren alone. Darius, the only thing I ask of you is, when you get that MVP award, dedicate it to Maxine and all the people with HIV and AIDS."

CHAPTER 58

Honey

Grant stood, kneeled before Jada with London in his arms. *Let me get my child.* I took London from Grant. Held my baby with one arm. If Grant proposed to Jada, I'd take off my shoe and hit him in the back of his head. Why did I feel so violent? Was I angry with Rita? Grant? Jada? Myself?

My mother called me "Lace." That was what she'd named me. I wasn't that person anymore. Who was I?

Grant held Jada's hand. I held my breath.

"Jada, I'm so sorry. I apologize with all my heart. You've helped me to mature. You've helped me understand what love is. And what love is not. I was wrong for proposing to you. You're beautiful, successful, intelligent, and deserving of having a man who appreciates all you have to offer."

Including that dry pussy he'd told me about? That was good enough. Grant could stop there. I paced behind him with London.

Grant continued his apology. "Thanks for helping me understand that love is irreplaceable. I tried replacing Honey's love with yours and instead of my being happy, I messed up so many lives. Yours, your son's."

He'd better say my name.

"Honey's—"

Jada said, "Apology accepted."

Guess she didn't want to hear him mention my name again. Thank God that lame apology was over. "Now we can get down to some real business?"

Officer Austin said, "If it's okay with you, Ms. Tanner, I can take everyone's statement here or we can all go down to the station."

Jada approved of Officer Austin taking statements from us at her house.

While rocking Luke, Rita recapped what happened. It was incredible. The last thing she'd said was, "Last time I seen Bambi was earlier today when she drove up this driveway and left them babies in front of the door."

When she said, "Bambi," Grant's face froze again. Hmm. There was more to this story.

Jada said to Grant, "I don't have anything to say except I told you I never took your babies."

Please, no more apologies. Enough already. You're right, okay. But that bitch better not let me find out she'd paid her personal assistant to kidnap my boys. Same difference. I'd kick both of their asses.

Officer Austin said, "Ms. Tanner, if you fully cooperate with us and give us all the information you have on Bambi Bartholomew, I'll make sure all charges against you are dropped."

When Grant didn't apologize to Jada again, I kissed him, then said, "I love you." As selfish as it may have appeared, I did not want to share Grant with Jada for another second.

"Well, Honey, I can't put that public display of affection in the report," the officer said.

I walked over to Jada. "You're wrong. I do owe you an apology." There was no reason to tell her I was the one who told Grant to file charges. "I hope you can forgive me." I realized I was angry because I was holding on to wanting to be right, when I knew I was wrong.

Jada looked at Grant, then at me. "I forgive you and ask that the two of you forgive me. I was looking for love, clinging to my insecurities about my age. I was tired of being alone, and I was selfish. I didn't want Grant. My truth is, I didn't want to be lonely."

"Long as we doing confessions," Rita said. "Honey, I apologize for being a lousy mother. I'm proud of you. And I love you."

I cried on London. My tears wet his blanket. All my thirty years of living my mother had never said she was proud of me and she never told me that she loved me. Acceptance and love was all I wanted from my mother my entire life.

Now I had two babies of my own to love. I promised God I'd be the best mother I knew how. I guess that was what my mom had done at the time. I was learning not to judge people. I was blessed. I had my babies back. And if I were lucky, maybe I had my mom back too.

Officer Austin said, "Off the record, Ms. Tanner, I'd love to take you out," then handed her his card. "Now let's get these two to the hospital for checkups. We've alerted Long Beach Police to issue a search warrant for Bambi Bartholomew's home and a warrant for her arrest. We'll get her, hopefully before she gets someone else. Everyone is dismissed."

Jada said, "Bambi isn't hard to find."

Sapphire said, "No worries. I'm on Bambi's case. She can't outsmart me." Sapphire looked at Jada, then said, "Sorry about leaking those photos of Darius with that woman to the press. I was certain you were involved in the disappearance of Honey's twins. I was wrong. Anything I can to do clear your son's name, let me know."

Jada said, "All of you get out of my house."

Glad this part was over, I had no apologies for my years of prostitution, being a madam, or unconditionally loving Grant. I kissed Grant, whispered in his ear, "Have you fucked Bambi?"

CHAPTER 59

Darius

Bad luck was a bitch. But I wasn't going to be a bitch for bad luck.

The plane trip back to LA gave me time to refocus on what was important, my wife, family, and team. The ride alone in my Town Car from LAX to Cedars made me miss being with my teammates. Couldn't wait to get back in the game.

Mom called the minute my driver parked near the hospital's entrance. Now that I was back in LA, guess I wasn't so popular. There wasn't any media madness at the airport or the hospital. Hated losing my popularity. Bad press was better than no press.

The driver opened my door. I answered, "Hi, Mom. I lost. Ashlee has permanent custody of DJ." I was too excited about seeing my wife to be mad at Mom. Maybe it was best Ashlee had DJ a while longer. She was right. She deserved more time with my son but she wasn't keeping him. I was getting my man back.

"Well, I've got some news that will cheer you up. Where are you?"

"At the hospital getting ready to go upstairs and visit Fancy. But I could use some good news. What's up?" I settled myself in the back-seat, motioned for the driver to close my door.

"One, all of my charges were dropped. Two, they found the twins. And three, I know who's responsible for your car incident, and you were right, it was no accident."

My heart stopped. I stopped, I sat still. "Who, Ma?"

"Bambi—"

Had to cut Mom off. "Your personal assistant? Why would she want to hurt us? She could've killed us." Damn, a chick went through my mom to try to harm my wife, my kid, and me. Why?

"There's more to the story. Go visit Fancy. Come see me tomorrow after Fancy is discharged."

"Ma, text me Bambi's address."

"Darius, no. Let the police handle this, please. You don't need any more bad press."

"Ma, text me her address." Soon as I left the hospital, I was paying that chick a personal visit. If Ma didn't text me Bambi's address, I knew where to find it.

I got out of the car, picked up a pass from registration, and went to 3117 thankful this was my wife's last night in the hospital. I was glad I'd made it back in time for her discharge. I was looking forward to our alone time to give her my uninterrupted version of the madness before the paparazzi bombarded us first thing in the morning.

Tap. Tap. I knocked, then opened her door. That was the Ladycat I was accustomed to seeing. The hospital gown didn't detract from her beauty. Her hair flowed over her shoulders, her face was radiant. When she noticed me, Fancy sat up in her bed. No smile or hello. She was reading *Be Careful What You Wish For.* A woman in a white wedding gown was on the cover.

Jokingly, I said, "Hey, I hope that's not a sign of how you feel about me."

The book left her hand, whistled through the wind, pages fluttered, the spine hit me in the head. "Ow!"

"Get out!" she yelled. "Get out of my room and stay out of my life!"

I rushed my wife, covered her mouth, then shook my head. "Keep it down before the nurses make me leave again. I'm not going anywhere. You can't get rid of me that easily. Don't you want to hear my side?"

Not my wife too. I already felt like shit after listening to Ciara and Maxine's mom back to back. At least Ashlee had forgiven me, I hoped. Under no circumstance was I letting my wife leave me. Had to have my star player on my team.

"I'm not staying married to a male whore. You can't control your dick, Darius. I get sick for a week and you're cheating on me. And that lady from the restaurant came here, to my hospital room, and tried to kill me. I could be dead! Twice! Next time I might not be so fortunate. You're not worth my losing my life over your mistress. She can have you."

I shook my head. "That's not true. I don't have a mistress. Is that what they printed in the paper?"

"To hell with what's in the paper, I'm talking about the woman who came here and . . ." Fancy stopped talking and started crying.

CHAPTER 60

Bambi

Where was my Darius? What was taking him so long to come to me?

Relaxing in my oversized tub, I enjoyed my candlelit bubble bath. That two-headed lady did say, "Darius will come to you." When? How long was I supposed to wait? Where was I supposed to be? That two-headed lady had better not be a double scammer. I'd hunt her down if her love spell didn't work and she'd better not think I'd forgotten about my engagement ring either.

"Since you can read my mind, you thief, give me back my ring."

I scrubbed my body with a loofah sponge three times over. Inserted my finger into my pussy, cleaned myself out. I got out of the tub, into the shower, shampooed and conditioned my hair. Filled the tub with cold water, dipped my body to tightened my skin. I massaged my body all over with aloe and almond body oil, toweled dry, then applied Victoria's Secret Vanilla Shimmer body lotion.

I lay across my bed, gazing toward the ceiling. The room was black. I couldn't see the space in front of my nose. I meditated, cleared my mind, recapped my conversation with the two-headed lady.

I'd done my good deed. Actually, I'd done more than two. Dropping off the twins at Jada's made my good deed quadruple. The babies were safe. Honey and Grant were grateful. Bailed Jada out—she didn't have to stay in jail awaiting her court hearing. Plus I'd heard on the news earlier her charges were dropped. The two-headed lady should give me extra credit.

Once my cell phone started ringing back to back, I knew Rita had sold me out. I didn't care about that old woman, her daughter, grand-babies, Grant, Honey, Fancy, or Jada. All I cared about was my Darius.

It was time for my love spell to do the damn thing.

My body felt like satin, pussy was sweet as cotton candy. Closing my eyes, I'd channeled my thoughts toward Darius. I massaged my breasts, spread my thighs, craved and visualized his body on top of me. His dick head stroked my lips. He put his head inside me. I could feel it growing bigger and bigger.

I moaned, "Say you love me. Say my name. If you can hear me, I'm waiting for you at . . . in Long Beach." I repeated my address three times. I concentrated all my energy on connecting with Darius. The house was quiet. I had no distractions, no Rita, no whining babies.

Surrounded by Darius's pictures and posters, I hugged his body pillow. I wrapped my legs around the pillow imagining what I'd do when I had the real thing. I prayed Fancy wasn't keeping Darius from me. With Darius's bad press, that bitch Fancy should be on my team. I tried to patiently await my lover, my future husband, and my friend.

Two hours later I heard a humming sound in my driveway. I sprung from my parents' bed. "He's here! He's here! I did it! It worked!"

I ran to the front door, opened it. There was my Darius getting out of his car . . . police car?

I slammed, then locked my front door. If the cops come up in here, I might have to do a Kathy Bates, except I didn't have a basement. I'd have to toss my dad's remains in the ocean, squeeze the police officers' dead bodies in the coffin. I was not going to jail.

I went to my closet, got my semiautomatic, stood in my living room. If they entered my home, I was prepared to kill them.

CHAPTER 61

Darius

I heard a voice in my head. "Darius, you need to take care of that bitch, Bambi." That fucked me up. No one was in the hospital room but my wife and I. But that sound interrupted my thoughts. It was as though a person spoke directly into my ears. That voice was crystal clear. I jammed my pointing fingers in my ears deep as I could, rattled my head, then yanked my fingers out. I admitted to myself I wanted revenge.

My wife narrowed her eyes, stared at me, then said, "Don't try to play crazy with me. I'm not falling for it, Darius."

I slid a chair next to her bed. "Our love is stronger than this. I don't know what mistress you're talking about." I hadn't tried to find or thank the woman I'd picked up at My House but I was grateful she still hadn't spoken to the press. Maybe it was best to let that situation slide and pray it didn't haunt me later.

With the twins being found, the charges being dropped against my mom, my situation should slowly dissipate and return to normal. Maybe someone would be a bigger fuck-up and the media would focus on them.

The voice returned. I scratched the back of my head, frowned. "Darius, you need to go take care of that bitch."

I told Fancy, "Baby, I gotta go."

"You're not going anywhere."

First she demanded I leave, now I couldn't go. I didn't want to go. I had to. Something was summoning me and I couldn't control myself. "Darius, what are you tripping about?"

I whispered, "I'm on my way." Aw, man. Was this shit for real? I scratched the back of my head again. Okay, settle down. You want revenge on this chick so bad it's driving you nuts.

"Darius, you're on your way where?" Fancy asked.

I shook my hands in front my chest. "I said that because I know who's responsible for the accident, all right." What the fuck was going on inside my head?

"What has gotten into you? So the media is printing lies about you?" Fancy asked, stuffing her pillow behind her back. "You're not going to sit here and play crazy with me. You are going to answer my questions."

I heard, "If you don't go now, she's going to get away." I frowned. This shit was weird. Rattling my arms, I shook it off, then said, "I don't need Bambi."

Fancy said, "Bambi? Who in the hell is Bambi? Forget I asked. Don't answer that."

Fancy opened the drawer facing her bed, pulled out a business card, handed it to me, then yelled, "Who in the fuck is Bambi and why was her card on my stand?"

I took the card, tore it in half, threw it in the trash. I'd put a card on my wife's stand after that nurse's assistant . . . Fuck! What the hell was happening here? "I don't know that bitch!"

"Darius Henry Jones, why did you call her by her name?"

"What are you talking about? I was telling you about DJ."

"You never mentioned DJ, Darius. Stop lying! Just stop it."

Wow, this was my way out. "I didn't tell you? I lost custody of DJ today."

"Today? You're telling me you lost custody of our son today? Oh, so now you're trying to drive me crazy. First, Bambi. And now . . . How the hell did you lose custody of DJ?" Fancy stared into my eyes. Her eyes shifted side to side, scanning mine.

"My mom asked Ashlee to watch DJ for a while. Ashlee took him back to D.C. and filed a petition for custody. With all the bad press on my back, she won. That would've never happened if the accident hadn't happened. The good news is we know who's responsible." I'd hoped to take the focus off me.

"Who, Darius? Who's responsible?"

Suddenly, the name hit me and I couldn't tell Ladycat. "I don't remember. I have to double-check with mom." I checked my iPhone. Mom hadn't texted me Bambi's address.

Fuck, this shit was getting creepier by the minute. The same person who tried to kill my wife was my mom's assistant? And she'd tried to kill my wife twice. And she's been around us the entire time and we were clueless. Damn.

Fancy snapped her fingers. "Earth to Darius. I'm over here. You lost our baby to her? I'm getting my baby back. Ashlee is unfit."

"How you gon' take care of my son and not be with me?"

"You should've thought about that when you were getting your dick sucked."

True. But no woman wanted to hear a man's truth. At that time I was thinking with the wrong head. Getting my dick sucked felt incredible. I wish I could trade places with my wife for one blow job so she could understand.

CHAPTER 62

Bambi

The police officers backed away, stood outside my front door. "We know you're in there. Bambi Bartholomew, come out with your hands up."

I thought that kind of shit only happened on television. I'd wait them out. I kept standing in the middle of my living room floor. They weren't going to catch me off guard.

This is the thanks I got for helping Jada and paying Rita to keep her damn mouth shut. That was okay. I had a plan for them.

I couldn't have a healthy marriage with Darius if I had to keep the police off our backs all the time. Maybe when the love spell took over, Darius would fall in love with me, and I could relax. How long would that take? I had too many unanswered questions.

The police messed up my fantasy. After I finished making love to Darius, I had to text that two-headed lady.

I sat in a chair facing the door. It was quiet outside my home. Too quiet. I pictured Darius undressing me. I came instantly when he bit my nipple. I wanted so much from this man. I imagined his dick deep inside me. Prayer wasn't a part of the spell but I prayed to conceive his baby tonight. How, I didn't know and I didn't care. As long as I had Darius's baby growing inside me, I'd be happy.

My eyes rolled to the top of my head. My entire body tingled. I came again. Trying to speed things up, thoughts of Ashlee ran interference. She crept into my mind. Darius withdrew from me. Redirecting my thoughts to Darius, I relaxed as I held him in my arms. We'd make love again and again. I lay my head on his strong chest, held him tight, dozed off. If he moved, I'd feel him.

I awakened, still sitting in the chair in my living room. I peeped outside. It was still nighttime. The police were gone.

"She lied to me!" I texted the two-headed lady, What happened here? When is my love spell going to work?

She texted, You forgot something.

I texted her, You're lying to me and you stole my engagement ring. I want it back.

This trick was playing games.

She texted, Bambi, you create your own illusions. Let's see if what's going to happen to you next is a game. Don't contact me again.

She wasn't the boss of me. *What if I do?*

She texted, Try me.

I put on my sweat suit, tennis shoes, and stuffed my Ho-on-the-Go bag with lots of cash. I peeped outside. All was quiet. Shit was complicated. This was the last time I'd be in my parents' house. I gripped my semiautomatic in one hand, tote in the other.

Something told me not to open my front door.

CHAPTER 63

Darius

"I'll tell you everything, if you promise not to leave me. I know we can work this out." I'd tell almost everything. That part about Ashlee sucking my dick, no way would Fancy forgive me for that one.

"I was sad the last time I left the hospital. Ashlee came in your room, in here, acting a fool. I got dumb with her. Then the nurse told me I couldn't come back. That night I went to the Playhouse."

Fancy interrupted. "First off, you've got your days mixed up so I know you're lying. Second of all, the Playhouse, Darius? For real you went to the Playhouse without me, knowing how those scantily dressed women are?"

"Baby, listen. Things happened so fast it's a blur. My days are overlapping in my head. I do know that there was this one woman. She followed me all night. She offered me every part of her body but I refused. I got out of there and went to My House."

Sarcastically, Fancy said, "My House. I can see where that was a better choice of scantily dressed women. Get me my book."

"You!" I didn't mean to raise my voice at my wife. I took a deep breath, lowered my voice. I ground my back teeth, tightened my jaw, then picked up Ladycat's book off the floor, placed it at the foot of her bed. She wiggled her fingers. Reluctantly, I put the book in her hand hoping that was where the book would remain.

"You act as though I'm not human. I am. Do you follow me every place I go on the road to keep watch over me? Is that what you're doing? Or are you traveling with me because you love me?" Again, I had to shift the conversation to avoid telling her the truth.

She opened her book. "You don't have to worry about my following you any place else ever again." Tears fell between the pages.

"I don't mean I don't want you with me. I love having you with me but if it's for the wrong reasons . . . I thought you trusted me."

"I've heard the scandalous stories about groupies. I don't want that for us. I want to be available to sex you, to keep you satisfied. As your wife, Darius, that's my job. I know it's hard for you. Me too." Calmly, she continued, "Tell you what. You go back to being with the team, I'll work on getting DJ back, and we'll revisit whether we should stay married after the season is over."

How did we go from my wife planning a second wedding after the season to contemplating divorce? I wasn't debating that proposal. That was a good package deal. Before the end of the season, I know I'd convince my wife not to leave me. Sometimes all a man needed was a chance to make things right. MaDear was in heaven watching out for me.

I heard the voice again. "Darius, get over there and take care of that bitch Bambi right now!"

I reached into the trash can, got both halves of Bambi's business card, kissed Fancy, then said, "Baby, I gotta go."

CHAPTER 64

Fancy

I had a lot on my mind.

I sat on my bed at ten in the morning waiting for Darius. I almost lost my life and he cheated on me. Why? Wasn't I his everything? I was the best wife I knew how to be. Traveling with Darius was fun. Not being Darius's wife, what would I do? He was my soul mate, my everything.

"Hey, Ladycat," he said, handing me a black tote with long straps. "I left your cell at home. It's on the nightstand." He handed me a hanger with slacks and a nice button-up blouse. He was short on words and I didn't know what to say to my husband.

Inside the bag was a pair of flat shoes. I was ready to leave but not excited that I was going home with him. Had to sort out my situation. Didn't want to talk to my mom, told her to meet me at the house later. Venting would help me feel better emotionally but I didn't want my mom judging my husband or giving me advice I knew she wouldn't accept if she were in my position. Resolving my marital problems was my responsibility. I handed Darius the bag.

I wasn't asking my husband where he'd gone last night. Didn't want to know. Hoped I didn't turn on the news at home only to hear more bad news. Had enough of that. But I did want to know, "Where are my wedding and engagement rings?"

"At the house, in the bag with your other belongings," he said. "I'm leaving today to join my teammates in Miami. I'll be back in two days to check on you. I think you should stay in LA and not go to Atlanta right away."

Why? Did he have a mistress in Atlanta too? Did he have unfinished or unresolved business in Atlanta? Was he really going to Miami?

"No problem. Go be with your team. That's your obligation. I'm staying in LA until after the season," I told him. "I have things to do."

Darius frowned. "Things to do? All right. Cool. So you forgive me?"

"There's nothing to forgive you for. Right?"

He shrugged his shoulders, quietly escorted me from the hospital to the limo out front.

I hated the tension between us. It was like Darius was someone I knew but had no real feelings for. He didn't seem like my friend, my lover, and definitely not my husband. He'd hurt me so much, my feelings for him had dissipated.

Was this our future? Was this how happily married people ended up miserable or in divorce court? I wanted to scream, to cry, to pound on his chest . . . I wanted to disappear, for a moment.

He held my hand. "Ladycat, I love you. I don't know what I'd do without you."

He should've thought about that before he'd had sex with another woman. "I love you too." I did love my husband.

The limo arrived at our LA home in the valley. I didn't wait for the driver to open my door. I got out. Went inside. Never realized how much I missed DJ until now. I smiled thinking of him. There was innocence in a child's spirit. The sound of DJ's feet running through the house, his laughter, and his unpredictable words, I missed that already. His birthday was coming up in a few days. I wanted him here with me.

The limo left our house with Darius in it. He texted me, Seems like you need some alone time. Going to check on my mom. Be back in a few hours.

I didn't respond. Darius was grown. If I had to make him be with me, he could stay gone long as he'd like. Avoiding confrontation that he'd created was my husband's way of escaping reality. I knew Darius.

He figured if he stayed gone long enough, I'd forgive him or forget about it. When he returned home, he'd act like the scandals never happened.

Walking to the mantel, I picked up our wedding picture, let it slip from my hands. I left it on the floor. Had more important things to do. I went to the bedroom, got my cell, called Ashlee's mother Ashley.

She answered, "Hello?"

I inhaled. Quietly exhaled. "Hi, Ms. Anderson. This is Fancy, Darius's wife."

Coyly, she said, "I know who you are. Guess you're calling to speak with DJ."

I had to contain my excitement. "Yes, I am."

"DJ, Fancy's on the phone."

"Hey, Fancy. Where you at? You coming to get me? Where my daddy at?"

Softly, I said, "Hey, baby. You want me to come get you?"

"Yep." That was his last word.

The next voice I heard was Ms. Anderson. "Please, come and get him so he can see his daddy."

"I'll be there tomorrow." I knew Ashlee. I knew she didn't have him with her.

When my mom got here, she could stay here until I got back. I packed my bag and made a copy of our Dallas custody order. If Ashlee wanted custody of DJ, she'd have to go through me.

CHAPTER 65

Ashlee

"Mama, what the hell you mean you let Fancy have DJ? You give away shoes and clothes, not my child. Why didn't you call me? If you didn't want to keep him, all you had to do was say so. I would've come and got him. You could've left him here with me."

Dang. My mother created a battle of the custody orders. I could handle Darius in the courtroom but that bitch Fancy would make me act a damn fool in front of any judge. Why, oh, why had Darius made me swallow his cum? His second child could be growing inside me. If Fancy wanted a child so bad, she should have her own.

"Ashlee, baby. You asked me to come get DJ because of your mental instability. Remember? Like it or not, Fancy is doing you a favor that I'm not willing to do permanently. I raised you. I am forty-five-years young. This is my time to shine in the sun."

I wanted to hang up in my mother's face. "When, Mother? When did she come? Sound like I hear him in the background." I tried listening to what my mother wasn't saying. I swore I heard DJ's voice while my mother was talking.

"They just left about fifteen minutes ago. I'm not having this conversation with you. You're hearing things. Take your meds like you're supposed to, Ashlee, and let DJ stay with Fancy and Darius."

"What airline are they on?"

"I don't know and I don't care. Ashlee, you had better not. You hear me? I know what you're thinking."

I hung up on my mother, before she'd hang up on me. I went online, Googled a list of phone numbers for all the airlines. I started with United reservations.

"Yes, I'd like to cancel my reservations for today from DFW to LAX." I gave the booking agent Fancy's and Darius's names.

"I don't have my confirmation number in front of me. Can you look it up by my address?" I gave them Darius's Atlanta address.

The agent said, "Sorry, I'm not showing a reservation for Fancy Taylor or Darius Jones Junior."

Idiot rep! Ending that call, I phoned Delta, Continental, US Airways, Northwest, Southwest. I called JetBlue and all the other airlines that flew out of DFW. I could not find that bitch's flight information.

I called Baldwin. Thought of what to say while I was hold.

A minute later I heard him say, "What now, Ashlee?"

What the fuck was this, national beat down Ashlee day? "I need you to tell me how to get my son back."

Sighing heavily in my ear, Baldwin said, "I thought he was with you."

"He was but my mom came and got him."

"Probably best. You're not stable, Ashlee. What are we going to do about the Jay Crawford case?" he lamented.

"I don't give a fuck about no Jay Crawford, you hear me! I want you to get my son back here immediately or you're fired!" Did he forget who was paying his mortgage?

"Ashlee, I wish you the best. I can no longer represent you. Let my secretary know when and where to transfer your files."

"You can't quit on me! Hello? Hello? You're fired, Baldwin. You hear me! Fired!" Baldwin was long gone before I'd finished my end of the conversation.

I sat on my sofa, cried. Jumped up. Paced from one living room window to the other. Peeped out the window. Jay's bitch was going inside with her son. Didn't want to kidnap his bad ass again. "Ahhhhh!" I put my hands over my ears.

Fuck that bitch Fancy. I was going to confront her ass. I went online and bought me a one-way ticket to LA. I packed my bags and headed to Washington-Reagan National.

Nothing and no one would keep me away from DJ and Darius.

CHAPTER 66

Darius

Halfway to my front gate, I had my driver take me back to my front door. Getting out of the limo, I entered my garage, got in my Hummer and left. Fancy hadn't come home. Her mom was at our house but Fancy wasn't. What was my wife trying to prove?

"They'd be a fool to slam into this baby," I said, cruising in my Hummer. To avoid traffic on the 405 or bring back memories of the day of the accident, I got on the 110S with no particular destination. Driving at times helped me to clear my head.

Night before last was a blur. Last thing I vividly remembered was my wife hitting me upside the head with a book. I left the hospital in transit to . . . I couldn't recall. Definitely wasn't the Playhouse or My House but I woke up in my bed fully clothed, shoes on my feet. Lady-cat wasn't happy to see me when I'd picked her up from the hospital. I kept quiet in the limo on our drive home from the hospital 'cause I knew I'd fucked up.

Aimlessly driving I found myself at Shakey's Pizza at Avalon and Del Amo. Too early for pizza but I ordered a large Shakey's special to go. Made my way over to Juice-C-Juice for a smoothie. By the time I downed the smoothie I'd be ready for my pizza. Must've stepped in this place by MaDear's divine intervention because it was also an African-American bookstore.

"Hey, my man," I said to the young dude behind the counter. No sooner than I'd said, "my man," I missed DJ. Was he okay? Was Ashlee being a good mother? Didn't want to focus on her too long. Why had she sucked my dick? Where was my wife?

"Hook me up with a large banana, peach, honey, mango, and throw some strawberries in for color contrast."

I wondered how old he was. Didn't seem old enough to be on payroll but he seemed confident hookin' up my drink. "My man. What's your name and how old are you?"

"Christopher but everybody calls me CJ," he said, turning on the blender.

Felt a tap on my shoulder, turned around, looked down. Damn, she was shorter than shortie from the Playhouse. "What's up?" I asked, praying she wasn't a groupie.

"Hi, I'm Lori Carter, the owner of Smiley's Books. I want you to read this," she said, handing me a strange-looking book with a black stickman straddling an ankh on the cover.

"I'm good," I said, taking my smoothie. "CJ, hook me up with two ounces of wheatgrass."

"Give me two minutes of your time," Lori said. "By the time your wheatgrass is done, I'll be done talking with you."

I stood, nodded. "Two. Go."

She put the book in my hand. I sat it on top of my pizza box, handed her a twenty. She gave it back. I put the twenty on the counter for CJ.

"The book is on me. I've seen you all over television. Heard about your wife's accident. It's no accident that you came here. Your chakras are out of alignment."

My what were what? Chakras were out of alignment? What the fuck was she pushing? She better not break out one of them Body Magic for men.

"You're wondering but don't know how to solve your problems. Read the book, brother." She said "brother" with depth that moved me. Like she was a black woman who actually cared about a black man's state of well-being.

CHAPTER 67

Darius

"You are a king," Lori said as she looked into my eyes. I knew I was "the man" but no woman had told me I was a king before.

"To whom much is given, much is required. You've taken a lot from lots of people but haven't given much in return. That's why your life is out of synch. You can't undo your past but you can control your destiny. Start paying it forward. Start a nonprofit in your name. You have the resources to help those less fortunate than you. It's my responsibility to give you the book. The rest is up to you. You know the saying. 'If you want to keep getting what you're getting—' "

"I know, 'keep doing what I'm doing.' "

"And one last thing—get rid of your bad vibes. Cut your locs. Give yourself a fresh start."

I downed my double shot of wheatgrass. "Thanks, Lori," I said, clenching the book under my arm and my smoothie in my hand. Could this book really change my life? I put the book and my pizza in the car, went next door to the barbershop. I desperately wanted a new beginning. I sat in the chair. "Let's do this. Cut 'em off."

Dude didn't ask no questions. He talked nonstop until he'd cut my last loc. I collected each loc, put them all in a Ziploc bag. Let him line me up, paid and got outta there. Headed down the strip mall in search of a Yankees cap, made my way back to my car. I felt free at last.

Driving to Mom's, I said aloud, "It couldn't hurt to read this here joint."

I parked in Mom's driveway, cracked the spine. I scanned the table of contents. My eyes stopped on, "Fear of Failing" and "Chakras, Our Energy Centers." "Wow." I let myself in. "Ma! Where are you?"

"In my office," she called out. "Come here, sweetie."

I dashed in the kitchen, poured a glass of cranberry juice for my mom. Grabbed the container for myself so I could wash down that thick smoothie. Found mom in her office.

"Sit," she said, smiling. "What are you reading?"

I set her glass on a coaster away from her laptop. "Nothing, yet. Stopped by Smiley's. Picked up this book. Lori Carter said it would help me to center myself. Figured I needed clarity in my life. You should read it with me."

Mom took the book, flipped it over, read the back. She flipped through the pages, stopped at the back, scanned the table of contents, read the title, "Hmm. *Just Cause I: Moving from a Mundane Existence Into a Deliberate Wholeness*, by Shannette Slaughter. Never heard of her but looks like a thought-provoking read. If I'd known you were going to Smiley's, I would've had you bring me a smoothie and some wheatgrass."

Mom loved that stuff, got me hooked on it too. Although I felt like I was at my lowest point, couldn't go any lower, being at Mom's house made me feel better. Hearing Ciara and Maxine's mother tell me the truth about myself hit me in my gut. There was no way I could ignore what they'd told me.

How would I have felt if Maxine was my daughter and she'd contracted HIV? Or if a man pushed my pregnant daughter down, made her hit her head, then left her for dead? I thought about how I'd treated Heather, Miranda, Ginger, Zen, Ashlee, the woman who'd sucked my dick the other night.

"Ma, you haven't said anything about my hair."

"I love it. I can see your face. You look happier. Any regrets?" she asked.

"Not a one."

CHAPTER 68

Darius

I'd taken *Just Cause I* from Lori to learn more about myself. Did having money all my life make me arrogant? Why had I treated women so badly? The worst part was, it never dawned on me how heartless I was, until recently. I wanted to change. I never wanted to hurt another female that bad. Now those niggas on the court, they had royal ass whippings coming from me. I couldn't wait to get back to basketball.

Ma said, "I've got great news. But first, how's Fancy?"

I reclined on Ma's chaise, put my hands behind my head, crossed my legs. "She's cool. I guess. I dropped her off at home yesterday. Haven't seen her since."

"You left her by herself?"

"Ma, she's not home. Her mother is at our house but my wife isn't home. Trust me, with her bad attitude, she's fine. Give me the great news, Ma."

Saw a tweet from my boy Christopher Henderson. Celebrating my Grammy nom with fam and friends 2nite at GLC at the BC. Come through.

Posted to my Facebook profile, Congrats, Chris. B there round 6.

"Can you put down that iPhone long enough to hear what I have to say?"

"Sorry, Ma." I put my phone in my lap, stared at my mom.

My mom's eyes lit up. Hadn't seen that in a while. Felt good. She said, "I got all the pics of that night from Sapphire."

"So. What difference does that make? The media already has the pictures posted everywhere. That's old news." I sat up, moved closer to my mother. Officer Lawrence Austin's card was on her desk.

"But they don't have the legal right to continue airing them or what happened. They have no proof. You have no charges. And the woman involved, I found her. All she wants is an apology from you."

"I'm good at that. So this dude helped you," I said, picking up the card.

Mom smiled. Felt good to see a genuine smile lighting up her face.

"You could say that. We're going out."

"As in on a date?" I asked. "You're going out with a police officer? Really?"

"Really," she said. "It's a first but he might be fun. And he's definitely a better choice than my hiring Bambi."

She wasn't lying about that. I had too much going on. Mom was right. I was going to let the police do their job and pray they found that crazy chick.

"Ma, I called Ciara and apologized to her. She gave a million reasons why she'd never forgive me. Called Maxine." I paused. Didn't want to get into a conversation about Maxine's death.

"Tell me the truth. Am I that bad of a person, Ma?"

CHAPTER 69

Honey

"Honey, let me make our reservations to go home," Grant said. Home? "And where exactly is that?" I asked him, breast-feeding Luke. Ms. Waters had shown the best hospitality but Grant was right. The time for us to make arrangements to leave was now.

I inserted my pinky finger into Luke's mouth, broke his suction. His mouth repeatedly opened. Realizing my titty was not there, he frowned. His face turned red.

Grant laughed. "You'd better hurry up."

"He's so greedy. He sucks in my titty soon as he feels it. Let him cry. That way I can put my nipple and areola in his mouth properly this time. His greedy behind is not jacking up my breasts." I placed my pointing and middle fingers at the top and bottom of my areola, then eased my nipple directly into Luke's gapped mouth.

Knock. Knock. "It's Sapphire. I know y'all not in there fucking. Open the door."

I opened the door. Sapphire handed me two large gift boxes. I motioned for her to sit the boxes on the coffee table, then said, "You are so crazy. I love you. Come in." When appropriate, I'd decided to replace my "thank you" with "I love you" as a constant reminder to let those closest to me know how I felt about them.

"I'm not coming in for long. Hi, Grant," she said, standing in the doorway waving. "When are you leaving Velvet's and heading back to Atlanta?"

I answered, "We were just having that conversation. In a few days, a week tops. I'm ready to sleep in my bed."

Losing my boys for a few days made me appreciate how precious life was. If I couldn't help someone, I wouldn't hurt them.

Sapphire hugged me, then said, "Be at Jada's house tomorrow morning at ten. We have to watch the surveillance tapes with Officer Austin. Just in case he needs additional information for this Bambi chick, give it three days before you leave LA. I'm heading out in about a week. Maybe sooner. Gotta get back to my husband. I'm overdue for a tune-up on this pussy."

Grant and I both laughed. "I second that," I told her.

Having my boys was a blessing but I'd been without dick for too long. I gazed into Sapphire's eyes. Told her, "I can never repay you." Being a detective would always be in Sapphire's blood. Every time she tried to quit, something else happened. First she helped Velvet, then her own mom, now me.

"Ba—" I stopped speaking. Grant's frozen expression interrupted my thoughts.

Nervously, he asked Sapphire, "Will Bambi be there?"

"We wish. No," Sapphire said. "They haven't caught her yet but that's one of the reasons we're meeting tomorrow. Honey, that boy has fallen asleep with your titty in his mouth. Carry on."

I closed, then locked the door. Stared at Grant. "Don't embarrass me in a room full of people. You might as well tell me now and tell me the whole truth."

"What?"

"Your face tightens whenever that woman's name is mentioned. Don't you think you've hurt me enough? Tell me now." I peeped inside the two decorative boxes. Sapphire had bought me two outfits. *Thank goodness no more wearing maternity clothes.*

"There's nothing to tell. I promise you I don't know her. So you're going to let me make our reservations to leave in three days?" he asked.

I wanted to cry. I knew he was lying to my face while his was straight. I stood in the center of the floor praying he'd told me the truth. Grant had a place in Rosewell and D.C., my house was in Buckhead. All of my former escort girls lived with me in Atlanta. I couldn't wait to show them the twins, especially my play-sister Onyx. My girls had become my family.

If Grant had told the truth, we could've stayed with him. I was taking the boys to my house. If for any reason things didn't work out between Grant and I, I wasn't packing up belongings for four people. I'd told my mom she could stay a few weeks and help with the boys but I wasn't leaving her or anyone alone with my kids.

"Will you please trust me to make our reservations?" Grant asked.

"Sure." Wasn't like I couldn't change the reservations if I didn't agree with his decision. I burped Luke, then lay him in the middle of the bed next to London.

"Honey, come sit on the sofa beside me."

I looked at Grant. He was so fine and still the only man I'd ever loved. I sat next to him, kept my eyes on the boys. I'd decided I didn't want to change my name back to Lace. Honey suited me. Inside, I knew who I was.

Grant held my hand. "I'm so sorry for all the things I've done to hurt you. I never want to hurt you again. I don't want any surprises. Truth is—"

Defensively, I said, "What?" I felt a confession coming on. I knew he knew more about that Bambi woman than he'd told me.

CHAPTER 70

Honey

Grant said, "Truth is, I want to take you and our boys to D.C. to meet my parents. The right way this time," he said. Softly Grant kissed my lips. "You are so beautiful."

I became quiet. He knew what he wanted but what did I want? Did I want to meet his parents? Would they accept me? Would they judge me? Would they welcome my boys as their grandchildren but reject me? "I'm not sure I'm ready to meet your parents. Why don't we wait a few months?"

"I don't want to wait," Grant said, French kissing me. His tongue danced in my mouth. I sucked his tongue, put my tongue in his mouth. We alternated for a few minutes. I was so hungry for this man breast milk leaked from my nipples.

Grant touched my pussy. I know he wasn't trying to get me to make love to him. Backing away from his tongue and moving his hand, I told him, "Six weeks for that."

He shook his head, laughed. His large white teeth were perfectly aligned, breath fresh. His caramel kiss tasted so sweet. I wanted his dick inside me. I rattled my head, dried the milk streaming down to my stomach. I hoped our boys would have perfect teeth too. Didn't want to make a bunch of trips to a dentist for braces for two kids.

"That's not what I had on my mind but since you brought it up, does that include oral sex? I can give you a pussy massage, if you'd like."

"What is it that you don't want to wait for? I'll suck your dick later." I would. My pussy had stitches not my mouth. And he was right. There were other ways we could pleasure one another until the doctor said it was okay to have sex. I was not going to be one of those women who went back for their six week checkup and found out they were pregnant again. I was happy with two boys. Should've had my tubes tied.

Grant knelt before me, held my hand. "Honey, I love you with all my heart."

I sniffed, blinked back tears. The sincerity of his words penetrated my heart.

"I don't want to wait to ask and I don't want to take you home to my parents as my babies' mama. Honey, will you marry me?" His face was so innocent, his heart vulnerable.

I didn't want to raise our boys alone. Didn't want to be a single mom. I didn't want to live my life without Grant. We'd been through a lot. And this was the only man I ever wanted to be "in love" with. I deserved love. Deserved to be loved. I looked at my boys on the bed, then looked at Grant.

I knew he hadn't had time to buy a ring. And although we were both millionaires, I didn't need a ring to prove to the world I had a man or a husband. I only had to prove to him, and him to me, that the love in our hearts would bond us through the toughest times and unite us during our best of times.

"Yes, Grant Hill, I will marry you."

CHAPTER 71

Jada

This time Darius, Fancy, Sapphire, Grant, Honey, Rita, Ashlee, and Officer Lawrence Austin gathered in my entertainment room to review the surveillance footage from the hospital, BOA Steakhouse, and CUT. Ashlee had flown in again at my request but this time she was not going to take DJ.

Another Lawrence had entered my life. I admired him. Sacrificing his life on a daily basis to keep our city safe. He loved his job and I was enjoying getting to know him.

"Make yourselves comfortable," I said. "There's plenty to eat and drink, help yourselves. Ashlee, you come sit by me." I had to stay close to her, keep her away from Fancy and Darius. Ashlee didn't know but Fancy's mother, Caroline, was upstairs in my guest bedroom watching DJ.

Officer Austin was a real gentleman. I'd take my time before sexing the man behind the uniform. I'd gotten vaginal estrogen pills to help lubricate my vagina. Didn't want to relive the shredded wheat episode that I'd had with Grant. I chuckled inside. My pussy was on the pill. Wasn't falling in love or lust. Well, that wasn't completely true. The womanly side of me craved Lawrence's body. I'd fantasized about ripping that uniform off him, handcuffing him to my bedpost, then masturbating while making him watch. Then I'd give him the best blow job before taking off the cuffs.

"Thanks for coming. For those of you who haven't met me, my name is Officer Lawrence Austin," he said, handing out his business cards. "I know each of you have survived hardships, some more tragic than others. Let's all pray watching these tapes today will help us find Bambi and keep her from harming anyone else."

Next time I hired a personal assistant I was doing a background check to the background check. Bambi could've killed all of us if she wanted to.

Ashlee blurted, "Darius, where's my son? I know you got DJ. That bitch went to my mother's house and stole my child. Officer, arrest her." Ashlee pointed at Fancy.

What I'd learned this past week was innocent people could easily end up behind bars. I didn't believe Jay Crawford raped Ashlee. It was paramount that witnesses did not casually identify individuals as criminals. And it was equally important that I never put myself in a situation to be victimized. If I hadn't chased behind Grant, I wouldn't have been arrested for kidnapping or trespassing. I was thankful I didn't stay in that hellhole overnight. Moving forward, I wouldn't quickly judge anyone.

I looked at Lawrence. He said to Ashlee, "Miss, you're going to have to cooperate or I will have to ask you to leave," then said to the group, "If any of you recognize Bambi in any of these clips say, 'That's Bambi' and I'll make a note of it."

Before he started the video, I asked, "Any updates on Bambi's warrants?"

"Bambi is a chameleon. She's clever. Like Ms. Rita St. Thomas said, the officers confirmed two coffins were in her parents' bedroom." He nodded, then continued, "Her mom was in one and skeletal remains were found washed up on the shore by her home. We believe it's her father's remains. But Bambi is nowhere to be found. Yet."

I looked at my son. My heart smiled. I did like his haircut.

When Ashlee didn't move, Officer Austin dimmed the lights and started the first clip. Fancy's new heart-shaped engagement ring with pear-shaped diamonds on both sides sparkled in the dimly lit room. After Fancy realized her ring was missing, I told my son to order a duplicate. No telling where Fancy's ring was and, even if it was found, I told Darius, "If one person tried on your wife's ring, she doesn't need that energy on her finger." I was proud of Darius. I'd seen personal growth within my son already. His spirit was calmer. He was considerate of others' feelings and opinions.

The clip of the nurse taking the twins from Valentino played. Ashlee, Rita, and I said at the same time, "That's Bambi." I knew someone was missing. Where was Valentino?

When the clip of a nurse entering Fancy's room then leaving with a teal bag played from my projector, Ashlee and Rita said, "That's Bambi."

Next we saw the woman seated at the bar at BOA. Ashlee and Rita said, "That's Bambi."

When the video from CUT played, Rita, Ashlee, and I said, "That's Bambi."

Honey gasped, then asked, "Grant? You lied to me?"

Grant said, "No, I didn't," but the longer the clip played the angrier Honey became. We all watched Grant open the door to a hotel room that Bambi entered. He carried a tray with two martinis.

Honey said, "So happy hour was in my room? I asked you to go get my things and you're in my room fucking Bambi?"

Grant remained silent. We watched as, a half hour later, the door opened and Bambi left but Grant didn't leave with her. Honey stood.

Sapphire said, "Sit down, Honey. You can deal with Grant later. This is about Officer Austin finding the woman who stole your babies."

Four hours later, after the video viewing ended, we all seemed mentally exhausted. Grant followed Honey out of my house. *Yeah, take it outside,* I thought. Better her than me. For real. I was glad Honey didn't start fighting in my house. Sapphire thanked Officer Austin and then left. Had a feeling she had to save Grant from Honey.

I hope Honey choke him good.

CHAPTER 72

Darius

"Darius, wait," Officer Austin said. "Where are you headed next?"

Fancy asked, "Why?"

I looked at Lawrence. "Dropping in on my friend Christopher Henderson at Grande Lux Café at the Beverly Center. Why?"

Officer Austin said, "I've got a feeling Bambi will show up wherever you are. When the officers searched her house, she had every news article on you since high school, a life-size body pillow, posters . . . you name it, she had it. All you."

I shook my head. "I still don't remember her."

"Yes, you do," Ashlee said, handing him a photo of Bambi from kindergarten.

I frowned. "Man, that's her? The chubby chick? Damn! What a difference a few years make. I still don't remember her."

Ashlee stood nose to nose with Fancy. "I know you got my son. I came to get him. Where is he?"

I put my hand between Ashlee and Fancy, stood in front of my wife, then said to Ashlee, "Leave my wife alone. You have DJ."

Fancy tapped on, then spoke into her cell phone. "Ma, send DJ downstairs."

My lips curved high, I took Fancy's phone. "Ladycat, what's going on?"

DJ came dashing down the stairs. Ashlee opened her arms. "Baby, come to Mommy."

DJ ran straight to Fancy. "Hi, Fancy. Hey, Mommy. Daddy! Daddy! I miss you!"

I kissed DJ on the forehead long and hard. "Daddy misses you too, my man. I love you." I kissed my wife. "I need you. Don't ever leave me. I love you."

Ashlee reached for DJ. He leapt into my arms. "No, Daddy. Mommy doesn't feed me and she puts me on time-out. I stand in the corner all day. Please don't make me go."

Ashlee's eyes turned red. "This isn't the end of this, Darius! I won't stop until I get you back." She stared at Fancy. "Have your own baby, bitch! And next time *you* suck your husband's dick! Bet he didn't tell you he fucked me when he came to D.C. And I'm pregnant with his next child."

Fancy took DJ from me, then said, "You handle her, so I don't have to," then went upstairs.

DJ gave me an upward nod. I smiled, then said, "My man. My man."

Ashlee stormed out of my house. What the hell? Now I understood why my wife didn't want Ashlee to have custody. I remained calm. I didn't go after Fancy or Ashlee.

"Seems like you're quite the man," Officer Austin told Darius. "I want to plan a stakeout. If Bambi shows up at Grand Lux Café, we'll catch her. Hopefully we can get one of these females off your back."

CHAPTER 73

Honey

"Why did Grant have to lie to me?"

He hadn't said a word since we'd left Jada's house, walked into Velvet's house. He took the boys in the bedroom, then closed the door. I wasn't following him. He'd fucked up, not me.

I sat in Velvet's living room talking with Sapphire. "After you dropped in, gave me this outfit, then left, Grant asked me to marry him. I asked him repeatedly about that Bambi woman. He stared in my face and lied to me. Said nothing happened with that woman. I knew he was lying." I cried in Sapphire's arms. "I'm not marrying him. I'd have to be a damn fool to go through this shit with him again."

"Hush, Honey. You're upset. You are going to marry Grant."

Who's side was she on? I'd forgotten she'd fucked Grant too. Tried to take him away from me. Velvet had fucked Grant too. The memories I'd buried about Grant resurfaced. I tried rationalizing his promiscuity but only became madder. He was a male whore.

"I'm not staying with him. Would you marry him?" I asked her.

Drying my tears, Sapphire said, "Here's why you're going to marry him."

I placed my hands in my lap and listened. I had to hear what ridiculous reasons she had floating in her brain. Just because she was married and happy didn't mean I could have the same. Not with a man who was a liar and a cheat.

She smiled, then asked, "Do you remember when we first met?"

I nodded. It was at the hotel New York New York in Vegas. Sunny Day was my number-one escort. And Sunny was also Sapphire's friend. Sapphire wanted Sunny to get out of the prostitution game. I was close to but wasn't ready to let Sunny go. Maybe if I had let Sunny go with Sapphire, she'd still be alive.

It was hard for me to say, "Yeah, I do remember." My throat ached.

"Do you remember when I took Valentino's hundred million and gave you half?" she asked.

Where was she going with all these questions? Of course I remembered that too. But I'd made my own millions before she gave me fifty. I smiled without parting my lips. We were some bad and bold bitches. I'd bought all twelve of my escorts one-way tickets to Atlanta. Eleven of them came right away. I bought us a big house. Helped each of them start their own business. I never wanted them to compromise themselves for anyone else. And I wasn't compromising myself for Grant or any man.

I nodded, thinking, *What's next?*

"Do you remember when Valentino and Benito kidnapped you from your home in Atlanta?"

That was some wild shit. I was scared to death and brave as hell at the same time. I escaped, not unscathed though. My ass was sore, feet worn out from hiking to I–75 South in my stilettos. I'd forgotten about Ken, the man dressed like a woman who'd offered me a ride, then drove me to a cemetery and tried to make me suck his dick. The bullet I put in his balls said he'd never do that retarded shit again.

"I do. What else?" I asked Sapphire. I was no longer sad or angry. Strange how I'd forgotten the number of people I'd trampled on since Rita had kicked me out.

"One more thing," she said. "Even if Grant did fuck Bambi or Bambi fucked Grant, however you want to look at it. My point is, nobody's perfect. And all the men that you fucked when you were a prostitute, not one of them . . . Look at me," she insisted. "Not one of them gave a damn about you. None of them loved you. You have a man in that bedroom who loves you. And you love him. All the things he's done that hurt you, he's done with someone else. Grant has never put his hands on you. You go in there, forgive him for whatever happened in that hotel room, and you tell him you want to be his wife. If you let him walk away, you're going to be the miserable one, and don't call me crying. I'm done." Sapphire got up, extended her arms, hugged me, then left.

I let go of my ego, tucked away my pride, and opened the bedroom door. Grant was in the bed playing with the boys, gently rolling them around. "Can we talk?"

"If you don't want me, let me have a relationship with my boys," he said.

I sat on the bed, then said, "There's nothing I want more than to be your wife and for us to be a family."

Grant hugged me. He cried. We cried.

"Honey, you complete me. I'll never lie to you again," Grant said, kissing me.

Did I believe him? No, I didn't.

Did I love him? Absolutely.

CHAPTER 74

Darius

I parked in section 3B, headed toward the elevator for Blooming-dale's at the Beverly Center. I bypassed the parking pay machine, trotted down two sets of moving escalators, and hooked a right into the bar area of Grand Lux Café.

I was about a half hour early. The bar was crowded, so I asked a young man sitting alone at a table for two in the corner, "Mind if I sit here?"

"Hey, Darius. Not at all, man. May I have your autograph?"

I smiled, signed the back of his yellow receipt. "What's your name? What are you doing with your life?"

He smiled. "I'm Christopher Watson."

Three Christophers in two days. That was wild. I scribbled, "To 'My Man Chris,'" above my signature.

"I work here but I'm going to become a dancer," he said.

"That's what's up. Stay in the arts. Just remember, to get and stay on top, you must do what others are not willing to do. Never get comfortable. Become the master of your craft. Work hard every day. You can do it," I reassured him. The book Lori gave me helped me understand people looked up to me. My words were powerful. I saw Christopher Henderson's mom, dad, and his dad's new wife walk in.

"Thanks, Chris," I said, leaving the bar, heading into the dining area.

I scanned the room. Officer Austin and a few of what I assumed to be his counterparts were dining at a table for four. I nodded.

"What's up, Darius? Glad you made it, man. You have no idea how much your being here means. Thanks," Christopher said. "This is my man Richard C. Montgomery. Anything you need tonight, you see Richard."

I held Richard's hand; we bumped shoulders.

"Be my guest of honor," Christopher said. "Sit next to me."

At first I started to decline sitting next to him because he was seated on the booth side of the table. Chris was five-eleven. I was six-eleven. But it was his day. He was the Grammy nominated honoree.

"Congrats, man. 'Blame It' is going to win. No doubt," I told him. I sat with my back against the booth. Tried to stretch my legs. Couldn't. "I'ma have to take a chair across from you, man."

When I stood, she walked in. I'd seen enough pictures of her to recognize her dark deep-set eyes and bangin' body. The jet-black hair flowing down to her ass didn't fool me. She strutted to Chris's table. She sure as hell didn't look anything like the chubby girl in kindergarten. She was all woman. I understood how Grant fucked her. I wouldn't have fucked her but I sure would've let her give me brain. I stayed cool, pretended I didn't recognize her.

"Hi, Christopher. Congratulations." Bambi slid between the opening of the table. Sat next to Christopher, faced me. "Darius? Oh, my God! What have you done with your hair! I'ma get that two-headed bitch. She made you do this, didn't she?"

Christopher stood. "She with you? I don't know her."

I raised my hand in the air, looked over the booth, behind her back, made eye contact with Officer Austin, then pointed. Lawrence and his friends pushed their chairs from underneath them and ran in my direction. Guess they didn't want to scare the patrons because none of the officers drew their guns.

Bambi slid under the table, slid between my legs. I grabbed her leg, then let go when her ass hit me with a stun gun. She ran toward the bar area.

"Oh, this here shit is superpersonal now." I ran after her. Martini glasses crashed to the floor. Somebody's Long Island iced tea fell on my foot.

We chased Bambi out the door. Two of the officers ran across La Cienega Boulevard, got in separate police cars. One ran to the right. Officer Austin and I ran up the escalators behind Bambi. I was on his heels. In five-inch heels, Bambi sprinted three steps at a time to the third level. Turned around, sprayed Mace in the air, then disappeared.

Officer Austin and I coughed. I stopped at the top of the second escalator, closed my eyes. *Damn, that girl is good.*

Officer Austin said, "Get in your car. She has to come out of the garage. If she follows you, I'll follow her."

I hadn't been in the garage long enough to have to pay so I headed out the exit. I turned right onto La Cienega, kept straight. At the light, I saw Bambi in a black Dodge Charger at the cross light. I stayed on La Cienega.

Officer Austin's car sped in the lane to my left, zoomed toward oncoming traffic, swerved between cars, avoided collisions. He stopped in front of Bambi's car.

She backed into another police officer's car that was behind her, dented the door. She slammed into Officer Austin's car, backed up, hit the car behind her again. Four police cars now surrounded her car on each side. Bambi opened her car door, ran between two cars.

She was not getting away. I got out of my car, blasted off like I was doing a suicide run. In seconds I passed the officers, was closing in on her ass. She looked over her shoulder, saw me.

"Damn." Just when I reached out to grab her, she tripped and fell into a baby stroller.

The baby's mother pushed Bambi to the ground and started beating Bambi's ass. I was cheering on the baby's mother. I'd never seen four guns in a chick's face but if one of the officers would accidentally shoot Bambi, I didn't see a thing.

CHAPTER 75

Bambi

I fucking hate kids.

I stood in a fucking lineup at the precinct like those bitches on the other side didn't know who the fuck I was. I knew Darius was on the opposite side of that window with all the rest of those bitches.

"Talk to me face to face. Stop being bitches," I yelled. Got me over here turning side to side like I was a criminal. Crimes of passion didn't count. Darius made me fall in love with him. And that two-headed bitch pulled a three-card molly on my ass. I was never going to win Darius's heart and she knew it.

An officer pulled me out of the lineup. "Your accusers demand to see you face to face," he said. "They're glad you asked."

He escorted me into a large cold room with no windows. I hated the orange jumpsuit. This fruity color orange never was my color. My ankles were chained. I had to take small steps. My wrists were hand-cuffed behind my back. I knew what they didn't. I had the best attorneys on my team.

I sat at the rectangular table, in the only chair in the room. Darius, Fancy, Jada, Honey, Grant, Rita, Sapphire, and Ashlee stood against the wall as though they had traded places with me. They were my lineup. If I had my automatic, I'd eliminate all of them execution style.

"When I get out of this bitch, I'm coming after every last one of y'all including those twins. I'll be out by morning. And I'm pregnant with your baby." I watched Darius's and Grant's faces. "That's right, yours. You heard me."

Darius shook his head. "Not mine."

Grant remained silent.

Honey stared at Grant. The she walked up to the table. *Slap!*

Get that bitch's hands from around my neck. Arrest her! Arrest her!

None of those bastards stopped her. She let go. *Slap!* The bitch hit me again.

I had something for her ass. "Go on, Grant. Tell Honey how you gave me those babies. How you set this whole thing up for me to take the twins so you could win her back and be her hero. Tell her how you called Rita and asked her to help me out."

Rita's country ass said, "You keep Rita's name out yo' mouth."

"Or what? You gon' slam your truck into the back of Fancy's car again?" I said. I had something on all their asses. "Y'all making Grant's baby inside my stomach kick."

Calmly Ashlee said, "Stop lying, Bambi."

"I'm not lying. I am pregnant with Grant's baby."

"No, you're not," Ashlee said. "You're not pregnant at all. I can see straight through you. You've been following Darius since we were kids. You come to all of his games. You were the one who tried to kill Fancy. You stole Honey and Grant's babies, now you're trying to save your ass from prison. You're not the only one with evidence. If you don't leave Darius alone, I will personally bury you alive in a coffin."

CHAPTER 76

Darius

I was glad to have the madness behind me. Thought the season would never end. I was back on track with my game. Fadeaways. Three-pointers. Jumpers. Steals. Blocks. Dunks. My team made it to the championship. I was determined to win MVP. But even if I didn't, I was still the man.

I had to give Ashlee credit for having my back but she made me nervous when she'd told Bambi in front of everybody, "If you don't leave Darius alone, I will personally bury you alive." As long as I had Ladycat on my team, Ashlee didn't stand a chance of bringing me down again.

My wife and son were seated courtside. DJ sat on Fancy's lap cheering for me the entire game. My mom was next to them. The three most important people in my life were back in my life. Lawrence was seated next to my mom. Funny she ended up with another Lawrence. Lori was seated with them too. Couldn't thank her enough for giving me that book.

With twenty seconds left in the game, the ball was in my hands. We were down by one. I told myself, "I got this."

The other team was going to either foul me or give up a W. By any means necessary, my team was winning this game. I drove to the basket. Three seconds remained. That was plenty of time to get off the final shot. I was in the air, headed toward the hoop, then I heard the referee's whistle. My opponent flopped to the floor like a fish. Ref better not make the wrong call. *Do not say this was a charge.*

His hands hit his hips. "Block! Two shots. Atlanta."

They said it comes in threes. My wife had already given me a shot. Now I had to make two more. I stood at the free throw line. Bounced the ball three times. Bent my knees, raised my hands, flexed my wrists, then released the ball.

The crowd cheered as I tied the score. Hit it once, I could hit it again.

I bounced the ball three times. Bent my knees, raised my hands, flexed my wrists, then heard a voice whisper in my ear, "I hope you miss."

Aw, fuck. I released the ball. That shit wasn't anywhere near the rim. The crowd chanted, "Air ball. Air ball. Air ball."

Bambi's lawyers were good but they weren't good enough to get her out. Were they? Of course not. DJ might have grandkids before Bambi could be considered for parole for good behavior. But I'd seen that chick in action. She could be in the arena. I looked over my shoulder, DJ nodded upward. Although I'd missed the game-winning shot, DJ still cheered for his dad.

I mouthed, "My man," then heard my wife say, "Darius, wake up. Wake up. Today's our wedding."

I opened my eyes. Ladycat was there. Wasn't it bad luck to see the bride on her wedding day? I guess that didn't apply to renewing our vows.

"Yeah, Daddy. I'm the ring bearer, remember? Get up," DJ said, tugging the covers away from body.

I hugged my wife, kissed my son, went downstairs. Moms was cooking all of us breakfast. "I love you, Ma." She'd started my nonprofit. I made sure Lori was on the board. I'd learned from the book I had to surround myself with good people.

Today I was remarrying not just my wife, but my family. I stood in my living room, looked at my MVP trophy on the mantel, smiled.

"Who says you can't have it all?"

THE END

FOR REAL?

Discussion Questions

1. Do you believe Darius truly loved Fancy? Do you believe people can have sex outside their marriage and still be committed to their spouse?
2. At what point in a man's life is he ready to love and be loved? Have you been "in love" with a person that wasn't "in love" with you? If so, how did you handle the situation?
3. If a person's skeletons are revealed later in a relationship, why should it matter? How well do you know your family, friends, and lover(s)? What are things you must know about a potential mate?
4. What were Jada's top three mistakes in her relationship with Grant? Are these common mistakes you feel women make in relationships? If you were in Jada's position, what would you have done differently?
5. Do you believe Bambi is pregnant with Grant's child? What makes people engage in casual sex? Why do married people have sex outside their relationship?
6. Should a married person who's not committed to the marriage wear a wedding ring? If you were Fancy, would you have worn your rings after the accident?
7. The two-headed lady is waiting to cast your spell. Would you meet her at the cemetery at midnight? Do you believe in telepa-

thy? Who would you like to cast a spell upon? What would the spell be?

8. Should Rita have gone to jail for causing the car accident? Should she serve time for not reporting that Bambi had kidnapped the twins? Would you stay in a house that had two coffins in one of the bedrooms? If Rita were your mother, would you trust her with your babies?

9. Did Honey do everything possible to find her boys? What are the major things people should do the moment they realize their child is missing?

10. What character is crazier, Ashlee or Bambi? Do you believe they have mental disorders? Or do you think they are in control of their behavior? Do antidepressants hinder or help people who are battling depression or a bipolar disorder?

11. Where do you believe Valentino will end up? Should he try to reunite with his family? What type of relationship would Valentino and Honey have had if they'd married?

12. Were Darius's apologies sincere? What impact, if any, did his apologies have on the outcome of his streak of bad luck?

13. If you apologized to one person today, who would it be and what would you say?

Poetry Corner

True Love

True love is amazing
Love is priceless
Love smiles inside your heart
Love shines through your eyes
Love trusts
Love weathers the storm
Love hurts when you hear the truth
Love heals when you're hurting
Love celebrates your accomplishments
Love feels likes your spirit is floating
Love sees no shape, size, or color
Love accepts you for who you are
Love has no guarantees
Love does not judge
Love smells like the freshness you inhale after the rain
Love tastes like tears of joy
Love washes away your troubles
Love is vulnerable
Love is You.
Love starts with You.

Love is forever inside of You.
Love is the Creator's divine gift to You
God gave You Love to share with others

No One

No one should treat me better
No one will treat me worse
The way that others treat me
Is a reflection of my self-worth

If I don't know that I'm Worthy
If I don't believe in me
I can't expect others
To see what I don't see

I have to find my inner strength
I have to lead my way
I have to denounce the people
That come to me to prey

It's up to me to tell them
Please go away
I don't want you in my life
Not for another
Second, minute or day

I lift my head to the sky
I open my heart to receive love
I know that I am Worthy
I know there is a God

No one will treat me better
No one will treat me worse
The way that others treat me
Is a reflection of my self-worth

Thinking of a Master Plan

Ladies, always know what you want from a man.
Because he certainly knows what he wants from you.

Thinking of a Master Plan
Sitting on the couch with his dick in my hand
I've got to figure out
What I want from this man

Do I want
A husband
A lover
A friend

I wanna get paid
He wants to laid
We on the same page?

Should I kiss it
Lick it
Tease him
Please him

I've got to get paid
Before he gets laid

Should I suck it
Fuck it
Stroke it
Or choke it

Thinking of a master plan
Sitting in his lap with his dick in my hand

I'm not searching for a 9 to 5
Cuz the one thing that I despise

Is a man who wants to bust a nut
Inside of me
For free?
Dude

I need a pair of shoes
A dress that's new
A bill paid
Maybe two
I need some dead presidents
Jefferson, Grant and
Some C-notes
Boo

To keep on my cell phone
and my lights
to turn you on
All through the night

Thinking of a master plan
Sitting on the bed with his dick in my hand
I kiss it
Lick it
Suck it
Rub it

He grabs the back of my head
I go down down down
Swirling my tongue
Round and round

Pussy might be his favorite dish
But until I get paid
It's still his wish

I tightened my lips
To his dick

I go deeper and deeper
Touch the spot
That his girl can't hit

Just when he's ready to cum
I'm done
Thinking of my master plan
I say boo
What I need from you
Is ten grand

Get money

His eyes get wide
His chin drops low
I know what he's thinking
Fuck this ho
But he's got a big ego
And a hard dick

So I lick it
Kiss it
Suck it
I go deeper and deeper
Touch that spot
That his girl can't hit
Make him shiver
Before he screams
Aw shit!

I'm paid in full

Take the Bambi Challenge

I enjoyed the research I've done for *Darius Jones*. I think we can agree that Bambi is crazier than Ashlee. We'll know for sure provided Jay Crawford ever gets his day in court.

Just for fun, I want your book club members to do a makeover contest. If you're not in a book club, you can independently do this makeover. From head to toe, each member will change her hair, body shape and size, glam up or tone it down. The person who makes the most dramatic change wins your contest.

Send your Bambi Challenge "before" and "after" group and individual pictures to me at contest@marymorrison.com. We might surprise your book club with something super special.

See if you can outdo Bambi. Create your alter ego. Incorporate some of these spy gadgets and become a detective, diva, dominatrix, or stalker. I'll share the web sites I used but see if you can find and create something jaw-dropping.

Another challenge is to see if you'll readily recognize me as I undergo extreme makeovers for each of my book signings and events.

I used the following web sites for research and fun. And I visited as many of these places as I could:

• Dream Girls | http://www.dghair.com

- Zarawigs | http://www.zarawigs.com

- Takeouts | http://www.herlook.com/takeouts-better-boob-job.html?gclid=CLSLmP-Tm50CFSn6agodpTQX_Q

- Bubbles Bodywear | http://www.lovemybubbles.com

- Silicone Body | http://www.siliconebody.com/

- Dominatrix Lingerie | http://www.dominatrixlingerie.com/index.php?cPath=53

- SM Boots | http://www.smboots.com/

- Loud 'N Clear | https://www.tryloudandclear.com/17/index.asp?refcode=1002

- The Spy Corner | http://www.thespycorner.com/index.php?l=product_list&c=1&gclid=CMmU2LHh2Z8CFQwpawodoFwTHw

- DynaSpy, Inc. | http://www.dynaspy.com/spy-cameras-c-66.html?osCsid=h6jd55aas2q0t98nueeoj4vnh3

- Spy Gadgets | http://www.spygadgets.com/undercover-cameras/sunglasses-camera.html

- Self Defense Weapons | http://www.stungunsandtasers.com/

- Love Spells | http://www.everythingunderthemoon.net/love-spells.htm

- The Universe and Multiple Reality | http://www.manyuniverses.com/indexS.htm

- The Playhouse | http://playhousehollywood.com/

- My House | http://www.myhousehollywood.com/

- BOA Steakhouse | http://www.boasteak.com/balboa/index.htm

- CUT Beverly Hills | http://www.fourseasons.com/
  beverlywilshire/dining.html

- Roscoe's House of Chicken 'n Waffles | http://www.roscoeschicken
  andwaffles.com